# The Unloved Mate

**A ROMANCE NOVEL**

*written by*

**SKYLAR**

Copyright © 2024 Skylar

Skylar has asserted her right under the laws of Singapore, to be identified as the Author of the Work.

All rights reserved.

No part of this book may be reproduced or transmitted in any form by any means, graphic, electronic, or mechanical, including photocopying, recording, taping or by any information storage retrieval system without the written permission from the copyright holder.

This is a work of fiction. Names, characters, businesses, places, events, and incidents are either the products of the author's imagination or used in a fictitious manner: Any resemblance to actual persons, living or dead, or actual events is purely coincidental.

Design and composition by CRATER PTE.LTD.

First Edition 2024.
Published by CRATER PTE.LTD. Singapore

To my family, who saw the future I couldn't see and believed in me.

And my best friend, kirtika who opened the doors to this fantastical world to me.

Thank you. I hope I made you proud.

# AUTHOR'S NOTES

My creativity in writing stemmed from my passion for reading. I still remember that day in 10th grade when I read my first book and life was never the same since then. The need to read, sometimes specifically tailored to my needs, was what drove me to write my first book, The Unloved Mate.

I wrote it because nothing else was left to satisfy me at that time. As they say, "Write what you want to read." It happened to me and I wrote it with my clumsy imagination. I wrote it with zero expectations and on an app where fiction was in abundance. My story was like a drop of water in an ocean.

Unexpectedly, the story was discovered by readers and I was motivated to make it better. Before I knew it, the story made a small name for itself, and I was found by a Dreame editor.

It was a life-changing event for me. I started to write more, learn more, and achieve more. My editor at that time, Betty, was the sweetest and helped me navigate through the new journey I was venturing into.

Dreame/Stary has been my friend since 2019 and I wouldn't have it any other way. Five years later, I am still working to improve myself, and I know there is no stopping in this world.

This is the world I chose to create for myself, just like the fantasy I write.

It's full of plot holes and problematic characters, but it's mine.

# Table of Contents

**AUTHOR'S NOTES** ................................................................................. iii
Chapter 1 ................................................................................................. 1
Chapter 2 ................................................................................................. 4
Chapter 3 ................................................................................................. 8
Chapter 4 ............................................................................................... 10
Chapter 5 ............................................................................................... 13
Chapter 6 ............................................................................................... 15
Chapter 7 ............................................................................................... 17
Chapter 8 ............................................................................................... 19
Chapter 9 ............................................................................................... 22
Chapter 10 ............................................................................................. 25
Chapter 11 ............................................................................................. 28
Chapter 12 ............................................................................................. 32
Chapter 13 ............................................................................................. 35
Chapter 14 ............................................................................................. 42
Chapter 15 ............................................................................................. 46
Chapter 16 ............................................................................................. 51
Chapter 17 ............................................................................................. 54
Chapter 18 ............................................................................................. 58
Chapter 19 ............................................................................................. 60
Chapter 20 ............................................................................................. 66
Chapter 21 ............................................................................................. 71
Chapter 22 ............................................................................................. 75
Chapter 23 ............................................................................................. 78
Chapter 24 ............................................................................................. 83
Chapter 25 ............................................................................................. 87
Chapter 26 ............................................................................................. 91
Chapter 27 ............................................................................................. 97
Chapter 28 - Part 1 .............................................................................. 101
Chapter 28- Part 2 ............................................................................... 105
Chapter 29 ........................................................................................... 110

| | |
|---|---|
| Chapter 30 | 115 |
| Chapter 31 | 120 |
| Chapter 32 | 123 |
| Chapter 33 | 126 |
| Chapter 34 | 132 |
| Chapter 35 | 136 |
| Chapter 36 | 140 |
| Chapter 37 | 142 |
| Chapter 38 | 146 |
| Chapter 39 | 150 |
| Chapter 40 | 153 |
| Chapter 41 | 156 |
| Chapter 42 | 160 |
| Chapter 43 | 163 |
| Chapter 44 | 168 |
| Chapter 45 | 172 |
| Chapter 46 | 177 |
| Chapter 47 | 181 |
| Chapter 48 | 185 |
| Chapter 49 | 188 |
| Chapter 50 | 192 |
| Chapter 51 | 196 |
| Chapter 52 | 200 |
| Chapter 53 | 204 |
| Chapter 54 | 208 |
| Chapter 55 | 213 |
| Epilogue | 218 |
| Bonus Chapter #1 | 220 |
| Bonus Chapter #2 | 224 |
| Bonus Chapter #3 | 226 |
| Bonus Chapter #4 | 229 |
| Bonus Chapter #5 | 231 |
| **ABOUT THE AUTHOR** | 236 |
| **ABOUT DREAME** | 237 |

# Chapter 1

**Isabella's POV**

It was 1:23 at night, or more like morning, and I was still cleaning the last few dishes in the sink. I have been working for twenty hours non-stop today.

I needed some sleep. I finished the last plate and sighed. Now I can get some sleep. Finally!

I am an Omega of the Howlers Pack. My parents are warriors in the pack. I don't know why, but no one loves me here. I am often called names and sometimes beaten up, too. I don't want to be here. But the only thing keeping me from running away is the idea of finding my mate. I know that he will love me and take me away.

I smiled at that thought.

*Just a week more, Bella. Then we will find our mate. He will love us and cherish us,* my wolf, Nora, said in my head.

*Yeah, hope so,* I said.

I walked over to the storeroom, which is also my bedroom. The Alpha said I'm no more worthy than the trash kept here, if not less. So I have to stay here in the dark and dirt. I am really scared of the dark. But I can't object to the Alpha's order.

I walk up to the storeroom and walk in. All my possessions are scattered around. Not that it's anything new. Some cruel members do this all the time to trouble me. It's not difficult to sort things because all I own is a couple of baggy old clothes, an alarm clock, and a torn-up rug on which I sleep. I don't even have a blanket to keep myself warm.

I clean up everything and go to sleep.

*Goodnight, Bella,* Nora says.

*Goodnight, Nora,* I said.

# The Unloved Mate

**A week later...**

I woke up with a smile on my face, which did not happen. At all. I am happy because today is my birthday and I will find my mate. I quickly get up and shower in the common shower, which is for the Omegas. It's 5:00 in the morning so no one will be up right now.

I went to the kitchen and prepared breakfast for the pack. In an hour, I have the whole thing ready. Bacon, eggs, toast, fresh juice, and apple pie.

I hear footsteps, and I hide in the kitchen corner after setting up the table. They don't like to see my face in the morning. All the pack members occupy the three long dining tables and serve themselves. I am hungry, too, but I'm not allowed to eat breakfast. Only lunch, and that two pieces of toast, a cubed-sized chicken piece, and a cup of water. They give it to me so that I don't die.

After everyone is done, they leave for school, work, or anything they must do. I clean up the dishes. I put them in the sink and started cleaning them. After I'm done, I go clean all the rooms.

When I reach the second floor, I smell something fresh. Chocolate and mint. It is refreshing.

Nora starts to howl happily.

I think I just found my mate.

I followed the scent which led me to the Beta's room. I touch the doorknob to open the door. But as soon as I do that, I feel a stabbing pain in my stomach. I ignore the pain and plaster a smile on my face. I don't want my mate to see me in pain.

I opened the door, and my smile fell off my face. My mate. The one who is supposed to love me is butt naked on top of a similar butt naked girl, whom I recognise as Morgana, the pack's favourite person, the Alpha's daughter.

They both sense me and look at me. Mason, the Beta, looks at me and frowns while Morgana covers both of them with the blanket.

Realisation flashes upon his face, soon replaced by rage and disgust. Tears are flowing down my cheeks. I leave the room and run towards my room and cry.

# Chapter 1

After ten minutes, the door opens, revealing Mason. He throws at me on the floor and without warning, kicks me on the sides. Then, a punch in the face. Kick. Punch. Kick. Punch. It goes on until I fall limp on the floor. The last words I hear are more painful than the beating I just received for no reason.

"I, Mason Jonson, reject you, Isabella, as my mate," he spat. "I don't know why the moon goddess would do such a thing as to pair me with such a trash like you. I have a true mate. Morgana. She will lead me to the Alpha position and keep me happy and satisfied, which you can never do," he continued.

Then I blacked out…

# Chapter 2

**Isabella's POV**

I feel like my life is slowly being sucked out of my body and leaving me more lifeless than I was before. Being abused and not loved is a different thing, and being rejected by your mate is an entirely different thing.

A week has passed since that day, and no one knows what happened. Mason threatened me.

Now, he beats me openly, and no one does anything about it. They join in sometimes. My life has been worse than it was. I tried to kill myself sometimes, but Nora did not let me.

I have to survive all this. I am afraid. Of everything. The men that beat me. The women that burn me. Everything. I do not speak. I don't scream. I only silently bear the pain they inflict upon me in hopes that death will be finally bestowed upon me to release me from here.

**That same day…**

**Damien's POV**

Sometimes, I think I have the worst case of bad luck in the entire universe!

I have to work non-stop. Pack meetings, travelling to other packs, different events that Alpha is forced to attend, etc…

I am a cruel Alpha. I agree, but I don't want my pack to suffer. I want them happy. But still, a very important part of me is missing. My mate. My pack's Luna. I am twenty now, and I am still looking

# Chapter 2

for her. I think I should give up. I travel a lot in hopes of finding her. But I guess I will have to stop now.

Today, there is a get-together among the Alphas of different packs. It is held every year at a different pack. This time, it's at the Howlers Pack. Honestly, I am not a fan of that pack. I have heard the Alpha was the pack's beta and received the position after mating with the Alpha's daughter, which is cheap of him because she is not his real mate.

I stand in front of my full-length mirror and adjust my suit. When I'm satisfied, I walk in my closet for my watch and wallet.

I look at my closet and sigh. About a month ago, I was on a run around the city border when my wolf started screaming 'mate' in my head, and I was this close to finding her, but I lost the scent. In hopes of finding her, I had emptied half of my closet for her.

I took my necessary things and exited my room. I put on a stone-hard face. No one has seen me smiling except for a few close ones, and I intend to keep it that way. I meet my Beta outside the pack house.

We reach our destination in an hour. We exited our cars and were welcomed by Alpha Mason and Luna Morgana. We greeted each other and were soon joined by other Alphas, their Lunas and Betas.

We were seated in the big living room. Drinks were served, and all were engaged in small talk. I was incredibly bored. I needed to get out of here. No one was talking to me. They were terrified of me, and I liked it that way. I mind-linked Nate, my Beta that I'm going out for a stroll.

I excused myself. I was finally free. I walked out and instantly got lost. This place is like a maze!

I don't know how, but I ended up in the kitchen. I looked around and caught a scent. Honey and cinnamon.

*Mate,* my wolf yelled in my head. I started doing a happy dance in my head. I frantically looked around, but nothing.

Then I focused on the scent. It's coming from a cabinet in the kitchen. But that's not all, the scent is mixed with a metallic smell

# The Unloved Mate

of blood. I mind-linked Nate, and within five seconds, he was with me.

I quickly opened the cabinet, but what I saw broke my heart. My mate.

I carefully pulled her tiny body from the cabinet and set it on the floor. Her body was covered in blood. Black and blue bruises were on her body. Her breath was short and ragged.

I took her unconscious body in my arms and went to the living room. Nate followed closely behind me. As soon as I entered, I heard people gasp.

I laid my mate's fragile and tiny body on the couch.

"SOMEONE CALL A DOCTOR!" I yelled at the people who were staring at my unconscious mate in shock.

After a minute or two, a lady in a lab coat came in. It must be the doctor.

She pulled a chair beside her and started examining her.

After examining her, she called for us. I ran towards my mate and held her hand instantly.

"What's wrong with her? Is she fine? What happened? When will she wake up?" I asked the doctor desperately.

"She is fine, Alpha. She has multiple bruises on her body, and I guess the injury on her head led to her passing out. Her six bones are broken, and she is extremely underweight. Her tiny frame isn't helping either. And staying in the cabinet for too long cut off her oxygen supply temporarily. She should be conscious by tomorrow morning," she explained.

I nodded, and she bowed and left.

That's when I realised something. Why the hell does she have bruises? Why was she in the cabinet? And the main question... Who did this to her!?!!

My sadness was soon turned into anger at the thought of anyone harming my gem of a mate.

I rapidly turn around to face the Alphas. Specifically Alpha Mason.

"What is the meaning of this, Alpha Mason?" I said extremely calmly.

## Chapter 2

He gulped.

"Uhm… she… she is clumsy and keeps falling o-on thin a-air. And about the cabinet… some kids might h-have p-pranked her maybe?" he said

"Who did this to her!?!" I yelled I had enough of his lying already.

He remained silent

"Answer the Alpha! Who did this to our Luna?!" Nate yelled in protection of his Luna.

"Luna?! She isn't the Luna! She is an Omega! She—" Before he could continue, I grabbed his throat and backed him to the wall.

"A word against her, and I will rip your head off your body!" I growled.

# Chapter 3

**Isabella's POV**

I was woken up by the sound of yelling and things being thrown. I opened my eyes and took in my surroundings.

I was on the couch in the particular living room. But how did I get here? I was thrown in the kitchen cabinet after today's beatings so that I don't bother them.

I looked around and saw someone holding Alpha Mason by his neck.

"A word against her, and I will rip your head off your body!!" the person growled.

I tried to get off the couch but fell on my face. My ankle is sprained.

"LUNA!" a boy said. I looked around, confused. He was looking at me but calling for Luna Morgana. Weird.

I tried and failed to get up. Suddenly, a pair of strong arms picked me up by my waist and sat me on the couch. And the weirdest thing is I felt a tingling sensation where he touched me.

I looked at the person, and my eyes widened. He is easily the hottest person I've seen or will ever see. He had thick, inky black hair, which I wanted to run my fingers through. He was very well built but not in a gross way, just perfect. His face was so beautiful that models would be cowering.

He sat beside me with a concerned look on his face. I looked at him, confused.

He cupped my face and smiled.
I kept my blank face.
He frowned.
I frowned.
He smirked.
I still frowned.

# Chapter 3

"Hi, sweetheart. Are you okay now?" he said in a deep and husky voice.

I gulped and hesitantly nodded.

"Good! What's your name, sweetheart?" he asked with a small smile.

"Isabella." My voice was barely above a whisper.

"A beautiful name for a beautiful gem, I see," he said with what looked like love in his eyes.

"Damien?" Luna Morgana's voice said from behind.

I quickly got off the couch and bowed to her. She ignored me and threw a flirtatious look at the person 'Damien' who sat beside me seconds ago.

Damien gently pulled me back to the couch ignoring the looks Luna Morgana was giving him. He made me sit impossibly close to him. I was practically sitting on his lap.

He was huge. I looked like a kid in front of him. It was like comparing coconuts and plums. The difference is significant.

Damien looked at me and wrapped his hand around my waist. He smiled in satisfaction.

Then he looked at the Luna with a glare. And I seriously don't want to be on the receiving side of it. It was that scary.

"It's Alpha Damien to you, Luna Morgana," he said

As soon as the word Alpha came out of his mouth, I stood up from his oddly comfortable embrace and ran to the storeroom terrified.

He was Alpha Damien! The Alpha Damien!

I don't want any other Alpha in my life. Ever again…

# Chapter 4

**Isabella's POV**

I don't know what to feel. The person who tortured me is my mate. The person who was holding me was the Alpha Damien.

Alpha Damien was well-known in the werewolf community. He was like a king without a crown. Everyone feared him. His pack is the biggest one so far. He kills anyone that threatens him or his family. He also has a golden wolf, which is abnormally powerful. That's why most fear him; they know he can single-handedly take an army.

But then, why was he here? And why was he holding me? And the look on his face? I'm confused!

My head started to hurt. I saw the door of the storeroom being opened and a silhouette of a man coming towards me...

And I blacked out... for the third time today!

**Damien's POV**

Why would she run away?! Have I done anything wrong? For the first time in my life, I feel nervous about what other person thinks of me.

*She's not a random person! She is our mate! Go to her!* my wolf, Dom, was yelling in my head. I was about to follow her, but Mason stopped me.

"Alpha, I don't understand! Why are you behaving like this?" Mason, the moron said. Yep, that name suits him.

"I don't need to answer to anyone. But if you are so curious, then listen. She's my mate!" I growled

Everyone gasped.

Mason shook his head and laughed.

# Chapter 4

"But that is not possible, Alpha! She already has a mate! But he rejected her on sight," Mason said.

I was shocked! She had been rejected! By her mate! Who in the right mind would reject a gem like her? But a tiny part of my non-existing heart that belongs to my mate is happy because now Isabella can be mine and only MINE!

"Why did he reject her, and who is he?" I growled. I need to know who inflicted such pain on my Isabella.

"It was me!" Mason said proudly, with a victorious smirk on his face. What is he so happy about?

"Why?" I asked again

"Because she's an Omega! I was the Beta! I did not want people to look at me any other way. I want respect! And with that filthy little thing by my side, I would never get it!" He growled.

I had enough of it. I have to see if Isabella is okay.

I stood up and mind-linked Nate. *Show them what happens when someone disrespects or hurts your Luna.*

I walked out of the room, not missing the smirk Nate gave me before a slight nod.

I follow my mate's scent, and I reach a room. I sniff the air, and I smell her again. Honey and cinnamon. But... mixed with salty tears.

I open the door and enter. I saw her looking at me through hooded eyes. She was about to say something, but she passed out. I ran to her and picked her up. She is light as a feather!

I took her outside and asked a random person to tell me where I could find the pack doctor. He took me to the small clinic thing in the mansion and left. I went inside, and the doctor from earlier was beside me in a flash.

"What happened?" she asked, looking at Isabella with concern and worry in her eyes.

I told her everything.

"Okay, lay her down on the bed. And please wait outside while I check her," she said, and I went outside without protesting. I don't want to delay her treatment because of me.

I sat on a chair outside, which was not comfortable. I waited for what felt like hours. The doctor came out, and I ran towards her. "What happened? Is she okay?" I asked

"Alpha, Isabella had an injury on her head when I treated her before, and it had not healed properly before a lot of stress was inflicted on her. Her wolf is weak, so it will take time. But she will heal. Just make sure not to stress her out. It can cause serious damage to the brain. And she might wake up in an hour or two." She bowed and left.

I walked in and sat on a stool beside her bed. She looked pale and unhealthy.

"I will make everything better, baby. Trust me, I will treat you like a princess. My princess. Just give me a chance, and I will make everything better," I promised her.

# Chapter 5

**Isabella's POV**

I groan as I wake up from my deep slumber. My head hurts! I try to open my eyes. It takes a lot of effort, but eventually, I succeed. The first thing I noticed was that I was sleeping on a bed. I look around and see cream-coloured walls and ceiling.

A girl comes in. I observe her. She is Nurse Shaylea, who works with the pack doctor. She hates me. Once, I was severely beaten and came to her for some medicine for my pain. She gave me 'hyperalgesia' which increases pain. That was the last time I took any medication.

She noticed me awake and gave me a disgusted look like always.

"Oh, so the little bitch is awake?" she says in a hushed tone. I look at her, confused. Why is she not talking in her usual shrilly, high-pitched, annoying voice and gaining the only thing she loves—attention.

She shakes her head at me. That was when I noticed a huge figure sleeping on the small sofa beside the bed. I could not see the face, though.

Shaylea walks to the man and runs her hand up and down his arm. I try to say something, but my throat hurts. I see a bottle of water on a table on the side and take it. I gulp down the water and finally feel at ease.

I see Shaylea getting irritated when the man— Okay, now I'm also getting irritated by calling him 'the man'.

I'll call him... Eddie!

So Eddie is not waking up, and Shaylea is whispering something in his ear. I reach out for his hand and touch it. Electricity shoots through my hand. Eddie jolts awake.

He frantically looks around, and I finally see his face. And I'm not thrilled.

Alpha Damien is Eddie.

Eddie is Alpha Damien

"Aaahhh!" I scream when I see him. I am supposed to run away!

His eyes widened with worry and concern. I shut my mouth, realising what I had done.

Then I felt something moving on my toe. I slowly unwrapped myself from the covers. I was carefully keeping eye contact with Alpha Damien. I looked at my toe and screamed.

"Aaahhh!!! Spider!!! Spider!!!!!!"

I closed my eyes and screamed some more. I hate spiders! Those filthy little things scare me!

A hand was placed at my mouth.

"Shhh, princess. I will get rid of it for you. Don't be scared. Okay?" A soft voice spoke. I opened my eyes and saw Alpha Damien. I see him a lot. His hands are still on my mouth as he bends down to pick up the spider. He held it between his fingers and tossed it out of the window.

I closed my eyes again. The hand was removed from my mouth, and I opened my eyes. I saw Alpha Damien very close to my face. I was smiling like a kid in the candy store with a twenty-dollar bill.

He looked at me expectantly. And you know what I did? Guess? No?

I screamed!

"Aaahhh!!!"

# Chapter 6

**Damien's POV**

I watched helplessly as she screamed. I don't know what to do! I have never been in a situation like this. I usually smile and laugh when others are afraid of me. But I don't want HER to feel terrified of me.

I hung my head low and sighed dejectedly. I am useless. I can't even make my mate feel good!

After what felt like hours, she quieted down. It took a lot of effort. I'm being pushed into the corner. A couple of bottles of chilled water. And a few nurses.

When she calmed down, I cautiously stood beside her. Her eyes were closed, but I had a feeling she was not sleeping.

I sat on the chair as quietly as possible. I rubbed my eyes and sighed. I have not spoken to Nate yet, so I don't know what happened with Mason, the moron. But I have a positive feeling it was not good for him.

I felt a hand rest on my shoulder. I turned my head and saw the nurse from before. The dirty look she was giving my mate before didn't go unnoticed. I looked at her in anger and confusion.

*What the hell does she want now?!* my wolf Dom yelled in my head.

*My head is already pounding! Don't you yell and make it worse, Dom!* Honestly, he can be a big pain in the ass sometimes.

I remembered the nurse looking at me, and I looked up. She was smiling sweetly. Too sweetly. I inwardly cringed. I don't like her, not her attitude and confidence. Absolutely not!

I shrugged her hand off my shoulder, and her smile flattered a bit.

"What the hell do you want?!" I whisper. I don't want my mate to be disturbed by some silly creature.

"You! I want you, baby. I know you want me to. Why are you wasting your time on this thing when we can spend it together?" she said in a seductive tone. She failed miserably. It sounded like someone was choking her.

I stood up and faced her.

"How dare you?! The person sleeping on the bed has a name. Isabella. She is not a thing. And if you think I will leave a precious gem like her for a good-for-nothing-blonde-bimbo, then you can't be more wrong! I saw the looks you were giving her. I kept my anger at bay because I didn't want my Bella to be any more afraid of me than she already was! But you crossed the line now. Get out of my sight right now, or so God help me. I will rip you to shreds. Literally!" I said in a slightly raised voice.

I would have yelled at her full-on, but my Bella is still resting.

The girl scrambled out of the room.

Are all the members of the pack stupid!?

First, the slutty Luna. Stupid

Then, the Alpha. More stupid.

And then the nurse. I can't get any more stupid!

I sighed and ran a hand through my thick black hair.

That's when I heard it. I froze on my spot. Turning around, I saw my Bella, and I swear I heard my heart break into pieces. My Bella was crying. And I don't know why. Most importantly, I don't know what to do.

I started crying, too…

# Chapter 7

**Isabella's POV**

I instantly stopped crying when I heard him sniffle. I looked up and saw tears streaming down his cheeks and sniffing.

He saw me looking and slowly walked towards me. He sat on the small stool and took my hand. Electricity flows through.

He wiped the tears and ran his big hands in my hair. I don't know what came over me. I raised my hand and wiped his tears, too. That brought a slight smile on his face.

"Why?" I asked

"Huh?" He looked at me, confused

"Why are you doing this for me? Why am I feeling like this? Why are you here with me?" I asked.

"I'm doing this because I want to make you happy and make sure you are okay. And I feel what you feel. Those sparks, I feel them too, princess. And I'm here for you. I don't give a damn about anyone," he said

"Oh" is all I said

"Why did you cry?" he asked

"You defended me in front of her. No one has ever done that. I was never important enough," I said and started crying again.

He wiped the tears away and pulled me into a tight hug.

"Hey. Don't say that. You are very important to me. And I will make sure that you are always happy. I promise. I will make everything better, baby," he said.

"But why are you doing this?" I said, pulling away from the hug and immediately feeling cold.

"Because you're my mate!" he said.

I froze. "No, this can't happen! I had a mate! You can't be my mate," I said.

He cupped my cheek and looked into my eyes.

"I know, baby. I know everything. Mason, the moron, told me. He rejected you. It's your second chance mate, and I want you to be happy. I want to give you all the happiness he couldn't. I feel blessed to have you as my mate, princess. Please give me a chance. I will do anything. Please," he begged.

I was finally having a chance to be happy with my mate. I want to be happy. But I can't trust him fully yet. I want to give him a chance. But... Ugh, this is so confusing.

*Give him a chance, Bella,* Nora said

"Okay. I'll give us a chance. But I still don't fully trust you. You have to gain my trust," I said. My voice was barely above a whisper.

I saw his face transform from nervous to shock to extreme happiness.

He had such a big smile that I was worried it would split his face.

He pulled me on his lap and hugged me like his life depended on it. "Baby, I promise I will gain your trust, and I do anything for it. I will treat you like a princess. My princess. Oh, my God, I can't believe I finally found my mate. I'm so happy!" he exclaimed

I don't know if what I did was right, but I'm happy.

# Chapter 8

**Damien's POV**

I can't explain how happy I am. My mate is willing to give me a chance. I couldn't believe my ears. I was doing a Jumbo happy dance in the head, or else Bella would think I was crazy.

I was looking down at her and smiling softly. She smiled back. A small smile, but better than nothing. Oh, my God! She's so tiny! So adorable! Oh, God, now I sound like a girl!

I remembered I had to ask her something. "Hey princess, how did you end up in the kitchen cabinet earlier today? And please don't tell me some pup pranked you. I know that's not true," I said, looking at her in the eyes. My voice could not get any softer.

She started shaking slightly. I could sense her fear and anxiety.

"Hey, hey, it's okay. If you don't want to talk about it, then we won't, but please don't stress yourself," I said while stroking her hair.

"I'm sorry, Alpha. I can't talk about it right now."

I noticed how she called me Alpha. "Baby, call me Damien or anything you want, but not Alpha. You are my equal, princess. You have full power over me. Don't forget that, okay?" I said softly but sternly.

She nodded her head, and I smiled.

The doctor walked in with a warm smile. She is the only one who likes Bella in the whole pack house.

"Hi, Isabella. I'm glad you're awake. I'm the pack's senior doctor, Lucy. Alpha has been worried sick for you. He even scared off a nurse." Why can't she keep her mouth shut?

"I'm sorry, doctor," Bella said.

"Why are you saying sorry, Bella? It's not your fault," I said "So... Isabella, I'm giving you some medications to make you healthy again. Those are to increase the blood in your body and provide missing nutrition. You are too thin and weak. I suggest

## The Unloved Mate

you eat as much healthy food as you can—vegetables, fruits, nuts, etc. A bit of fat consumption now and then, but not too much."

I listen to her every word and plaster them in my brain. I'll do it in a heartbeat if it is good for my princess. I mind-link Nate to come here.

Nate walks in with a frown on his face. He was probably thinking why I called him.

He looks up and sees Bella awake, and instantly, the frown is replaced by a one thousand-watt smile, and there are those weird twinkles in his eyes. I roll my eyes. He always does that when he is happy, even when Mom gives him cookies!

"Luna! You're awake! You can't imagine how happy I am! I finally have a Luna! Now you can save all our butts from the Alpha. When you were not there, he used to go all caveman on us and make us work overtime! That's plain mean of him, isn't it!?" He finished with a pout and big eyes.

What is it with everyone? All are dead set on embarrassing me in front of Bella today!

Bella gasped softly, and her eyes widened. "Is that true?" she asked in a whisper.

I gave her an unnoticeable nod and looked down on my lap. Suddenly, the shape of my fingers seemed fascinating.

"You should not do that. Everyone needs rest. What you do is mean. You won't do it anymore, would you?" she asked.

"I promise!" I said instantly.

She smiled slightly. I'm happy she's not mad at me.

"I'm sorry to interrupt, Alpha. I need to talk to you about something. In my office," the doctor said.

I saw Bella yawning, and I gently made her lie down, and she instantly closed her eyes. I smiled and tucked her in. I kissed her forehead and walked out with Nate.

We sat on the chairs in front of the doctor.

"Alpha, there is something you need to know about Isabella. She has been treated like a slave since she was only ten years old. She was very young. She had to do all the work for the pack. The

## Chapter 8

pack house has about seventy people living in it. She has been soaking all the pain, mental and physical.

"She received a regular beating. I never saw her without bruises or cuts. The pack had done everything to break her, but she didn't in the hope of finding her mate. That will care and protect her. But that last ounce of hope was snatched away when he rejected her. So I have a suggestion.

"Don't take her to your pack right now. She couldn't handle meeting new people. She will become more closed off. I suggest you stay here with her. Show her that no one can hurt her while you are here. Show her she's not alone. Make her believe she can do what she wants, not what people force her to do. Be there for her. Make her confident."

The words she spoke brought tears to my eyes. Tears of sadness. That she went through so much. Tears of disappointment. That I could not save her from this. Tears of anger. On people who did this to her.

I heard a slight sniffle and saw Nate with an emotionless face. His face held no emotions, but his eyes said everything. They had tears, too. Anger was burning in them. Hunger for revenge for his Luna was clear.

I blinked back the tears and gave a slight smirk.

"Don't you worry, doc. I will do anything for Bella. I will make her happy again," I said. I turned to face Nate. "While we are at it, we can have our fair share of fun, don't you think?"

Nate smirked in response. "Absolutely, Alpha."

# Chapter 9

**Isabella's POV**

I was sleepy. When Damien laid me down, I was out like a light. But my peace didn't last long.

A crashing sound woke me up. I sat up and saw Luna Morgana glaring at me.

I gulped inaudibly.

She grabbed me by my arms and threw me off the bed. I crawled into a corner and brought my knees to my chest. I was shaking from fear of what she was going to do to me.

She stood before me and crossed her hands in front of her chest. "Look at you, being your pathetic self, can't even defend yourself! Do you think you can make Damien punish Mason for what he did to you? Well, you couldn't be any more wrong. He will choose anyone over you. Do you know how useless you are? I'll tell you. No one loves you. Your parents abandoned you. Your mate rejected you. Your pack hates you. Damien will also leave—" Before she could say anything, the door crashed open.

I didn't dare look up. Maybe someone else wants to beat me too. There was silence for a few minutes before I was pulled onto someone's lap. I relaxed when I felt the sparks.

It was Damien.

I hugged him with all of me. I don't want him to leave me. I need someone in my life, especially him.

"Shh, don't cry, baby. I'm here now. No one is going to hurt you. Shh," he cooed at me.

His voice was very soft. It's almost like velvet. Sweet as chocolate.

He stood up with me still in his arms. I was clinging to him like a monkey. My arms were around his neck, and my legs were wrapped around his torso. My face was buried in his shoulder.

# Chapter 9

He walked out of the room. I took a sneak peek at his face and saw an angry expression.

He was angry. At me?

"Don't you even think that!" he said to me.

"What?" I said, confused.

"That I'm angry at you. I'm not angry at you. How could I? You're so cute, and you are my mate, and you haven't given me a reason to be mad at you," he said, smiling slightly.

"Then why are you angry, and at whom?" I asked

"The stupid pack members. I'm angry at all those people who ever hurt you in any way. And the fact that they hurt you," he said in an icy cold voice.

I gulped. Someone's going to get hurt.

We went to a clearing where all the training was done. Almost all pack members are present here. I feel myself getting anxious. I try to get off Damien, but he holds me tighter. His Beta was on stage, and when he saw us, he gave a big grin and waved. I gave a small smile in return.

Damien finally put me down on my feet. But he kept his hand on the small of my back. He gently nudged me forward.

I walked onto the makeshift stage, and everyone went quiet.

Damien took the microphone from Nate and looked— more like glared at everyone.

"As you all know, my name is Alpha Damien. I, along with my Beta, came here to attend the get-together. But I found my beautiful mate here. I'm her second chance mate, and I'm proud to be because I will get the opportunity to mend her bruised heart. I would like you to meet my mate, Isabella." He brought me forward. I kept my eyes downcast.

I was not allowed to make eye contact.

Damien put a finger under my chin and held my head up. I saw him smiling at me. He gave me a reassuring nod. I smiled at everyone. I received only glares and dirty looks in return.

"I have heard about many things you all have done. I don't know why you all did, but now it doesn't matter. I'm staying here with my mate for a while, and while I'm here, we will have fun with you. I'm going to make you pay all right, but much worse than I planned before," he finished with a smirk, and everyone went pale.

What is he up to?!

# Chapter 10

**Damien's POV**

I was mad. Really mad. That bitch scared my Bella! Bella thought I would leave her! How can I not be mad? But I will not punish them right away. I will kill them slowly. They will experience all the bad things they made Bella go through.

I smirked when I saw everyone's face going pale. I walked down the stage and extended my hand for Bella to come down. We make our way towards— Wait, I don't know where to go.

"Hey, Bella, let's go to your room. We can spend some time there," I said with hopeful eyes and a smile.

"You won't like my room. It's horrible," she said, not looking at me.

"Hey, as long as you and I are together, I don't mind if we spend time in a hut! Just want to spend time with you," I said. "Now lead the way!" I said, bowing dramatically. I saw her smile.

She hesitated but shrugged and started walking. "I know you will not like it. But if you insist."

We were walking for two to three minutes when she stopped in front of an old-looking door. I recognised the room. It was where I found Bella crying.

Is this her room? "Is this your room?" I voice my thoughts.

She just nodded. She opened the doors. The door made a squelching sound when it opened.

The room was not habitable! The room is more of a storeroom! Trash is thrown carelessly around the room. I can't believe Bella put up with all this bull shit for God knows how long!

"How could you live here? This place is not fit to stay in! It's a trash room! Not made for someone like you!" I said, horrified at the thought of her living here.

"Well... that's not what they said," she mumbled under her breath, clearly not meant for me to hear, but anyway I did.

"Who are 'they'?" I asked

She looked down and didn't answer.

"Who, Bella?" I asked again.

"Pack," she mumbled again.

"What did they say?" I asked

"Nothing," she replied.

"Bella!" I said sternly

"They said I was not worth more than trash. So they gave me this room to stay in," she said.

I looked around the room again. There was no mattress. Where does she sleep? "Where do you sleep? There is not even a mattress here," I asked. God, I sure have a lot of questions today. But I need answers.

"On the rug there." She pointed towards the 90% torn and rough rug.

"Come with me!" I said and took her hands in mine. I made my way to the Alpha's room.

I knocked once and didn't wait for them to open it, I pushed the door open. And as expected, both were half-naked on top of each other. I quickly covered Bella's innocent eyes and glared at them. They scrambled around the room to find clothes. Once they were dressed, I removed my hands from Bella's eyes and kissed her forehead.

It didn't go unnoticed how my baby was shaking in their presence.

"Alpha Damien, what are you doing here? At this late hour? Is something wrong?" Morgana asked.

"As you know, I'm staying here for a while. And being used to the comfortable lifestyle I lived in, I don't think I will be able to sleep in any ordinary bedroom of yours. I need a spacious and bright room," I said.

"Okay, Alpha. We will have the best room ready for you in fifteen minutes. By that time, you can do whatever," Mason said and mind-linked someone.

## Chapter 10

"And one more thing. What were you thinking when you generously gave that storeroom to my mate to sleep in?" I asked.

"Alpha, she was an Omega at that time, and that's to the lowest one. No other Omega wanted to share a room with her so we kept her there," Morgana reasoned.

"Omega or not, she's still a pack member! An Alpha and Luna are supposed to be a fatherly and motherly figure to the pack! Be their guardians! And not act like bullies! Like you did! I want you to apologize to Bella. Now!" I exclaimed.

"What!?" both of them said, looking at me as if I was crazy.

"Now!"

"We're sorry, Bella," they said in unison.

"It's Isabella for you. Only I can call her Bella!" I said and left for the new and comfortable room, which I demanded for Bella.

I couldn't care less if I had to sleep on the couch to make my Bella comfortable.

# Chapter 11

**Isabella's POV**

Damien demanded for a more comfortable room. I don't understand what was uncomfortable in the previous room. I would die of joy if anyone gave me that room to stay in! I guess, Alpha's rooms are like 'king quality' rooms.

We soon reached the room, and an Omega came our way and gave Damien the keys, not before giving me a slight glare. It didn't go unnoticed, though.

"What are you looking at?!" Damien spat.

"Nothing. Sorry, Alpha." He bowed and ran.

Damien unlocked the door and held out his hand.

"Come on, princess," he said, smiling.

"What? Why would I go in there? It's your room," I said, confused.

"It is, but we are sharing it. I know you don't feel comfortable sleeping on the same bed with me, so I told Nate to add an extra bed in there," he said, grabbed my hand, and pulled me inside.

The inside of the room was divine! It was spacious and cozy at the same time. I looked around the room in awe. I saw Damien staring at me. "Why?" I asked

"So you don't have to stay there. You deserve much more, princess. And once when you're comfortable enough, I will take you to my pack. There, you will be treated the way you should be treated, like a queen. But for now, we have to settle for this, your highness," he said, smiling slightly.

The thought of meeting his pack scared me. My pack hates me. Yes, hate is a huge term. But that's exactly what they do. So how can I expect his pack to treat me as their own? As if sensing my fright, Damien came to me and held my hand.

## Chapter 11

"Everything will be fine, baby. Trust me. I will never force you to do anything. We will go to my pack whenever you want. It's your choice. Promise," he said, looking in my eyes. That's how I knew he was sincere.

He won't force me. My opinion matters to him. I matter to him.

"Baby. It's late. We should have something to eat before bed. But first, change into something comfortable," he said.

I looked down at my outfit. I was wearing my three-year-old baggy T-shirt and black leggings. I don't have any more comfy clothes. I only own three T-shirts, four leggings, and three pairs of under clothing.

"I am comfortable in these. And you can have dinner. I will wait for you up here," I said, smiling slightly—a forced smile.

"Well, they don't look comfortable enough. And why are you not coming for dinner? Are you not feeling good? Do you need something?" he asked suddenly, worried.

"No, no, it's fine, I'm fine. I just don't eat dinner," I said, looking down at my feet.

"Why?" he asked, shocked at the revelation.

"Not used to it."

"Bella, how much did they feed you? How many times?" he asked seriously, with a no-nonsense face.

"Once a day, mostly lunch," I replied.

"What and how much?" he asked again.

"A couple of toast, some cube-sized chicken, and a cup of water."

"How are you so brave, Bella? You have been coping with all this shit for so long. I'm so sorry you had to endure so much pain, baby. But not anymore," he said, hugging me tightly as if I'd vanish.

He held me at arm's length and looked at me in the eyes. "Now you will have breakfast, lunch, evening snacks, and dinner! You will eat everything you like and how much you like. No one will stop you. I'll be there," he said sternly but smiled at the end.

## The Unloved Mate

He took my hand and gently dragged me down to the dining area. Then it hit me. I didn't make dinner! What will EVERYONE eat!?

I walked speedily to the kitchen, Damien following close behind me.

"What are you doing, Bella?" Damien asked. I had no time to respond. I looked around the kitchen to see if, by any chance, anyone had cooked something. Nothing! Absolutely nothing! What will everyone eat now?

Forty-five minutes until dinner starts.

I went to the pantry and found packets of spaghetti. I placed them on the counter and heated a big boiler.

"Baby, what are you doing?" Damien asked from behind.

"There is nothing to eat, Damien! I was supposed to make dinner today, like every day. But I forgot! Now, I'm trying to make something edible for everyone to eat. Or they will all starve. No one here can cook to save their life!" I ramble.

"They did so much, gave you so much pain, but here you are making dinner for more than a hundred people," he said

"If I do the same things they did, then what will be the difference between them and me? And I don't want myself to turn out like them," I said while making meatballs.

"Well, I want to be like you, so I'll help you!" Damien said and putting the second flame on and putting a saucepan on it.

"But I don't know how to make it. Be my instructor."

I told him what to do and it seemed as if he was absorbing everything I was saying. Within thirty minutes, spaghetti and meatballs were ready for everyone. Two of the Omegas came into the kitchen. Both of them looked at Damien and bowed.

"Take the food and place it on the table," Damien ordered them.

They quickly took all the dishes and left the kitchen.

By the time Damien and I cleaned up, everyone was already at the table. Pack members looked at me, some confused as to why I was there, some with glares, and some simply surprised. I noticed how only one seat was left at the huge table. At the head. I let Damien come before me, and he sat there. I stood beside him.

# Chapter 11

He looked at me and then at the table. He then let out a breath. Everyone carefully watches every activity.

"I guess there is no room left," he said and suddenly pulled me down on his lap.

I squealed a little in surprise. I tried to get up, but he held me tighter and moved a little so we both were comfortable. My back touched his hard chest, his strong arms around my stomach, and his chin resting on my shoulder. He was very happy with the position.

He took a plate and piled up loads of food in it. How could he possibly eat that much? Everyone had also fixed a plate for themselves. I noticed my parents are looking at me with disgust. I lowered my head.

Then, all of a sudden, there was a fork full of spaghetti in front of my mouth. I saw Damien looking at me and smiling. He looked at me expectantly.

I opened my mouth, and he fed me. It continued that way. He fed me, then himself, then me again. Occasionally, he brushed his fingers at my sides, and I let out a loud giggle. I was very ticklish.

Throughout dinner, no one spoke other than my occasional giggles and Damien's small laughs.

The dinner nearly came to an end when Alpha Mason spoke.

"Omegas did a great job today. The food was good."

The Omegas didn't hesitate before smiling and saying thank you and taking all the credit.

I let them pass like always, not like I could do anything. But Damien had other plans.

"Actually, my mate Isabella and I made all the food today, Alpha Mason. Your Omegas were either a bit too late for their work or they are dependent on my Bella," Damien said.

Alpha Mason cleared his throat.

"Well, the food is delicious, Alpha Damien and Isabella," Alpha Mason said.

"It had to be! We made it together, so there was a lot of love in it!" Damien said with a closed mouth smile

Well, this is awkward...

# Chapter 12

**Damien's POV**

"It had to be! We made it together so there is a lot of love in it!" I said with a forced smile. I want everyone to know.

I noticed Bella shifting uncomfortably, looking down on her lap. I know she's not used to eating with everyone and gaining attention, but I just couldn't help it. I want to show everyone that she is not something to be walked all over. She is worth more, and I will practically print it in their brains if I have to!

"Baby, you want more? You only ate, like, five forkfuls of it," I asked her.

"She doesn't eat even that. We have tried our best to make her eat a real meal, but I guess she's just being conscious of her weight," a walking, talking cake said.

At the corner of my eye, I saw Bella unconsciously rub her flat tummy.

"And why should she be conscious about her weight? She is underweight if anything, she needs to eat food," I said, gritting my teeth.

"Obvious, isn't it? She's fat! Have you seen her stomach and thighs? God, so fat! Look at me, skinny and perfect size," she said

"Do you know who you are talking about and who you are talking to?" I growled

"Yes, but this girl does not deserve to be your mate. You two don't match at all! You and I would be perfect together, Damien!" she exclaimed, standing up.

"It's Alpha Damien to you. I didn't give you the authority to call me by my name! And no one disrespects my mate! No one!" I said, dangerously calm. I saw everyone shiver.

"Alpha, I guess we need to teach them a lesson," Nate said from where he was seated.

## Chapter 12

"Of course. Teach one, and others will learn automatically. Take her to the dungeons and treat her like my Bella used to be treated before me. Make her pay!" I said, glaring at her. Her eyes widened, and she started shaking.

"No, no. You can't do that!" she exclaimed as Nate dragged her out.

I did not respond. I don't need to.

I returned to my senses and looked at Bella with a smile, only to change it into a frown. Tears were filled in her beautiful eyes.

"Baby, why are you crying? Don't cry. I don't like it when you cry." She did not stop. Instead, she hugged me and sobbed more.

I ran my hand through her hair and kissed her head. "Baby, do you want to go to bed?" I asked.

She just nodded. I got up with her in my arms. We entered our room, and I tried to lay her on the king-sized bed. Tried. She did not let go of me. Not that I mind. I sat down on the bed and lifted her head. Her eyes were slightly red, and her bottom lip was trembling.

"Baby, why are you crying? Did I do something wro—" She cut me off by hugging me tightly again.

"No, you didn't do anything wrong. But you did something that no one had ever done for me. You stood up for me. No one ever did. Not even my parents." Her voice was muffled.

Wait. Her parents?!

"Your parents?"

"Yeah, they are the warriors; they stopped caring when I was five. Left me on the mercy of the pack." I never thought of her parents until now.

But how can someone do that to their child? If my mother knows about this, she will throw a fit about it. She is a typical mother. Now I think I'm so lucky to have loving parents and a pack—some don't. But my Bella won't come on the list.

She will be loved.

"Baby, don't be sad. The sad expression doesn't suit you. You look good when you're happy. And I'll do anything to see that

## The Unloved Mate

smile on your pretty little face. Come on now, smile, smile, smile," I said and tickled her sides. She immediately started to giggle.

We talked for a while and got to know each other more. We both have something in common. Our favourite colour is white. Our favourite fruit is banana, and we both are each other's favourite.

I smiled at that one.

After some time, she fell asleep. I tucked her in and kissed her forehead.

"Goodnight, baby. Tomorrow morning will be the start of a new chapter of your life. Which will be filled with love, care, and affection."

I changed into some basketball shorts and lay down on the extra bed facing Bella. I stared at her beautiful sleeping face. I was probably looking like a creep. But who cares?

She looked so peaceful. So calm. No fears, no tears. The way I like.

I sighed and eventually fell asleep. Dreaming of my Bella.

# Chapter 13

**Isabella's POV**

I woke up at five in the morning, like usual. I looked around and realised I was sleeping on the big bed. It was like sleeping on the clouds.

I saw Damien sleeping on the extra bed. I got out of the covers and made my way to him. I tried to contain my giggle when I saw him. He was so cute! He sleeps like a baby. Mouth slightly open, eyes lightly closed, and hopelessly tangled in the covers.

I didn't want to wake him up, so I went on my day. I took a quick shower in the Omega's bathroom and made a beeline to the kitchen.

Before I could enter, a strong hand gripped my wrist. It hurt. The person turned me around and pushed me to the wall behind me. It was Alpha Mason. I didn't dare look at him and kept my eyes downcast.

"You little piece of shit! You know what you have done!? You are so selfish! Because of you, my pack has to suffer!" He growled in a low voice.

"I-I don't k-know w-what your—" He cut me off by banging my head on the wall. I gasped as black dots clouded my vision.

"Don't give me that bullshit, you bitch! I know you convinced Alpha Damien to favour you! He is furious because we gave you what you deserve. You just had to gain his pity by acting as if you were in pain. But the truth is that you deserve all that you got!"

"Stop!" I heard a soft voice.

It was mine.

I spoke up. "Stop. I'm not worthless. I am precious. I have a mate that wants me. I don't deserve what you said," I said softly with a bit of confidence. I don't know where the confidence came from, but Damien said that I deserve to be treated like a princess, and you know what I think I believe him—a little.

"Did you just speak? Did you speak up to me? You bitch! How dare you?" He raised his hand to slap me. I hid my head with my hands in defense.

But it never came.

I saw a girl with short dark hair and blue eyes holding Alpha Mason's hand. She looked him in the eye. She was daring him. She did not look familiar; who was she?

"How dare you, you foul creature! Don't you have any sense of respect for women? How dare you raise your hand on her! I should kill for raising your hand on my Luna."

Oh? I looked at them, confused. Alpha Mason looked at her in confusion and anger. He raised his other hand to hurt her, but she kicked him. There. Hard!

Ouch! It must have hurt. He doubled over in pain.

The girl smiled in satisfaction.

"What is going on here?" Damien's voice came from a few meters away.

I stood rooted to the floor. He saw me standing in the corner, jogging towards me and hugged me. Then he turned towards the girl.

"Nina? What are you doing here?" he asked the girl 'Nina'.

"Oh, brother! When will you understand me? Were sixteen years not enough to know I like to give and get surprises?" Nina said.

"Well..." was Damien's smart reply.

Nina rolled her eyes at him and held her hand to me. "Hi, I'm Nina! Damien's sister. I'm four years younger, by the way," she said. I shook her hand.

"The mention of you being younger by four years was not required there," Damien said.

"Whatever." She waved him off.

"Anyway. Nina, this is my mate, Isabella, and don't you dare call her Bella. Only I can," he said the last part in a whisper. "And baby, this is Nina, my younger sister."

# Chapter 13

"Nice to meet you," I said quietly.

"OMG! I can't believe my idiot of a brother found his mate! I thought his mate would not be half as pretty as you! Oh, holy skittles! You're so pretty! You know I have so many funny and embarrassing baby Damien stories Mom told me, I can share them with you. Oh, God, we have to spend time together! We should go out for shopping tomorrow, or technically today—"

"Nina, breathe!" Damien said with a straight face

"Oh, yeah," she smiled shyly and hugged me, catching me off guard.

I eventually hugged her back.

"I already like you!" Nina said. I guess I got on her good side.

"But baby, what are you doing at such an ungodly hour? It's still dark outside," Damien asked.

"I wake up at this time every morning. To make breakfast. I didn't want to wake you up, so I just took a shower and came here," I said with a small smile.

"Why didn't you wake me up?" he asked. How can I tell him that 'Oh, actually, you looked cute while you were sleeping like a baby, that's why' absolutely not!

"Never mind this time, but next time at least inform me. I was worried," he said and I let out a breath.

"Hey, since I drove for so long, I guess you guys can take me out for breakfast. All three of us. Nate can join, too," Nina said.

"Hmmm, not a bad idea. We all can go and eat out at a diner or something. So Bella doesn't have to make breakfast," Damien said

"But I have to make it for the pack. You guys go, I'll be here," I said. I really want to go. I haven't stepped out of the house only once did I go to the city border. That too for groceries. A month ago.

"Oh, they are grown-ups now. They can cook their food. Come on? Please?" Nina said and pouted.

"Come on, princess! It will be fun! And we can get ice cream later!"

My eyes lit up at the mention of ice cream. I get ice cream once a year, on the Alpha's birthday. It's a tradition to give ice cream

## The Unloved Mate

after the buffet. I'm grateful for this tradition. I get ice cream. "Promise?" I asked

"Promise!" he replied.

I hugged Damien tightly.

"I take it. Do you like ice cream?" He chuckled.

"'Like' is an unimaginablely huge understatement! I fell into a deep tub of ice cream and loved it the first time I ate it!" I said.

"Okay, then."

Then his eyes landed on an unconscious Mason.

"What is this thwart doing here?" Damien asked.

"I was going to the kitchen when he grabbed and yelled at me. He was about to hit me when Nina saved me," I said, smiling gratefully at Nina.

"Damien, you should have seen her talking back to him. His face was priceless!" Nina said during a fit of laughter.

"Really? You stood up for yourself!" I nodded, and he pulled me into a big bear-wolf hug.

"I'm so proud of you, baby. You have to be confident like this all the time!" he said and kissed my hair, forehead, nose, and cheeks.

"Now I'll get you an extra ice cream for that," he said happily.

We talked a bit more in the bedroom where Damien and I are staying. Two hours. That's how much we talked. It was mostly Nina.

She is very cheery. She smiled a lot. She and Damien have nothing in common.

Except that both of them claim to like me.

After a while, we were getting ready to go out.

Nina gave me some of her clothes to wear until we go shopping.

I didn't look half bad. The green and white sweater was a bit big, but other than that, it was all good.

Nina was currently in the next room, which was given to Damien before. I came out of the bathroom and saw Damien casually lying on the bed with a pillow on his lap, flipping through different channels on TV.

He saw me and smiled. I smiled back.

# Chapter 13

"You know you look gorgeous when you smile. You should smile more often," he said and kissed me on the forehead before entering the bathroom.

As soon as he disappeared, I covered my face and giggled. He is so sweet!

At that moment, Nina barged into the room, fully dressed.

"Hey, girly friend! Let's get some food! I'm not going to die of starvation. I want my death story to be more interesting than that!" she said and sighed dramatically.

I raised an eyebrow.

"Oh, come on, where is my brother? I want to leave this place already. I hate it here," she said. Her eyes displayed pure hate and anger. But not towards me. For which I'm thankful.

These siblings can be scary when they want to.

"What happened?" I asked cautiously, not to offend her or, worse, make her more angry.

She sighed and chuckled. "Oh, nothing, just a walking talking poop bag and a toothpick came to me and started talking gibberish. They thought they were making fun of me, so I broke two eggs and poured flour on them," she said and laughed.

I couldn't help but chuckle. It would have been fun to watch.

Just then, Damien came out of the bathroom and stared at us weirdly.

"I'm not even going to ask. Knowing Nina, she might as well have dropped eggs and flour with a topping of jelly on someone," he said seriously.

That's when Nina and I lost it. We were full-on laughing now. Like when you laugh so hard, no sound comes out of your mouth.

I saw Damien staring at me with a smile. His eyes held adoration and love.

"What? Is there something on my face?" I asked shyly.

He shook his head and chuckled. "I was wrong. You look a thousand times more gorgeous when you laugh," he said, and I'm sure my blush could give tough competition to a fresh red tomato.

He disappeared into the closet and my attention went back to Nina.

# The Unloved Mate

"I have never seen him so happy. You mean a lot to him, Isa. He has searched for many years in hopes of finding a mate. Since he was a kid, he would tell us how good he would treat his mate. How he would shower her with chocolates, stuffed toys, or anything she would like," she said and laughed. But I know how deep the meanings those words hold. Even I dreamt those dreams.

"You know, once Damien came home with a crying boy. Damien found him at the park when he was eight and the boy was seven. He didn't have anywhere to go. Homeless. So Damien brought him home, took care of him, and told him that he could stay there all his life if he liked. He was Damien's first friend," she said with a smile.

"Who was the boy?" I asked curiously.

"Oh, you know him. It's Nate. His Beta. Our father's Beta did not have children, so when Damien took the Alpha position, he gave the Beta job to Nate."

"Ohhh" is all I could say.

"Yeah, my brother can be a thick head most of the time, heartless and cold. But from the inside, he is compassionate. More than anyone. But he never showed the emotions, though," Nina said.

Damien came out of the closet before I could say anything. "Come on, ladies; we will have breakfast, not lunch. Talk in the car all you want," he said while fixing his watch.

He looked hot!

*Really, Bella!? Where did that come from!?!*

He took my hand, and I grabbed Nina's hand, and we left the room.

The car Damien owned was like a dream. It was sleek black and had soft seats. I don't know much about cars, but I can tell this one was expensive.

I sat in the passenger seat while Damien drove and Nina at the back. I wonder why nobody was in the hall when we left. They should be up by now.

We made small talk throughout the ride, and after fifteen minutes, we reached a simple diner called Bellona's. We sat in a

# Chapter 13

booth, and while the siblings were boring their eyes with the menus, I took the time to look around the diner.

It had a modern and vintage look at once. I don't know how they managed to have this look. But it was working. It has a cozy and homey feeling. There are couches near the walls with big tables, and the rest of the space is filled with regular chairs and square tables.

"Baby? Have you decided what you going to have?" Damien asked me while looking my way.

"Uhh, I'll just have a cup of honey and cinnamon tea with a peanut butter and jelly sandwich," I said, looking at the menu.

"That's it?" Nina asked, tilting her head to the side. Her short hair dangling to the sides.

"Yeah—" I could not complete my sentence as a loud voice yelled in my head.

*WHERE THE HELL ARE YOU! WHY IS THERE NO FOOD IN THE KITCHEN!* Alpha Mason's voice rang in my ears. It felt as if someone had blown a trumpet in my ears. Then, the realisation hit me in the face.

I'm in some deep trouble.

# Chapter 14

**Damien's POV**

We were currently sitting at the diner and waiting for our breakfast. Bella ordered a PB&J sandwich and tea. She needs to boost her appetite.

"That's it?" Nina asked Bella.

Honestly, my sister eats more than me. So my mate ordering this tiny amount of food didn't process properly in her brain.

"Yeah—" Bella gasped and held her head.

What happened? I was by her side in a flash. Seeing her in pain is painful. Her eyes were unfocused, and I knew she was held in a mind link.

I cupped her face in one hand and massaged her head with the other. "Baby? Listen to me. Cut off the mind link. Come back to me," I said.

That worked. Her eyes were focused again, and I hugged her softly, cradling her gently in my arms. I let go and kissed her cheeks.

"Who was mind linking you?" I asked

"A-alpha M-Mason," she said, and I let out a low growl.

"What did he say?" I asked

"He yelled at me and asked me where I was and to come back this instant and cook breakfast. He sounds drunk." She was now sniffing slightly, and I started planning fifteen different ways to kill an Alpha and get away with it.

And being the most powerful helps.

I hugged her again, but it was cut short as I was ripped away. I was ready to kill anyone who dared to do this. I looked up and saw Nina standing in front of us.

"Damien, I guess we should go home. And Isa here sure needs a girl's time. So we head home now, and you take care of your stuff,

## Chapter 14

and we will plan something to cheer up our Isa here!" she said with a cheery smile.

The idea was not at all appealing. I didn't want to leave Bella when she was sad.

I was about to decline, but Bella interrupted me.

"I guess it could work. I never had anyone to spend time with. Nina and I will spend some time together," she said excitedly.

That brought a smile to my face. My mate and sister are so good with each other—two extremely important girls in my life.

"So you don't want me anymore! I get it! You want me for my sister!" I said in fake hurt and pushed my bottom lip out a little. I've seen people do that, so why not?

"It's not like that, Damien. I just thought spending time with you would be a good idea and you won't be disturbed by me. I am sorry, Damien if you felt left out and bad." I instantly regretted doing that. She looked like she was about to cry.

I just shook my head and pulled her on my lap, hugging her tightly. "Oh, Bella, I was just teasing. I have no problem with you and Nina spending time together. You can do anything you like, princess. No one will stop you. Okay? Now smile, smile, smile, smile!" I said and tickled her sides, making her squeal

We walked towards the front door. It was a little after the whole mind-link ruckus; we had breakfast peacefully and then left. The entire time, Bella was on about how we should eat fast and not anger out Mason, the monkey, any more than he already is. I tried to tell her that she didn't need to care. He can go to hell and fry himself to death for all I care. But then Nina convinced her to calm down by saying that we were already late, so being a bit late wouldn't do anything. And she reluctantly agreed.

Like the gentleman I am, I held the front door open for both the ladies. Once we were in, we were all surrounded by angry and hungry wolves.

I growled at them. They immediately backed away, except for one.

Mason, the monkey.

"What the heck! Where were you? You were supposed to make breakfast first thing every morning. But no! You have fun while we starve ourselves!" Mason yelled at Bella.

I was about to show him hell when Nina beat me to it.

"Oh, really? If you were so hungry why don't you tell your mate to cook something delicious for you? Oh, wait! She doesn't have it here to cook. Sure, she can't cook to save her own life. You pathetic excuse of people surviving today because of Isa over here. If it weren't for her, your pack would have been nothing but a pack of runts and down-class bitches and sluts!" She then showed them the finger, took Bella's hand, and made her way upstairs.

"Hey, wait a second," I called and jogged up to them. "Since I won't be allowed to your girl's day and I probably won't be seeing you till morning, I want to hug you good afternoon, evening, and night now." And with that, I hugged her with all my might. I kissed her forehead, eyes, nose, cheeks, and chin. I am going to miss her as hell!

She gave me a heart-stopping smile and turned to walk away, but I grabbed her hand and pulled her to me. "One picture? Please?" I gave a slight pout and said.

She nodded, and I brought my phone out. I took about six selfies together, three pictures of her alone. *These will keep me sane until you are back in my arms, Bella,* I thought.

Once she left, my smile dropped, and I heard a growl.

I turned and came face to face with Mason, the monkey.

"You have no right to take Isabella anywhere without my permission. She is my pack's Omega, and I will make her do whatever I like, Alpha."

"Well, we'll see about that. But honestly, I don't care what you think. You are the last person on my 'to care' list, if not there at all," I said, smirking.

"Yeah, and I don't want your care. Just keep this in mind. Don't mess with me and my pack." He growled.

"I am not here to mess with you. I'm here to make you and your pack a mess. And now, if you will excuse me, I have a very long and important day ahead," I said coolly.

# Chapter 14

As I walked upstairs, I turned around and smirked at him. "Bring it on, Alpha!" And with that, I turned around and started planning on how I could sneak on my mate. Or better yet, be a part of their plan!

# Chapter 15

**Isabella's POV**

When I saw Damien giving Alpha Mason that look, I knew it was the start of something terrible.

But before I could do anything, Nina pulled me upstairs to her room. When we reached the bedroom, Nina tripped on a stuffed panda and fell face-first onto the bed. She huffed and sat up Indian style and patted the place for me to sit. I sat next to her but could not get myself to focus on her words. What was going on between the two Alphas?

A light slap on my thigh stopped the train of thoughts in my head.

"I know you are not listening to me. What are you thinking about, Isa?" Nina asked softly

"What do you think is going on downstairs?" I asked back.

"I don't know what is going on there, but I can assure you that Damien knows what is good for us, and he will not do anything stupid. Relax, Isa. I can tell Damien would have already solved the problem and is now planning to sabotage our plan for girl's day!" she said confidently.

"How do you know what he is planning?" I asked.

"Oh, I know him! He is probably hunting for excuses so that he can see you," she replied.

"You can be wrong," I said, and she just shook her head.

"Okay, then. I will count to twenty, and I'm one hundred percent sure he will be here by then," Nina said.

I just shrugged.

"1... 2... 3... 4... 5... 6... 7... 8... 9..."

"Did you have your medicine, baby?" Damien said, poking his head from the door.

Nina burst out laughing. I let out a soft chuckle.

## Chapter 15

"Is there something wrong?" Damien asked, walking in.

"Oh, nothing. I just told Isa how you must plan to join us on girl's day. And here you are," Nina said, and I saw a hint of pink on Damien's cheeks.

"Ha, puff, why would I do that? I just came to check whether she took all her medicine," he explained.

"No, I forgot," I said, looking down.

"Baby, you have to take care of yourself. If you don't take your medication, how can you be healthy? I know eating bitter pills can be painful, but you have to take them," he said while searching the drawers for my medicine.

He handed me a glass of water and gave me three big tablets.

Eww!

I gulped them down individually and gave the glass back to Damien.

"Now that Isa has taken her medicine, you can leave. We are here to spend some girl time, FYI." Nina glared at Damien.

He sighed and came to me and hugged me one last time. He was squishing me in his arms. "I'll miss you. Don't have too much fun without me," he said.

"Ya, ya. Now go!" Nina pushed him out of the room.

"Don't forget about me, princess! I'll come back to get you!" he said dramatically.

"Bye, prince. Come back to me soon." I called after him.

He smiled, and I blew him a kiss. He pretended to catch it and kept it in his shirt pocket.

He was so cheesy and dramatic!

After some time, Nina and I were sprawled on the floor with blankets all over us and watching a show called *'Teen Wolves'*. It's really good. It's ironic.

We finished three tubs of ice cream that Damien dropped off earlier, as he promised—a few bags of chips and cookies. It was getting dark now. I checked the clock, and it said 5:30.

Nina and I cleaned the room, and before I could get out of the room, she grabbed my wrist and hugged me.

"Do you think we can go shopping tomorrow? You need clothes," she said.

"I'll ask Damien. Then we can go together," I replied.

"Okay, good night, girly friend!" she said

"Good night."

I entered Damien's room and the sight was hilarious. Damien was sprawled on the bed. His head is resting on the headboard. A sulking expression was painted on his face. When he saw me, his face instantly brightened, and he hopped off the bed and tackled me in a hug.

"I missed you!" he exclaimed.

"I was just next door," I said

"Still!"

He broke the hug and kissed me on the cheek. "You had dinner?" I asked

"Yeah, I brought my dinner here, I figured you would be already full from all the snacks. And just so you know, the food was horrible. Not edible. I had to settle for fruits and salad," he said, frowning and making disgusting faces.

"You must be hungry then! I'll go to the kitchen and make something for you quick!" I said and bounced to the kitchen.

I looked around and found some chicken. I made some grilled chicken and filled them in a taco with some sauce. I walked back to the room with the tray in my hand.

Damien was sitting on the couch scrolling on his phone. He saw me approach and smiled.

I kept the tray with tacos in front of him. He eyed them for a few seconds and then started eating.

He moaned at the taste, and I knew the food was okay.

"How is it?" I asked

He gulped the food and looked at me with a smile. "It's incredible! I have had a taco so delicious!" he said and kissed my cheeks.

He then continued eating until the tray was clean. I was about to carry the tray when he stopped me. He took both of my hands and kissed my palm and fingers. "These hands have magic in them.

## Chapter 15

Food was delicious," he said. The look in his eyes told me that the words were true.

I washed the tray and left it on the rack. I entered the room and saw Damien had already changed.

He came to me and gave me one of his T-shirts. I looked up, confused.

"Wear this. The material is soft. I know you are not comfortable in those clothes. You can wear my clothes till we go shopping for you. Here." He handed me the T-shirt and kissed my forehead.

I remembered something. "Damien, Nina was asking if we could go shopping tomorrow. If you agree. She wanted to go," I asked.

"Of course, princess. Be ready after breakfast. We can go after that," he said, smiling.

He smiles a lot. But it suits him.

I went to the bathroom and changed. The T-shirt reaches my knees, and the sleeves go past my elbows. I pouted. I am 4'8. I'm short, I guess. Or maybe, Damien is too huge.

I sighed and exited the bathroom. Damien laid on his stomach on the extra bed. I can tell he is not comfortable on the twin-size bed.

I sat on the foot of the bed and shook him lightly.

"Hmm," he responded, looking at me. "You know my clothes look better on you than me."

I blushed, and he chuckled.

"Damien, I think you should sleep on the other bed. This bed is small and uncomfortable for you," I said.

"No, princess. I'm very comfortable. You go and sleep there. I'm all good." He gave me a thumbs-up and rolled over.

"You know that bed is very big; we both can fit," I said, without thinking.

"What?" he asked, shocked.

"We can both share the bed. If you don't mind," I said.

He thought about it for a minute. "Are you sure? 'Cause I tend to cuddle with the pillows or maybe even you," he said, and his cheek became pink.

"Yeah, I'm sure we'll manage. Come on," I said and got under the covers.

Soon, he joined me. There was tension in the air. Both awkwardly lay on the bed.

Then Damien moved to face me and wrapped his arm around my waist. With my back against his chest, I moved closer and cuddled. We both relaxed and soon sleep took over.

# Chapter 16

**Damien's POV**

Sleeping next to my mate, holding her while sleeping, is the best thing in the world. I woke up before her and stared at her like a creep. She cuddled to my side, her head on my arm and her hand around my torso. I sighed happily and brushed the bangs out of her face.

*You are a treasure to me. Very precious.*

She stirred beside me, and I quickly closed my eyes, pretending to sleep. After a few minutes, I felt her soft fingers on my face. Her fingers traced along my forehead and nose, and when she reached my lips, I licked her fingers.

I heard a squeal followed by a thud and a groan.

I opened my eyes, and Bella was not there, then I looked down. Oh, God, she fell!

I poked my hand out for her to take. She gladly accepted it, and I pulled her up. She sat down but whimpered slightly. I guess she fell pretty bad.

"I'm sorry. I shouldn't have scared you," I said while rubbing the back of my neck.

She laughed beautifully and said, "Don't worry, I was just taken by surprise. So you were up the whole time, huh?"

"Umm, maybe, maybe not," I said and laughed nervously.

"Okay" was all she said and got out of bed. She got some clothes from the closet.

"Can I take a shower first?" she asked.

"Of course. No need to ask me, baby. You can do whatever you want," I said with a smile.

"Thanks."

I rolled out of bed and stretched a little. I went to the window beside the bed and looked out.

# The Unloved Mate

There was a big forest. I was about to turn back, but I saw something or someone.

Nina.

She was talking to a guy. He was not a rogue. He had to be from this pack. His back was facing my side, so I couldn't see his face. They finished their talk and left in different directions. Weird.

That's when Bella walked in, and I thought about talking to Nina later.

"You feeling good now?" I asked and took some clothes to change in after the shower.

"Yeah. I feel good," she replied and started to dry her hair with the help of a towel.

I had a nice warm shower and changed into fresh clothes. When I came out of the bathroom, I saw Nina with Bella. They were talking in a hushed tone.

"What are you planning, Nina?" I asked in a suspicious tone.

"Nothing!" She squealed and jumped in surprise.

"Bella?" I looked at her expectantly, hoping that she would tell me.

She just gave me the most innocent face she could muster, and I swear my heart turned into a puddle. Why does she have to be so cute?

"Okay, fine, don't tell me. Are you guys ready? We will leave after breakfast," I said, looking for my Oakley glasses. I couldn't find them. "Baby, have you seen my sunglasses anywhere? I can't find them!" I huffed and dropped myself on the couch.

"I guess." Not even a minute later, she was in front of me with my glasses in her hands.

I smiled at her and gave them a big, sloppy kiss on each cheek. "Thank you, baby."

I bounced downstairs, leaving the girls to do whatever they wanted. I sat on the living room couch and scrolled through e-mails. I also own a chain of hotels in different countries. What do you think I do for a living? I'm a freaking billionaire in the outside world.

# Chapter 16

My girls came down looking pretty as always. I stood up, and we made a beeline to the dining room. As usual, there were only two seats left, so Nina sat on one, and I occupied the other with Bella on my lap.

There was some minor problem back home, so Nate had to go back right then. So Nina is sitting where Nate sat the other day. These people don't listen, do they?

The food was served. The sight of burned eggs and mushy sandwiches made me sick.

*Are you seriously going to eat that thing? I'm out of this! I'm not touching this,* Nina mind-linked me.

I looked at her and nodded my head. I won't eat this shit, and nor is my mate! I lifted Bella off me and grabbed her hand before walking out. Nina follows behind.

"What happened? Where are we going?" Bella asked

"Did you see that food? It was not food. It was a pure disaster! I don't even give my enemies that kind of food," I said, completely horrified by the sight. Eating food is probably one of my favourite things, but they ruined it for me!

"So where do we go now?" Nina asked.

"Let's go to the mall, we can eat something there." And we drove off to the nearest mall.

# Chapter 17

**Isabella's POV**

While driving to the mall, I couldn't help but feel as if something terrible was going to happen. Aside from the bad feeling, I'm very excited! I've never been to the mall before. I only received a few old, used clothes from the pack, so I never had a reason to go.

Damien parked the car and got out. I was about to open the door when Damien did it for me.

"I'm a gentleman, remember," he said with a playful smirk.

I smiled and took his hand.

"Ya, be a gentleman for your mate and forget about your baby sister." Nina pouted, still sitting in the back seat, arms crossed.

"Aw, is my baby sister mad at me? Come on, Nina, I'm sorry. Here, you take my other hand." Damien extended his other hand and helped her out.

"Perks of being a baby sister!" Nina said quietly in my ear.

We giggled at her tactics. I wish I had a big brother, too, a caring big brother like Damien.

"Let's go, girls," Damien said, ushering us in.

The mall could be described in one word: amazing! It has everything I would ever wish to have.

As soon as we entered, Nina dragged us to Forever 21 to buy me some clothes.

Damien said to buy anything that caught my eye. Money is not a problem. But I can't just spend so much of his money on me, so I just picked a pair of flowy tops, one One Direction T-shirt, and two jeans. I placed my clothes on the counter. The person was about to pack the stuff when Nina came out with many clothes in her hands.

"Pack these, too." She huffed and dumped them on the counter.

"Nina?" I asked

# Chapter 17

"Oh, don't worry, these are your clothes. Damien chose all of them, and I just carried them here."

My jaw practically hit the floor, and my eyes were wide open. "They are probably more than one hundred pairs of clothing, Nina!" I exclaimed.

"Maybe more. Damien saw you pick only a few, so he made it a mission to buy everything that he thought would look good on you," she said with a squeal and bright smile.

"That would be two thousand sixty-seven dollars and sixty-five cents, miss," the cashier said, and my eyes widened.

"That's it?" Nina asked in confusion. "I thought it would go up to three grand or something, but anyhow. We have to find Damien to pay for them now."

"No need to find me, I'm here." Damien appeared with some more dresses in his hand.

"Damien?" I asked, my face showing pure horror.

"What?" he asked innocently.

"What are you doing?" I whispered.

"Shopping for my princess since she won't do it herself. You know, I think I saw a nice dress at the rack behind somewhere—"

"Don't you dare! You know how much that cost! Two thousand sixty-seven dollars and sixty-five cents! We can't add any more. We have to reduce some!" I said, pointing my finger at him.

He only gave me an amused look and told the cashier to pack the ones he brought. The person was more than happy to do that. I just pouted and crossed my arms.

By the time we almost finished shopping, it was already 3:30. And don't get me started on the money spent. I was exhausted, and my feet were killing me.

"Uhhh…" My legs almost gave out, but Damien, being my saviour, saved me.

"Baby, you look so tired. Let's go home, okay? We can continue another time," he said, holding me up by my waist. His touch spread warmth through my body, and I felt somewhat relaxed.

"But… but we didn't go to a very important place! It will be the last, I swear!" Nina said, bouncing on her feet.

"But I can't walk anymore, Nina. If I do, I'm sure I won't be able to walk for a month!" I said, giving a sad face.

"But it's important! Let's go!" she said and walked ahead.

"Come on, hop on my back. I'll carry you," Damien said, turning around.

"No. My weight will crush you!" I said. Yes, I gained so much weight in just a week. I gained three pounds!

"Baby, are you kidding me? You weigh nothing more than a feather!" He chuckled and lifted me on his back.

He placed his hand under my thighs and my hands around his neck.

Most of the bags were already in the car because we could not carry them all. And the rest were with Nina.

We soon found Nina. But the store where she stood made my cheeks burn like fire. She had to go to Victoria's Secret! She saw us and waved. I could tell that Damien was getting uncomfortable.

"I see you got yourself a ride, huh?" Nina said and wiggled her eyebrows.

I blushed and hid my face in Damien's shoulder.

"Her feet were aching, Nina. The least I could do is carry her," he replied.

"Okay, then, let's go inside," she said.

"And Damien, you can come with us if you want. But if not, why don't you make yourself useful and bring lunch while we are here?" Nina said innocently.

Damien reluctantly let me down and faced me. "Baby, it won't take long, okay? I'll be back before you know it. Just shop for whatever you want and meet me here, okay?" he said, and I nodded.

"And what do you want for lunch or late lunch?" he asked me.

I just shrugged my shoulder and smiled.

"I'll get pizza then?"

I nodded. Pizza sounds good.

He blew me a kiss and smiled before turning around.

# Chapter 17

I didn't notice when Nina came and dragged me to the store.

"He's whipped! Like totally. He can't get enough of you! But I can tell why. You are everything he wished for!" She gushed and picked a pair of underwear before making a disgusted face and putting it back on the shelf

"He wished for a mate like me?" Why would he wish for someone like me?

"He would tell us how his mate will be the cutest thing ever! She would be kind and generous. You fit perfectly in all of these. I wouldn't be surprised if he had already prepared the box full of toys and chocolates," she said, putting things in the cart.

"Huh?"

"It was on his to-do list for when he found his mate. He made it when he was six. Dad helped him; Damien said he would give his mate all his toys and chocolates once he met her. He kept all his toys as good as new till this date." She laughed.

I found it sweet. Damien looks so tough and scary from the outside, but from the inside, he is so soft.

I'm lucky to be his mate.

We continued shopping for more... underclothes when I felt the need to use the restroom.

"Hey, Nina, I'm going to the restroom, okay? I will come back fast." I saw her nod, and I went to find the restroom.

It was at the far end. I quickly did my business and washed my hands. I took a step out when suddenly a sharp pain shot up on the left side of my head. I touched it and saw blood dripping on the floor. My vision became blurry, and the last thing I saw and heard was a silhouette of a man and his laugh before I slipped into darkness.

# Chapter 18

**Damien's POV**

I didn't want to leave Bella, but the thought of entering that store felt uncomfortable. So I left to get the girls some food. I know Bella is tired, and I know how to take all the pain away.

I went to a local pizza house and ordered the food. In fifteen minutes, the pizzas were handed over to me. I was making my way back when I saw a jewelry shop. A small ruby pendant caught my eye. The ruby were cut in heart shapes and were shining in the light.

*It would look beautiful on Bella,* Dom said in my head.

*Yeah,* I replied.

I quickly entered the store and told the man on the counter to pack the set. I told him to wrap it in a nice gift wrap. I took the box and hid it under my shirt. I will give it to Bella when we reach home. I know she will like it. I reached the store and saw Nina standing alone, looking everywhere. Where is Bella?

"Nina, where is Bella?" I asked

"She said she is going to the restroom. But I guess she's taking her time," Nina said

But I don't have a good feeling about it.

"Let me just go and check," Nina said.

"I'll come with you. I'll stand outside."

"Okay."

We made our way to the restroom and were immediately hit by the scent of blood. I saw blood on the floor and sensed Bella's scent lingering in the air, along with a foul, pungent smell.

Rogue.

They took Bella!! Oh, God! Why did I leave her side? It's all my fault! She doesn't know how to defend herself. If they even touch a single hair on her head, I will burn them alive.

## Chapter 18

I snap out of my thoughts when I see Nina pick up something. It's a note. Nina reads it and starts sobbing. I snatch the note out of her hands and read it. My blood boils as I read it.

How dare he! He took her! Because of what happened years ago, which had nothing to do with Bella! He will pay!

*I'm coming to get you, Bella, hang on.* I mind-linked Nate to get the best worriers from the pack and meet me near the mall.

I will find her and end this stupid chase once and for all.

The note:

I know you are probably looking for your mate now, so to ease your worries, I left this note. I still remember that day three years ago, and I won't let you forget it too. You will suffer as much as I did.

Best wishes,
Adam

# Chapter 19

**Isabella's POV**

I woke up with a heavy headache. I sat up and groaned; I looked around the unfamiliar surroundings and panicked. Where am I? Then I remembered the attack. Someone took me! They kidnapped me. But I don't think kidnappers keep their victims in such a beautiful room.

The door opened, and a lady, probably around fifty, came in with a warm smile. I didn't know what to do so, I just kept a blank face. She came in with a tray and set it in front of me.

"I see you up, dear. I'm Linda. I brought you some breakfast. You should eat, you are very weak," she said softly and patted my head before leaving. I heard the lock click, and I knew the door was locked.

I uncovered the tray. It contained pancakes, bacon, eggs, and a small carton of milk. I didn't realise how hungry I was until I saw the food. I slowly ate the food, and when I was full, I kept the tray aside.

Where am I? Who took me? And why? Oh, God! Damien! Where is he? Will he be looking for me now? Ugh! I'm so confused!

The door opened again, and a man with brown and blonde hair entered. He had a slight smile on his lips.

"Hi, I'm Chris. I'm assigned to take care of you. If you want anything, you tell me. Okay?" Chris said cheerfully. His nature reminded me of Nina.

I just nodded in reply.

"Hey, listen, I don't know why you are here, but whatever it is, you can't leave. Just cooperate, and then no one will hurt you. The boss is not bad," he said and gave a reassuring smile.

# Chapter 19

"But I miss Damien and Nina." Tears start building in my eyes as I think about them.

"Hey, don't cry. I can't see a friend cry. That's my weak point," Chris said, looking worried.

"I'm your friend?" I asked, confused. He is my kidnapper, and he is not supposed to be my friend.

"Yeah. It's my talent. I make friends fast," he said and snapped his fingers.

"Okay."

"So, what's your name?" he asked. "I'm gonna be around, so I need to know your name."

"Isabella," I said.

And that's how I made a new friend.


**Damien's POV**

Nate and some of the best warriors from my pack arrived at the mall. They all were pissed. But at the same time, determined. They are already protective of their Luna.

"Alpha, what is the plan?" Nate said in a serious tone.

"We know the person who kidnapped Bella. All we have to do is find where he is and bring my Bella back," I growled

"Who took our Luna, Alpha?" a warrior asked.

"Adam!"

Growls were heard from every warrior.

"We leave in an hour. I have a vague idea where he could be. After all, he didn't forget what happened three fucking years ago!" I exclaimed.

They all bowed their heads and left to prepare.

That thick head, Adam. He just had to take her. Just when I found her, and started to become happy. I have to end this for both of us.

"It's all my fault. If only I had not left her. If only I had gone with her, this would have never happened," Nina cried on my shoulder.

I stroked her hair. "It's not your fault, Nina. Don't blame yourself. It will be all right. I'll bring her back."

In an hour, we were all ready to bring my mate back. We all settled in three cars. The place was not far away. It is where the incident happened, where Adam buried all his humanity and became a heartless beast, where his mate died, and where he killed her.

**Three years earlier…**

*Adam was the Alpha of the neighbouring pack. Adam, Nate, and I were best friends. We did everything together, but Adam found his mate when he turned seventeen. Quite early.*

*He had a mate to care for but still spent every Sunday with us. Little did he know his mate didn't love him. She was there with him because he was the Alpha. I knew this the day he introduced us to Kayla. The way she looked at us, we understood she was up to no good. She always pretended to be blindly in love with him.*

*Once, Nate and I caught her red-handed with some filthy rogue. She didn't even deny it. But when we told Adam all this, he didn't believe us. He broke our friendship. Kayla told him that we were jealous of him, and that's why we are doing this.*

*From friends, we become rivals. He did everything he could to take us down. But I knew he was under her influence, so we only defended him.*

*Then the day came. He saw his mate with someone else. That someone. She was kissing him. It was me. I had to do it. For him to see who she was. I had planned it all. I offered her the place as Luna, which was much bigger than Adam's. I told her I loved her. But I was cautious. And I let her kiss me so Adam could see. She admitted all her dirty deeds in front of him. And he was left heartbroken.*

# Chapter 19

*He killed her on the spot.*

*I tried to explain to him why I did it, but he didn't listen. He thought I did it to ruin him, and he promised to make me feel the same.*

**Present...**

He still thinks I did that to hurt him. He was my best friend! Why would I do that to him? I just wanted him to see the truth.

We arrived—at the manor.

It was a mansion for the three of us. We received it from our parents when we were ten. We named it 'the manor'.

I was right. He was here.

I walked in from the front door. I am not afraid. I went straight to Adam's office. He was casually sitting on his chair. He looked up and gave a small smile. It was not a cunning or evil smile. A genuine smile.

"Damien. I was expecting you. Come sit," he said as if we were friends. After that day, it was the third time Adam had done anything. The first two times were small attacks on my pack.

"Where is Isabella, Adam? I don't have time for bullshit like this," I growled.

"I know you want to see your mate, Damien, and not to waste time. So please have a seat," he said, now serious.

I sat across him and looked at him expectantly.

He sighed. "I want to know what happened," he said.

I frowned. What?

"I want to know what happened to our friendship. Why did you do that to me all those years ago," he said with sad eyes

"I didn't do it willingly, Adam. You were my best friend. I would never do anything to hurt you. Nate and I caught her with a rouge, and we came to tell you, but you didn't listen! You thought we were jealous of you! When she started doing it more, we wanted you out of her clutch, that's why we planned everything. I offered her the position of Luna in my pack. Of course, it was not

## The Unloved Mate

true. But she was convinced, and then you saw us. It was all part of the plan. To help you see the truth," I explained.

"I'm sorry. I'm sorry I didn't believe you. I'm sorry I broke our friendship. I'm sorry I kidnapped your mate, but I wanted to know the truth. And I sent a message to you, but there were no replies, so I had to do this," he said.

"But why now? So suddenly," I asked.

"I found Kayla's diary in her box a week ago. It had everything in it," he said sadly.

"It's okay, bro. I understand now how you felt. I found my mate a week back," I said and smiled.

"I know. I saw her. She's a gem. And don't worry, she is safe and resting now. We didn't do anything, we just wanted to solve this problem and hopefully get my best friends back," Adam said. He had tears in his eyes.

I stood up and hugged him.

"Forgot about me, you idiots!" Nate said from the doorway and tackled us.

We laughed, and I called off the attack. I want to see my mate now.

"Adam, Isabella?" I asked.

"Oh, yeah. I assigned Chris to take care of her. I'll just call him," he said, taking out his phone.

"What? Who is this Chris? And why is he with Bella, alone?" I exclaimed.

"Relax, he doesn't swing that way," he said, and I looked at him, confused. He sighed again.

"Chris is gay!" he said.

Oh!

Then, a boy waltzed into the cabin and did a small salute.

"Hello, boss. Hello, boss' friends. I'm Chris, but you can call me Chris," he said and did a wave.

"Where is my mate?" I said straight to the point.

"Oh. She's sleeping. Come on, I'll take you to her." And he walked out with us following him.

## Chapter 19

He led us to a room and opened it. It was a nice room. A normal room. I saw a small figure sprawled on the bed. Bella! I was by her side in a flash.

She was sleeping soundly. I brushed some hair that had fallen on her face and caressed her cheeks.

She stirred and stretched like a cat. She is so cute! I couldn't help but smile. Her eyes fluttered open and landed on me.

I smiled when her eyes widened.

"Damien?" she asked as if I was a dream.

I opened my arms and nodded. She flew in my arms, and I chuckled.

"I missed you!" she said

"I missed you, too, baby, more than you can imagine," I replied and stroked her hair.

She looked at me smiling, and before I knew it, she crashed her lips on mine.

# Chapter 20

**Isabella's POV**

I don't know why I did what I did. It just felt right to do. So I placed my lips on his. I don't know how to kiss, but I have to try, isn't it?

Damien stood frozen. I am not sure if it's a good or bad thing. So I moved my lips a little, which seemed to bring him out of the daze, and he took control.

He held my waist with one hand and pulled me closer. His other hand tangled itself in my hair. I moved my hands and wrapped them around his neck. He licked my bottom lip, then he squeezed my hips a little and I gasped. He took the chance and slipped his tongue in my mouth. He fought for dominance and eventually won. Soon, I was out of breath and in need of oxygen. He pulled away rested his forehead against mine, his eyes were still closed, and licked his lips, smiling.

"That was amazing," he said in a husky voice. I nodded and looked down shyly. He removed his hand from my hair and cupped my face, making me face him. My face was burning. I could feel the blush on my cheeks.

"Don't hide your pretty face from me, baby. Don't be shy. We will be doing that a lot now," he said, smirking. I could tell my cheeks were a replica of tomatoes. He chuckled at my reaction and pulled me in a tight, possessive hug.

"I was so worried about you. From this minute, I will not let you out of my sight." His voice came out muffled.

"Damien, who were those people? Why did they take me?" I asked. He pulled away a little and held my waist.

"I guess you deserve to know everything," he said and continued to tell me about Adam, their friendship, what happened three years ago, and why they kidnapped me.

# Chapter 20

"So, now it's all over?"

"Yes, princess, it's all over, me and Adam sorted out our differences and are back to being friends. You don't have to worry about anything, princess," he said with a smile.

"Lovebirds! Dinner is ready!" Nate yelled from the other side of the door.

"When did they leave?" Damien asked no one in particular.

Then realisation hit me in the face. They were here when I kissed Damien! Oh, God, kill me now! I hid my face in my hands and groaned. Warm hands covered my hands and pulled them off my face.

"What's wrong?" Damien asked softly. He is so sweet!

"I kissed you in front of all of them! What will they think of me now? I will not be able to face any of them for months!" Damien only laughed at my explanation and shook his head.

I pouted, and he kissed me again—just a peck.

"It's nothing to be embarrassed about, baby. It was just a kiss. And I'm sure they will forget about it by the time dinner is done," he said, giving a charming smile. "But I won't forget it. After all, you took my first kiss."

I looked at him with a shocked expression.

"Yes, it was my first kiss, too, I saved it for my mate. I was fascinated by the idea of finding a mate since I was a kid, so I wanted to have my first experience with my mate." Now, it was his turn to blush. I giggled, which earned a groan from him.

"Okay, now enough talking, let's get dinner, you didn't even have lunch. Don't want you to starve now, do we, princess," he said and pulled me by my hand.

We reached the dining room, and the chatter immediately stopped, and everyone turned their head towards us. I shifted closer to Damien and wished the earth would open and swallow me.

"Nina? What are you doing here!" Damien's words caught my attention. I looked around, and sure enough, a smiling Nina was sitting on a chair.

## The Unloved Mate

She stood up and tackled me in a hug. "I'm sorry, Isa. I should have not left you. I'm so sorry. Please forgive me?" she said, pulling back.

"It's not your fault, Nina," I said with a smile.

"You indeed have a gem of a mate, buddy," a voice said from behind. I turned around and saw a man with dark hair and eyes, the same age as Damien.

"Baby, this is Adam, the one I was talking about," Damien said.

He smiled and extended his hand for me to shake. I accepted it with a smile. "Nice to meet you, Isabella, and sorry for the inconvenience."

"It's okay," I said quietly.

We all took a seat at the table and served ourselves. There was mac and cheese. I took a small portion that I thought I could eat.

But as I was about to finish, Damien added a few spoonfuls more to my plate. I was about to question him, but he gave me a stern look and gestured for me to eat it. I pouted but finished with surprisingly little effort. I flashed a victory smile to Damien, and he patted my head like a puppy. Everyone laughed a little, and I joined too.

After dinner, we all sat in the living room, discussing anything. "Hey, Nina, you didn't tell us how you got here?" Damien asked. I was cuddled to his side, seeking warmth.

"Oh, I was worried about Isa, so I was constantly mind-linking Nate for your location, and he finally gave in, telling me you were here, so I came as soon as I could," she explained.

Damien nodded and pulled me closer to his side, kissing the top of my head. Adam came in with a plastic bag in his hand. "Hey, I guess we should watch some movies! While having ice cream!" he exclaimed, and I squealed excitedly at the mention of ice cream.

"So, is that a yes!" He looked around, and everyone nodded.

We debated which movie should be watched. I didn't know many movies so I just kept quiet.

Everyone eventually decided to watch *The Conjuring*. It was a horror movie, much to my horror.

# Chapter 20

I hate horror movies, but Damien got excited about the film, so for his sake, I agreed.

Throughout the movie, my head was buried in Damien's chest. I only had a few sneak peeks here and there. I couldn't even eat my ice cream myself. My hands were too busy covering my eyes. Damien had to feed me ice cream, but he was not complaining.

Somewhere in the middle of the movie, I had an urge to go to the bathroom. I was too scared. I had no other option, so I poked Damien on the cheek. He was so absorbed in the movie that he didn't notice. I poked him again and again until his attention was on me. Finally.

"What's the matter, princess? Do you need anything?" he asked.

I shook my head. "I need to use the bathroom," I said.

"It's right at the end of the hall when you exit the living room, princess," he said.

"I know, but I'm scared," I said in a whisper.

He raised his eyebrows and tried to hide his smile, but failed with a big F. "Okay, I'll come along then," he said got off the couch, and held my hand as he led me to the bathroom. He switched on the light and motioned for me to go in.

"You go in, baby. I'll be here."

Trusting him, I went in and did my business. I finished and washed my hands. "Damien?" I called. No answer. "Damien?!" I called again. This time, there was shuffling out of the door.

"Damien, is that you!?" My voice cracked at the end. I hesitantly opened the door. And I sighed in relief. Damien was leaning on the wall, and his eyes closed. He was sleeping. I shook his shoulder a little too harshly.

"Damien!" His eyes snapped open, and he looked around for danger. Then his eyes land on me. He smiled apologetically.

"Sorry, I didn't know sleep took over." He rubbed the back of his neck and chuckled nervously.

"It's okay, but don't do that next time. I was so scared," I said with a slight pout. He kissed my lips and held my hands.

"Sorry, it won't happen again," he said.

## The Unloved Mate

We returned to the living room but halted when we saw the scene in front of us.

Nate is sleeping on the couch with his mouth open. But that's not all.

Nina, and Adam. Lips locked.

"What the hell is going on!?" Damien's voice boomed through the house.

Oh, God…

# Chapter 21

**Damien's POV**

"What the hell is going on!?" I was utterly horrified by the view in front of me. My sister and my friend! This is unacceptable!

Both of them sprang apart. Both are breathing heavily, their lips swollen and their hair messy. If I were any longer late, I don't know what they would have done. Ugh! I don't even want to think about that.

I felt a soft, small hand on my arms, and I relaxed a little. Little. I am still furious. "If you don't want me to kill someone tonight, then explain what is going on!" I yelled.

Both had the same terrified expression. Adam opened his mouth to say something, but Nina beat him. And the words that came out left me speechless.

"He's my mate, Damien. We are each other's second chance like you are Isa's."

I don't know what to reply to that. Nina found her mate on her birthday, six months from today. When she turned sixteen. Just like Adam, she found her mate quite early. He was the chief of the pack house. He was a good match for her. Though they were opposite, they balanced each other. But one day, the rogues attacked, and he died, saving Nina. It had taken her quite some time to get back to her usual self again, but she did. And now this.

I didn't say anything and sat on a couch, my face emotionless. I felt Bella sit next to me, I pulled her on my lap and inhaled her scent: honey and cinnamon. I calmed down a bit.

I finally came to my senses. "When?" I asked

Adam sighed. "Today, I came to the Howlers Pack to meet the Alpha. He needed our help with something. For some odd reason, he told me to come from the forest side. When I reached it, I felt

## The Unloved Mate

my wolf howl, and a sense of happiness bloomed inside me. Then I saw Nina coming from inside the house, and I knew she was my second chance. And I was the one she was speaking to when you saw us," he finished and Nina continued her part.

"I was restless that morning, so I thought of running. Then I saw Adam coming from the forest, and as he described, I knew he was my second chance. He tried to convince me to accept him, but I was not sure. After all, you and Adam don't get along. So I told him I'd think about it and left."

I closed my eyes and sighed. I looked at Bella. Just looking at her face calms me down. She ran her fingers through my hair, and I groaned.

"Okay then, what can I do when you two are destined to be together? Now that I have found my mate, too, I know how it feels." Both of them had a smile on their faces. Then I turned to Adam. "But if you hurt my baby sister in any way, I will cause some serious damage."

He chuckled nervously and nodded. Then my eyes landed on a dead-looking Nate. Seriously, this guy sleeps like a log. The world could be ending, and he would still be found sleeping. I shook my head and chuckled.

"Continue what you were doing. We are going to sleep," I said, holding Bella in my arms. She squealed but didn't protest. I still remember my room in the manor. Second floor, third room.

I opened the door, and as expected, the room was the way I left it: plain blue walls, white furniture and a golden frame on my bed. I always wanted to have a big picture of my mate and me together, so I brought the frame. I can finally fill it. It won't be empty anymore.

I closed the door with my leg and placed Bella on her feet. She looked around the room and smiled. She liked the room.

"Is this your room?" she asked, and I nodded. "It's really beautiful."

"Hmm."

There was a knock on the door, and I opened it while Bella made herself comfortable on the bed.

## Chapter 21

Nina was standing there smiling.

"What do you want?" I asked and raised an eyebrow. She made a sour face and stuck her tongue out.

"I came here to give you some of Adam's pajamas. And also I brought Isa some clothes before coming here. Bye." She huffed and handed me two small bags before turning on her heels.

"Who is it?" Bella asked.

I turned around and closed the door. "Nina brought some clothes for you before coming here and some of Adam's clothes for me." I gave her the bag, and she smiled.

I kissed her forehead and told her to change in the bathroom, and I will change here. I stripped off and wore Adam's clothes. They were quite comfortable. Then Bella came out of the bathroom in short shorts and a crop top. She looked heavenly!

She sniffed the air a little and frowned. Then she looked at me and her lips formed into an 'o'.

"What happened, baby? Any problem?" I asked. She just came to me and took hold of the T-shirt I was wearing and sniffed it. I frowned. What is she doing? "Baby, what are you doing?" I asked her. Her nose scrunched up adorably, and I was almost 'awed'.

"Who's clothes are these?" she asked, ignoring my questions.

"Adam," I replied.

She just shook her head and said, "Don't wear it. I don't smell like you." God, kill me now! She's so cute and innocent!

"Your wish is my command, your Highness!" I did a little bow and she giggled.

I decided to sleep in my boxers tonight since my Bella doesn't want me to wear Adam's clothes. I stripped off to my boxers and saw Bella covering her eyes. Oh, God, what am I going to do with her? I mentally chuckled. I slowly removed her hand from her eyes and kissed her cheeks.

"Baby, if you feel uncomfortable, then tell me. I will sleep in my clothes then, okay? It's no problem at all," I said, and she shook her head.

"No, it's okay. It's just that I've never seen a man so naked before," she said quietly, looking at my face as if avoiding looking down.

"Okay then, let's go to sleep, okay? We leave tomorrow morning. We can have breakfast on the way to your pack," I said and helped her under the covers. It looked as if she was drowning in the covers. I kissed her nose lightly and lay down on the other side. Switching off the lamps, I turned around to face Bella and wrapped an arm around her tiny waist.

"Damien?"

"Hmm?" I mumbled, my eyes closed.

"Where are we?" she asked. I opened my eyes and felt her turn around to face me. I brushed some hair off her face.

"This is the mansion our parents gave me, Adam and Nate when we were young. It is like our headquarters. We hung out here we spend most of the time of our lives here," I explained and felt her nod.

"Goodnight, Damien."

A smile formed on my lips, and I kissed her forehead again.

"Goodnight, baby. Sweet dreams."

# Chapter 22

**Isabella's POV**

A loud thud woke me up, followed by a string of curses. I tried to ignore it and snuggled into the soft fabric of the covers. After a few minutes, a gentle hand brushed my cheeks, sending sparks through my body.

Damien.

His large hand caressed my cheeks lightly and brushed the hair from my face. I leaned against his touch and enjoyed the feeling. "Baby, wake up. It's time to leave." His soft voice made me sigh in contentment. How can he be called cruel? He is such a sweet mate!

I mumbled some words that made no sense to him or even me. I heard him chuckle and kiss my eyes. "Wake up, princess. Everyone left already. We are already late." At those words, my eyes flutter open.

The first thing I see is the bright smile on his face. He leans in and gives my lips a short and sweet kiss that makes my cheek burn. It will take some time to get used to the kissing.

"What do you mean everyone left? It's so early," I said and got off the bed to use the bathroom.

"It's already noon, baby. You slept in." He called behind me.

I froze. Never in my life have I slept in. Once I did, I learned my lesson and never did it again. I look at him. "Why didn't you wake me up?" I asked and stood in front of him.

He was sitting on the edge of the bed, fully dressed. He wrapped his hands around my waist and pulled me between his legs. "You looked so peaceful while sleeping. I didn't want to wake you up, so I told everyone to leave, and we would leave later in my car," he said, shrugging his shoulders. "Now, get ready. It's a three-hour drive. They must have reached the pack house by now."

I nodded, kissed his head, and ran to the bathroom. I heard him laugh and let out a giggle of my own. I did my business and brushed my teeth. I came out and saw a dress laid on the bed for me. I pick it up, and some underclothes from the bag and get into the shower.

After getting ready, I go downstairs. Damien is sitting at the dining table with a plate full of food in front of him, untouched. He sensed me coming and looked at me. His eyes skimmed me from head to toe, and he opened his arms for me. I didn't hesitate before going to him and leaning into his touch. He adjusted me on his lap to make me comfortable, and we both ate silently—a comfortable silence.

After lunch, I packed whatever things were left here and there and met Damien at the garage. We got into his car and drove off.

During the drive, he held my hand with one hand and gripped the wheel with the other. I turned on the radio. 'Love Me Like You Do' started playing. I liked the song, even if I never heard it before.

I dozed off sometime later and woke up when the car came to a stop, or more like jerked. I looked at Damien with a frown on my face. He smiled at me and got out of the car. I looked outside the window and realised that we were in the middle of a gravel path; it was an unknown area. There was no sign of civilisation—only a few trees and flat land. I could make out by the colour of the sky that it would be dark in a few hours. We have been on the road for so long?

There was smoke coming out of the bonnet of the car. I could barely see Damien opening it and examining what the problem was. After a few minutes, he closed the bonnet and came in. There were black patches on his face. I removed the box of tissue from the dashboard and wiped the patches. He gave me a sheepish look.

"What's the problem?" I asked.

"Uhm, the car broke down, and I have no idea how to fix it." He sighed and closed his eyes.

"You tried to call someone? Maybe—"

He cut me off by saying, "I tried, but my phone has no network in it. And also, the battery is low."

## Chapter 22

"We could walk. Maybe we will reach the pack house before dark."

"About that, uhm, actually, uhm, I have no idea where we are. I was following the GPS. But somewhere in the middle of the drive, it stopped working."

I gave him an 'Are you serious' look, and he bit and chuckled nervously.

"What are we gonna do now?" I said, on the verge of having a panic attack. Damien sensed my uneasiness and pulled me on his lap. He stroked my hair with his large hand and hugged me tightly.

"Don't worry, baby. We will stay the night in the car, and in the morning, we can start walking and maybe find some help. I guess I have some packed sandwiches in the bag on the back seat. We can have that and sleep for now. I'm here, don't worry." His words calmed me down a little.

We ate the sandwiches and cleared the backseat to sleep in. We kept all our bags in the front.

Damien laid down on the backseat, leaving no room for me. I stood there staring at him. He noticed me standing there and smiled. Suddenly, he pulled my hand, which caused me to fall on top of him. He closed the door with his foot and adjusted me on top of him. My head rested on his chest, and his legs tangled in mine. His left hand was under his head, his other hand wrapped tightly around me. Almost possessively.

He kissed my head and closed his eyes.

"Goodnight, Damien."

"Goodnight, princess. Dream of me." That earned him a smack on his chest. He just chuckled and held me more tightly.

The warmth radiating from him was comforting. And before I knew it, I was deep asleep.

# Chapter 23

**Damien's POV**

The first thing I noticed when I woke up in the morning was the soreness in my back. Sleeping in the backseat of a car and having your mate sleep on top of you is not a piece of cake. I shifted slightly to make myself comfortable, but that didn't go as planned. Instead, it woke up Bella.

She shifted and raised her head, which was shoved between my neck and shoulder. I smiled at her, not wanting her to see me in pain. "Good morning, baby! Did you dream of me, as I told you to?"

She gave me a bright smile, but it soon turned into a frown when she sensed my discomfort. She got off me and helped me sit up. She eyed me with concern. She grabbed my shoulder and turned me around, so I was back facing her. She pressed her soft hands on my back, the pain decreasing with every touch.

Her hands were magical. I needed it. An unconscious groan escaped my mouth. She continued to massage my shoulders for a few minutes.

"Baby, I'm feeling much better now. Thank you," I said, giving her a bright smile, which she returned. I grabbed her hands and kissed her fingers and both palms.

"It's the least I could do. You had to sleep uncomfortably so that I would have a nice sleep. So—"

I cut her off. "Did you have a nice sleep, Bella?"

"Yes, very!" she said brightly.

"Then it was worth it!" I leaned to kiss her, but she moved her head to the side, which made me kiss her cheek. I pulled back and groaned.

# Chapter 23

Sensing my frustration, she only giggled, which was music to my ears. I did my best to suppress the smile threatening to form on my lips.

"What? Can't a wolf get his good morning kiss now?" I asked and glared playfully.

"Morning breath!" she said and shook her head, covering her mouth with her hands.

I grabbed her hand and pried it from her mouth, giving her a quick peck. I searched for a bottle of water, and as soon as I found it, I gave it to Bella.

She got out of the car and rinsed her mouth at the side of the road. I stretched my hands and looked around. I could only see flat land ahead. I have to think of something and fast.

Bella reached over and handed me the half-full bottle, and I washed my mouth. In hopes of fixing it, I rechecked the car. It was a hopeless case.

*Why did you buy such a useless car, you stupid oaf?* Dom said mockingly.

*How would I know all this would happen?* I shot back

*Do anything. Mate is not happy!* His words were true though. Bella was scared but didn't show it.

"Bella! I guess we have to abandon the car and move ahead. We can get help," I said

She nodded and smiled at me.

"Wolf form or human?" I asked her. Even though I don't want her to tire herself by walking, it's her choice.

"Human," she said with a bright smile, and I raised an eyebrow. "I just want to."

"Okay, if that's what you want." I sighed and grabbed the necessary stuff from the car in one hand and Bella's hand in another.

We walked in silence. We were slowly making our way through the isolated path. But the presence of my mate held me together. Pulling her closer, I slipped my hand around her waist and kissed her cute button nose.

**After walking for three hours...**

Bella was regretting her decision now. She was too worn out even to stand straight. We are walking for three hours straight.

At first, she was excited about the 'adventure' we would experience, and now she was sitting in the middle of the road with her legs stretched out, groaning lightly.

I chuckled and sat down beside her. I fished a water bottle from the bag. Opening the cap, I raised the bottle to Bella's lips. She took a greedy sip and sighed in contentment. I placed her legs on my lap and massaged them gently.

"Damien! What are you doing!?" Bella said, trying to take her legs off my lap.

"Trying to make my mate's pain go away, as she did to mine a few hours ago," I said, referring to this morning.

She kept on protesting for some time, but gave in eventually.

After I felt content with my work, I mentally patted my back when I saw Bella back on her feet, bouncing like a rabbit.

It was getting sunny. The sun was full-on blaring, and we were sweating like crazy. I removed my shirt and slung it on my shoulder. But I couldn't feel better. How could I? My mate was sweating before me, and I couldn't do anything. I slipped the shirt back on. I cannot let my mate suffer all alone. I will suffer, too.

After an hour, we came upon a mutual decision to sit beneath a tree and eat something. After finding a reasonably shady tree, we sat down. I searched the bag and retrieved a plastic lunch box filled with cookies. Why is there a box of cookies in the bag?

I gave Bella a look, and silently asked if she knew anything about the cookies.

"Nina made some cookies the day before we left. She asked me to keep it in my bag, because hers was full. I guess everything happens for a reason," she explained, took the box from my hand and handed me a cookie.

# Chapter 23

I shook my head but ate it anyway. After we had enough, we packed the rest and started to walk again. The heat was not as bad now, as it was a few hours ago.

The sky was a shade of golden now. This indicated that it was evening and soon it would be completely dark. And as if God finally took pity on us, I spotted a small light a few miles away. It looked like a pub from here. You know where big and scary guys go? Yeah, that.

My suspicions were cleared when we reached the source of light. It was a pub. The loud music could be heard outside, and I didn't want to take Bella inside. But I can't leave her outside either. The chances of finding a phone were slim, but still there. I took hold of Bella's hand, holding it firmly in mine. I turned to face her.

"Don't let go," I said sternly, and she nodded.

I opened the wooden door and cringed at the strong smell of cheap alcohol. Bella stiffened beside me, and I gave her hand a little squeeze for reassurance. I pushed past the huge bodies of drunk people and made it to the small counter where a scrawny and bald man was serving alcohol. He eyed Bella, and I instinctively pushed her behind me and held her wrist lightly.

"What would you like to have?" he said, and smiled, showing off his disgusting yellow teeth.

"We would like to use a phone please," I said, being as civil as possible, with these people looking at my mate as if she were a piece of meat.

"Ah, yes, it's in the backside. Just through the door." He pointed to an old, beaten-up tin door.

"Thank you," I said, and placed a hand on Bella's back, going through the door.

I located the old telephone in the corner of the small room. I placed the holder between my ear and shoulder and pressed the keys. It started to ring.

"Hello?" Nate's voice came from another side.

I sighed in relief. "Nate!" I said happily. I swear I was never this happy to hear his voice in my whole life.

## The Unloved Mate

"Damien! Where are you, guys? We thought you guys eloped to Vegas to get married! We were worried!" he exclaimed.

I rolled my eyes, only he could get these stupid ideas. "Nate, don't worry. We didn't elope anywhere. My GPS stopped working, and we got lost. My phone has a little battery remaining. Track down my number and come to pick us up. We are near a small, freaky pub," I said.

"On it!" he said and hung up.

"Is he coming?" Bella asked, I smiled and nodded. She sighed in relief.

We left the pub and found a tree, comfortable enough to sit under, waiting for Nate. It was already dark, and I could tell Bella was tired and sleepy from all the walking. I laid her head on my lap and slowly stroked her hair. She slowly fell asleep. I kissed her forehead. Sleep didn't come to me. I was on high alert for any danger lurking around or any sign of Nate.

It's going to be a long night...

# Chapter 24

**Isabella's POV**

The sunlight shines in my eyes as soon as I open them. I blink a couple of times to adjust to the light. I rubbed my eyes and found that I was in the backseat of a car. I raised my head and realised my head was on Damien's lap. I sighed in relief. At least he was with me.

He had his eyes closed and mouth slightly parted. He was in a deep sleep. I know he didn't sleep all night. He was on high alert.

I got off his lap and sat next to him. I peeked in the driver's seat and saw that Nate was driving.

He saw me in the rearview mirror and smiled at me. "Good morning, Luna. Did you sleep well?" he asked.

"Good morning to you, too. And I slept well, thank you."

"When did you find us?" I asked

"Oh, a couple of hours ago. You guys managed to have a detour. You had to head towards the west, but you went the opposite direction. Now, it will take more than two hours before we reach your pack house," he explained.

"Was Damien awake the whole time? When did he sleep?" I asked while stroking Damien's hair lightly.

"He fell asleep as soon as he made you sleep on his lap. He said he was exhausted," he replied.

I feel bad now. He was awake all night, and I was sleeping peacefully. He must be really tired. I sat on the edge of the seat and pulled his head on my lap. It was time to return the favour. His hands wrapped around my waist, and he snuggled onto my stomach. I kept stroking his hair to make him feel at ease.

Nate passed me a bottle of water and a wrapped chicken sandwich, which I took gratefully.

## The Unloved Mate

I looked out the window and sighed. So much happened in just a couple of days: my kidnapping, Adam, Nina's second chance, us getting lost. I'm exhausted. Physically and mentally. I pulled Damien closer to me and rested my head on the seat.

After a few minutes, Damien's stirring caught my attention. I looked at him and caught him staring at me with a smile.

"Good morning, baby," he said in his deep, husky voice. He leaned forward and pecked my lips before resting his head on my lap again.

"Good morning. How are you feeling?"

"Good." Then he turned his head towards Nate. "How long till we reach?"

"One and half hours more," he replied.

Damien groaned and snuggled closer to me again. I rubbed his shoulders and felt him relax under me.

"You are so amazing, baby."

I blush at the compliment. No one has complimented me before. His words make me feel weird things in my tummy. "So are you," I said back.

He looks at me and smiles, then kisses my tummy, making it all tingly and closes his eyes.

Oh, God! What is he doing to me? He always makes me feel like this. His smile ignites a strange spark in my body, and don't let me start on the kisses! It feels like a freaking zoo in my tummy. I take a deep breath and compose myself.

Before I knew it, we reached the familiar driveway of my pack.

"Damien? Wake up, we arrived," I said in his ears, but he showed no sign of waking up. I tried again and again but to no avail.

"Try calling him 'honey'! Might wake up," Nate said and got out the driver's seat to get the bags.

I thought about it. Let's give it a try. It won't hurt to call him that. He will not remember me calling him that if he doesn't wake up. And if he does, then mission accomplished.

# Chapter 24

"Damien? Honey, wake up. We are back," I said softly and kissed his lips, I pulled away, but he held my neck from behind and placed my lips back on his.

That sneaky devil.

He kissed me softly as if I would break. I kissed him back and closed my eyes. I was feeling that tingling in my tummy.

"Hey! Not in my car, you two!" Nate yelled from outside.

I quickly let go, and Damien pushed himself off me. He rubbed his face and licked his lips as if seeking an aftertaste. I blushed and opened the door. I straighten my dress and get out.

Damien followed behind me. Literally behind me.

Nina is sitting on the couch in the living room, watching *Sponge Bob Square Pants*. I shake my head and giggle. It catches her attention, and she spots me staring. She smiles and throws herself at me. If it weren't for Damien behind me, I would have fallen.

"Where were you two? You know how worried we were! How could you get lost when you have a GPS in your car!" she exclaimed when she broke the hug.

"Uhm, I don't know how, but the GPS stopped working. I took a few wrong turns, and we went in the opposite direction, then my car broke down, resulting in us getting more lost," Damien replied to her and wrapped his hands around my waist, hugging me from behind.

"Alpha Damien, Isabella, we are glad you are back safely."

I turned back and saw Alpha Mason and Luna Morgana approaching.

"Yeah, we are glad, too," Damien replied, rolling his eyes.

"Yeah, well, lunch will be served in fifteen minutes. Hope to see you there," Luna Morgana said and left.

"Oh, God, just being in their presence gives me a headache!" Nina exclaimed, and all of us chuckled.

Damien and I cleaned up and went downstairs for a much-needed lunch. Especially for Damien. He didn't eat anything since morning.

We entered the dining hall, and to my surprise, there were two empty seats at the table. Damien sat at his regular seat, and I went to sit on the empty one at the other end of the table, but he had other plans. He held me by my waist, dropped me on his lap, and continued eating as if nothing happened.

"Alpha Damien, there is an empty seat where Isabella can sit. You don't have to trouble yourself," Luna Morgana said, touching his hands and giving him a concerned look.

Damien was a little too quick to remove his hands from her hold and dropped a glass of juice on her. She gasped and looked at Damien, eyes widened. The juice left a horrible shade of orange on her white dress.

"Oh, I'm so sorry, Luna Morgana," he said, not looking least sorry. "And it is my pleasure to have my gorgeous mate sitting on my lap. It's no trouble," he said with a smile, mocking her.

The silence of the room was broken when a warrior came in running "Alpha, Luna, we are under attack!"

And all hell broke loose…

# Chapter 25

**Damien's POV**

"Alpha, Luna, we are under attack!"

When those words came out of his mouth, everyone stood up and started panicking. Seriously, these people need a break. We Alphas are trained to always prepare before the war, during the war, and after the results of the war. And here are they, hopping like kangaroos.

I was seated in my seat, having my lunch peacefully. But then I felt Bella shaking. Why is she shaking?

*Because they are under attack right now, she's scared! You buffalo! Stop eating!* Dom yelled in my head.

*Yeah, I knew that! And I'm not a buffalo!* I shout back. Most of the time we talk, we only yell at each other.

I tighten my hold on Bella and turn her around to face me. Her expression was of pure horror and panic. That did it. I banged my hand on the table, sending all the plates and whatever flying around the room, and everyone froze.

I cupped Bella's cheeks and gave her nose a small kiss. I looked around. Everyone was looking at me with weird expressions: anger, confusion, frustration, fright, and even joy.

"The warrior that passed the message of an attack, come forward," I ordered.

The man came forward, stood before me, and bowed.

"Speak. What happened? Exactly what you saw," I said

"I saw around three unknown and unusual wolves running in our direction and crossing our boundary," he said.

"And you assumed they were attacking! How have you been trained? Just because some wolves run into your territory does not mean they mean harm!" I sneer. These pathetic wolves.

"But—"

## The Unloved Mate

"But what? Because of all this, my mate is terrified!" I said and looked at Bella. Her big hazel eyes stared back at me. I smiled at her and held her to my chest, cradling her gently. "Don't be scared, princess. I'm here. No one will hurt you. You trust me on this, right?"

She nodded, and I felt my wolf grinning in joy that our mate trusted us.

I stand up and lay Bella on her feet. I held her hand and went to the main door. As the boundary came into view, I saw three familiar wolves just outside the boundary line, panting. When they saw me, they stood up and bowed their heads. They are more powerful and larger than other wolves because they have Alpha blood in them.

I mind-linked them. *Go behind a tree and put some clothes on.*

They obeyed and went to change. They all came back wearing basketball shorts and jerseys. The twin boys, Jared and Jacob, returned with their friend Michael.

All are grinning like fools.

"Alpha Mason, I want you to grant them permission to enter your territory," I said, more like commanded.

He nodded his head and permitted them. They immediately ran to me and hugged me tightly. All of them broke into a fit of laughter. And I cracked a smile. They got off, and they greeted Nate and Nina. They were gone for a long time, but now they were back. And I was beyond happy.

"So what are you rabbits doing here?" I always called them rabbits, because when they were young, they would bounce more than they would walk—all three of them.

"Oh, Damien, quit calling us that now! You very well know we are not rabbits now!" Jared said

"What are you doing here?" I asked again. Then I noticed how Bella was not with me. I spun around to look for her and found her standing near Nina. I sighed in relief and opened my arms for her so that I could hold her.

She took small steps but came to me. I held her in my arms and looked at the three musketeers.

## Chapter 25

Their eyebrows shot up, mouths hanging open. And an absolutely shocked expression covering their faces. I held my urge to laugh at their faces.

"Close your mouth, idiots!" I told them, and they shut their mouth.

"You."

"Have."

"A."

"MATE!"

They said dramatically. Why is my life filled with crazy people? Of course, leaving my Bella. She is not crazy.

"Yeah, is that so hard to believe?" I rolled my eyes.

"Yes!" They are impossible.

"Come in. We can discuss all that stuff inside," Luna Morgana said.

I tugged at Bella's hand, and we started making our way to the house. On the way, Bella suddenly lost balance. I caught her just in time.

"What happened?" I asked, concerned.

"I think I twisted my ankle. It's nothing." She waved it off, but I wasn't having any.

I picked her up bridal style, and her arms wrapped around my neck. I pecked her lips and entered the house.

Everyone was seated in the living room, waiting for us. It looks like the three made themselves comfortable, sprawled upon two big couches.

"Would you explain why they are in my land, Alpha?" Alpha Mason asked, eyeing them.

"Hey! Don't look at us like that!" Michael said in an offended tone.

"They are here to meet me," I said and plopped down on an empty couch with Bella in my lap.

"And why?" Alpha Mason asked.

I didn't bother to answer that. I placed Bella beside me and pulled her leg onto my lap, examining it and looking for any kind of injury.

## The Unloved Mate

"Because we didn't see him for the past four years," Jared answered.

Oh, God, there is a small bruise forming.

"And why now suddenly?" Alpha Mason asked again. He has a lot of questions.

"Because we wanted to!" All three yelled in his face.

I paid only half attention, though. There was also swelling on her ankle. It can get bad if not treated. I picked her up again.

"Damien! What are you doing!?" Bella asked.

"You managed to sprain your pretty legs, Bella. We have to make it better. I guess there is a spray in our room for it," I said, making my way upstairs.

I heard footsteps thundering behind us, and I knew all three of them were following us.

I placed her on the bed and brought the spray out. I carefully sprayed it on her ankle and covered it with a bandage. I looked at her triumphantly, but she was not looking at me. She was looking at the door. I followed her gaze and saw Jared, Jacob, and Michael standing at the door, arms crossed.

"Who are they, Damien?" Bella asked in a small voice.

I sat beside her and kissed her forehead. "Baby, they are my brothers Jared and Jacob, the twins, and their best friend Michael."

# Chapter 26

**Isabella's POV**

How many siblings does he have that I don't know about? First Nina, and now the twins. He doesn't tell me anything about his family.

Jared, Jacob, and Michael enter the room with big smiles. "Hi, beautiful mate of my brother," Jared or Jacob says, holding his hand out for me to shake. I reply with a small "hi" and shake his hand. "By the way, I'm Jared, and that serious one is Jacob. He's always serious." His tone changes from funny to serious in a matter of seconds.

"Hi." I give Jacob a small wave. He smiled back and gave a wave.

"That hunk there is Michael. He's our guardian angel. Saves us from all shit," Jared said and wiped a non-existing tear from his cheek. So dramatic. But I think they are fun.

"Baby, why don't you spend time with Nina and Nate? I'll get to you as soon as I finish talking to them, yeah?" I nodded my head, and he kissed me.

"Bye." I wave at all of them, and they wave back.

I skip downstairs to meet Nate and Nina. I see them plopped down on the floor with loads of junk food thrown on their laps and some shoved in their mouths.

"Hey guys, what are you doing?" I ask and walk closer to them, eyeing their mess.

"Hey Isa, did Damien finally release you from his hold? Finally, we can spend some time now. Join us. We are thinking of watching the *Twilight* series. Seriously, that movie is shit." Nina throws her hands in the air and huffs. I slid next to Nina on the floor, and Nate didn't waste a second before dumping a heap of food on my lap.

I look at him, and he just blinks at me giving me an innocent look. I wave him off.

"Hey, you! Can you put the DVD on that TV of yours? Thank you," Nina yells at a random girl. The girl has no option but to do as she says.

And so we start watching and eating.

**Four hours later…**

The Twilight sucks!

Seriously! I prefer a werewolf over a dead man, even if I'm half asleep! Why would Bella choose Edward?

**Two hours later…**

Great! Now she is dead and turns into a vampire, too! What about Jacob? He is so lonely, poor wolf!

**Half an hour later…**

I can't take it anymore! I'm done!

"Guys, I don't think I can watch it anymore!" I finally said, with a huff.

"Thank God!"

"Finally!" Both of them say at the same time. I look at them, and they have bored and frustrated looks painted on their faces.

"We were waiting for you to say those words so that we could end this drama," Nate says, throwing a handful of popcorn in his mouth.

"Yup!" Nina leans against the couch behind her and rubs her flat tummy. "Where is Adam? I didn't see him when he came back," I asked.

# Chapter 26

"Oh, he went back to his pack. I had to kick him out. He wouldn't budge. I said I would join their pack once I'm done here," she said.

Then my thoughts drift to Damien. Where is he? I should check on him. Maybe he got himself in trouble? Not that I can do anything about it. But still.

I go upstairs and enter our room. The view in front of me was so beautiful, I was almost 'awed.'

All the boys are sprawled on the king-size bed. Half lying on each other. Game remote controls are thrown in different directions. All look so cute!

Bromance!

"Aww…" two voices say behind me. I turn around and see Nina and Nate looking at them with baby faces. I giggle but cover my mouth with my hand.

"Let's take some pictures!" Nate whispers, taking out his phone.

He snapped pictures from different angles. While taking a picture from the side of the bed, I slipped on something and fell on it.

Nina and I froze. All the boys were groaning from Nate's weight. Michael opened his eyes and immediately threw Nate off the bed to the floor. The others soon woke up, too. Damien saw me and smiled. I smiled back. The boys got off each other and stood up. We all looked at each other and broke into a fit of laughter.

"Oh, Okay. Brother, I think we should get going. Mom needs us by morning, so we should leave now," Jared said, and the other two nodded.

"Aw, but why so soon? I didn't even get to know you guys," I said and pouted.

"Don't worry, little bird, we will meet you soon. And when we do, we will get to know each other well," Jacob said, dropping his hand on my shoulder.

Damien frowned and, not so subtly, removed his hand from my shoulder and pulled me to his side. "Mine."

All started laughing at that. Oh, God, he is so possessive, but I love possessive. I love him.

# The Unloved Mate

We walk them to the door and see them off. When they reached out of sight, we bid each other goodnight and went to our rooms. Since we all had loads of junk food, we decided to skip dinner. Anyway, it was too late for dinner. It was nearly midnight.

Damien removed his shirt, giving me a full view of his suitable pack. Hmm. I just shamelessly ogle at his heavenly body. What can I say? My mate sure is an eye candy, but only for me.

Wait. Where did that come from?! What is happening to me? Why am I thinking like this?

*It's the mate thing, Bella. You will be more attracted to him. And as confident and comfortable you get, the more the mate bond will affect your thoughts,* Nora said.

So I'm a bad girl now? I've always thought of having a mate but never thought about what to do when I find him.

Until now, he has been nothing but sweet and caring. And I know he will not change in the future. I can finally accept the mate bond and accept him. I gave him a chance. A chance to gain my trust, respect, and love. He has achieved all of them in just a matter of weeks. He even stayed here with me. Because of him, I could take a stand against my bullies. He gave me his love and treated me as if I was the center of his world. What more could a girl possibly dream of?

He made my dreams come true.

I realised I was standing in the same place and staring at him. When he stood in front of me, a smirk plastered on his face.

"You done checking me out, baby?" he said, wiggling his eyebrows.

I blushed hard and avoided eye contact, thinking of an excuse. "Umm, uh, actually."

"Don't be shy, baby. It's all yours." He gestured to his body, which made my cheeks burn like lava.

I giggled and ran to the bathroom to change. I could hear his laughing all the way here. He seemed to be amused by this. Hmm. I'll give him a taste of his own medicine.

I slipped on my short shorts, which are short, and a crop top, which shows half of my stomach and is a spaghetti strap. I had

## Chapter 26

been reluctant to buy them, saying they wouldn't be useful since I wouldn't wear them. But they came in hand now, I will have to thank Nina later.

I walk out of the bathroom and see Damien in bed, mindlessly scrolling on his phone. I clear my throat a little, not trying to seem obvious. I ignore him, get to my side of the bed, and slide under the covers, shaking my hips a little. I turned the lamp off and lay down. I finally looked at him and saw him staring at me with eyebrows raised and mouth slightly open. I brought my hand up to his face and waved it. He blinked and took a couple of deep breaths.

He turned the lamp on his side and laid down, facing me. I faced the other side. He placed his hand on my waist and pulled me to him. My back touched his rock-hard chest. I could feel his hot breath on my skin. He was really close.

"What was that baby? Were you trying to tease me?" He whispered in my ear, sending shivers through my body.

"Was it working?" I asked in the same whispering tone. He started to place small feather kisses down my neck to my shoulder. I almost made a sound but held it in.

"You have no idea what you do to me, baby. You are so clueless about your actions. Just a smile of yours increases my heart rate. I am so lucky to have you in my life as my mate." His words send a wave of warmth through my body, and my heart skips a beat.

How can a man love someone so much? Is that even possible? I couldn't ask for a better mate. He is more than the best.

His lips continue their assault on my neck, and he grabs my shoulder, laying me flat on my back. He hovers over me, still kissing and sucking on my neck. His lips leave my neck and capture my lips. The kiss is soft and passionate. He plops himself on his elbows to keep his weight off me.

His right-hand slides to my hip, giving it a little squeeze. A moan escaped my mouth, encouraging him. He bites my bottom lip, and I open my mouth for him. His lips slipped into my mouth, and

# The Unloved Mate

I started exploring. My hands find their way to his hair. I weave my hands through his soft, thick hair and pull him closer.

After a few minutes, we pull away, breathing heavily, in desperate need of oxygen. But he continues to pepper kisses on my jaw, neck, and throat. He pulled away and looked at me through hooded eyes. His smile matched mine.

"That was amazing, baby," he finally says and drops beside me.

"Yeah," I breathe out

"Then we should do it more often, don't you think."

I laugh at that. "Why were your brothers here? So suddenly?" I asked softly while one of his hands slipped into my hair and another to my waist, drawing patterns.

"They came back yesterday from New Orleans. They had gone for four years for some wolf training. So when they returned, they came here to meet me and received the biggest shock of their lives, that I got my mate," he explains, ducking his head between my neck and shoulder.

"I love you, Damien," I blurted out, turning to the other side.

His hands on my body go stiff for a moment. I knew it was a wrong decision. I should have never told him. Then I was turned around roughly, and again, Damien hovering above me.

His warm hands caress my cheeks as he looks deep into my eyes.

"I have waited so long to hear those words from you, baby. I love you, too. I love you so much!"

Then he kissed me as if there was no tomorrow. I love this man-wolf.

# Chapter 27

**Damien's POV**

Oh, my God, was last night a dream? That was the first thought that crossed my mind when I opened my eyes. She told me that she loved me. All my dreams came true with those three words. And not to forget the hot making out. It felt like heaven. Just thinking about it makes me hard down there.

"Good morning, Damien." Her voice is so angelic. She turned over to face me and smiled. I smile back and kiss her little button nose.

"So the sleeping beauty is finally awake. Good morning, baby."

She nodded and said, "What are you thinking so much about?"

"Just about how lucky I am to be with you. What did I ever do to deserve a wonderful soul like you as my mate."

She blushed and locked our hands together. "I should be thankful, Damien. I don't know what I would have done without you. I was heartbroken. I lost all hope of being happy. At a point, I even tried to end my life, but Nora didn't let me. I guess she knew you would come. My knight in shining armour." She ducked her head on my shoulder, and I rubbed her arm soothingly.

"I'm sorry you had to go through all that shit. I must keep you safe and protected, but I didn't, but I will make it better. I will shower you with so much love that you will forget everything that happened in the past. Don't get me wrong, love, but a part of me is glad that Mason rejected you. Now, you can be mine forever, only mine. Mine to keep, mine to love." With those words said, I tightened my grip on her and closed my eyes, savouring the moment.

"I'm glad, too." Her voice was extremely quiet and cracking at the end. I loosened my grip and pulled away a little, just so I could see her cute little face, now covered with tears. I quickly wiped them off and cupped her cheeks in my hand.

"What?"

"I'm glad that Mason rejected me. No one could love me, as much as you do, Damien. You loved me when I was covered in blood and bruises. I am weak, and you are still here. Anyone else would have left me as Mason did, but you were still there. I love you." Her words felt like a pinch in my heart. My Bella is so fragile. How could anyone think of hurting her? But again, I witnessed it, so I can believe it. But what I can't believe is what I have done to avenge her. Nothing. Those people hurt her, and I was waiting for a perfect moment.

"What a pathetic mate I am."

"Don't say that, Bella. You are beautiful now and back then. I love you, I was in love with you even before I met you. I always dreamed of a mate like you. Sweet, caring, selfless, kind, shy. I can't describe my love for you. My love has no extend, no boundaries." Then I kiss her with everything in me, trying to prove my love to her.

Knock, knock

A knock on the door made me groan in frustration. Bella pulled away, giving me one last peck. She hopped off the bed and ran into the bathroom. I slipped on my shirt and was ready to give the person on the other side a little piece of mind.

I opened the door and was surprised to see a young girl, around six to seven, standing there with a food tray in her hands. The tray was way too big for her little hands. I took the tray from her and looked at her with a small smile.

"What are you doing here?" I asked softly. She didn't look up and kept her gaze on the floor. She was shifting on her legs, and her hands were now locked behind her back.

"You were late for breakfast, Alpha Damien, so Luna Morgana told me to deliver food to your room. I'm sorry if I'm late, Alpha," she said in a quiet voice, which reminded me of Isabella when I first spoke to her.

# Chapter 27

"Okay, you're not late. What is your name, and why did you bring the food? You should have told someone else, pretty girl." I crouched down to her level and lifted her face with my fingers. She is such a cute little thing.

"My name is Joey. They told me they would give me to the monsters if I didn't do it. If I told them that, I would not do anything, and my mommy hit me. I'm scared." Tears start to form in her big blue eyes.

I heard a gasp behind me. Bella stood there with a hand on her mouth, keeping herself from sobbing, her tears falling freely down her cheeks. She jogs up to the door and hugs Joey.

I know what she feels. She sees herself in the little girl. These people are monsters. They don't have any sense of humanity left inside them. She is no older than seven! She is a kid! It's her age to play and have fun, not cleaning other people's shit.

Bella pulls away from Joey and gives a small smile. Joey smiles back, a cute, girly smile.

"Joey, did you have your breakfast?" I asked, and she shook her head 'no'.

"They don't let me have breakfast till everyone is done with theirs," she said.

I pull Bella up and pick Joey by her arms. I balance Joey on my hips and give the tray to Bella.

"Let's go and have some breakfast then, shall we?" I sit her on the bed and place the tray full of food before her. Bella and I sit opposite her.

"Come on, eat up, Joey," Bella encourages her, and she picks up a small pineapple cube from the bowl. I sigh and pick up a fork and knife. I cut the chocolate chip pancake into a tiny bit size, and bring it to her mouth. She stares at me with her wide eyes.

"Open up. Eat," I said, and she opened her mouth. I fed her a couple more times before she started eating by herself.

Soon enough, we were full. Joey giggles at something Bella said in her ear while I stretch my hands and legs.

# The Unloved Mate

Another knock on the door grabs our attention, and I have to open it since the girls seem to be in their world. They were laughing and giggling.

I open the door and see a smirking Nate. I raise an eyebrow and silently ask, 'What'. I seriously don't need any interruption today. I want to spend some time with my princess. Is that too much to ask?

"Your mom called." And my knees almost gave out.

# Chapter 28 - Part 1

**Damien's POV**

"Your mom called."

Why did she call? She would throw a big fit if she knew I found my mate and didn't tell her. You see, my mom is a typical mother. She is protective of her children and their mates. She loves everyone. She is not capable of hating anyone. So I'm sure she will love Bella. What I'm worried about is me. She won't let me off the hook, and I know Dad will join her. He is the puppet of her hands.

*You don't say. You turn into a love-sick puppy when it comes to our Bella!* Dom said in my head.

*The same goes for you, too, Dom.*

*Never denied it.*

I sighed and looked back at Bella and Joey, who were cuddled on the bed. They must be tired after all the fun they had. That brought a smile to my face. But I have things to take care of. I have to talk to my mother first. Oh, God, help me.

I tell Nate to go, and I will handle things. I write a quick note for Bella and exit the bedroom. I don't want to disturb her sleep.

I go to the rooftop and call her. Two rings and she picked up the call.

"Damien Jameson Owen! What the hell is going on? You found your mate and didn't tell me!" Mom shouted.

"Mom! I'm sorry I could not tell you right away. The situation was not good, and we had some problems here. That's why I had to stay here for a while. But I promise I will bring her there soon."

"What is her name?" she asked in a much calmer tone.

I sighed. "Isabella." A smile formed on my lips just thinking about her.

"Oh, such a sweet name! What is she like?!" I could feel her excitement from here.

# The Unloved Mate

"Yes, Mom. That's what you said when I heard her name. And she is so cute! She is very sweet, caring, and kind and has everything it takes to be a perfect mate and Luna. She's the best," I said proudly. My Bella makes me proud, and I will show her off to everyone.

"Just bring her here, okay? I can't wait to meet her. For the time being, at least, send a picture of her," she requested. I know my mom is really happy.

"Of course, Mom. I'll send you her picture. Tell me if you like it."

I sent her the prettiest picture of Bella. I took this picture sneakily. She was outside in the garden, surrounded by flowers and the sun shining on her beautiful face. She looks like a goddess.

I waited for a minute before calling again.

"OMG!! She is so pretty! You are one lucky man, Dammy!" I groaned at the old nickname.

"Mom! Don't call me that! And I know she's pretty, very pretty," I said, and I knew I had a broad smile.

"Damien, your dad wants to speak to you, and you better bring her here this weekend. For you know what," she whispered the last part. It was my parent's anniversary on Saturday, and she was hosting a surprise party for Dad.

"I will ask her, Mom. But she is not comfortable around crowds. And if she doesn't want to come, I won't force her. She's been through a lot," I explained.

"Okay, but please at least try. I want to meet my future daughter-in-law. Now I'm giving the phone to your dad," she said.

"Hello, Damien. How are you, son?" My dad's happy voice always made me smile.

"I'm perfect, Dad. How are you?" I asked and paced around the rooftop. I want to check on Bella.

"Good. I heard you found your mate. And I saw the picture you sent. She is really pretty. I'm proud of you, son. Keep her happy," he said, and I nodded. Then I realised he couldn't see me, so I gave him a 'yes'.

## Chapter 28 – Part 1

"Okay, then, we will talk to you later. Hope to see you soon, son. Take care of yourself and Isabella."

"Bye."

I hung up and made my way back to the bedroom. I opened the door and saw Bella sitting on the bed, staring at the walls.

"Baby? What are you doing? And where is Joey?" I asked and closed the door behind me. She looked at me and smiled slightly. Not a bright smile. I frowned and sat beside her.

"She left, saying she had work. I couldn't make her stay."

"Baby, is something wrong? Tell me. Don't hide anything."

"Damien, why is everyone so bad here? First, they mistreated me; now, it's Joey. Then, someone else. This will keep going. I don't like it," she said in a sad voice.

"Baby, don't worry. I will set everything in its place. Everything will be all right. No one will suffer. I promise," I said and hugged her. I shifted her on my lap and buried my head in her hair. Her head rested on my shoulder, and I felt her nod.

"I trust you, Damien. I love you." My heart soared at her words and a big smile replaced my frown.

"I love you, too. So much." I give her a small kiss and pull away from the hug.

"Baby, can I ask you something?"

"Anything, Damien."

"Baby, there is a party at my pack this weekend, and my parents want you to come. It's their anniversary. If you don't feel comfortable, you can refuse. No one will force you," I said, looking at her face. She seemed to be thinking about it.

"Okay, I'll go. But will you be with me the entire time? I don't want to be alone," she said with a smile.

"Of course, baby. I'll not leave you for a second. I'm so happy you agreed. My parents will be overjoyed that you said yes," I said and kissed her cheeks. And before I could say anything else, there was a knock.

"What?" I asked

"Alpha, it's me! Nate! Open the door!"

## The Unloved Mate

I'm sure he does that on purpose. Come on, he always arrives at the wrong time. "Come in. It's open."

Nate strutted in. With an evil smile on his face. Now what?

"Alpha, I wish to speak to you. Alone," he said.

"Okay," Bella said and got off my lap.

I gave her a last kiss, and she left, much to my dismay.

"This better be good, Nate, or I swear, I will break all your bones."

"Damien, you know what is today?" he asked, avoiding my statement.

"Today is the seventh of February two thousand eighteen."

"Wrong! Today is Rose Day!" he said

"Rose Day?" He was looking at me as if I was an alien.

"Rose Day! Valentine's week!" Then it clicked. It's Valentine's week. Oh, God. How could I forget?

"Oh, God! What do I do now!? I forgot! Nate, help me," I said. I have always wished to celebrate Valentine's with my mate, and when the chance finally arrived, I forgot!

"Don't worry. You're my best friend, I will help you."

Then we spend an hour surfing through the internet about ideas. It was useless. Then I figured out that if I wanted to make Bella feel special, I should do something original. And I know precisely what to do.

"Nate, I know what to do," I said with a smirk

"And what might that be?" he asked, narrowing his eyes suspiciously.

I leaned closer and whispered in his ear. After narrating the plan, I saw a smile forming on his lips.

He nodded and bro-hugged me. "She will be flattered, Damien! This is so going to work!"

I rubbed my hands together.

Now, it's time to prepare for the plan ahead...

# Chapter 28- Part 2

**Isabella's POV**

I left Damien and Nate to talk and went to the kitchen. I love cooking, so let's make something. Gathering whatever was needed, I started to cook. As I was stirring some vegetables, I felt a presence behind me.

"So, what did Damien get you?" a voice said behind me. I turned around to face Luna Morgana. I decided to ignore her.

"I'm talking to you! Hello!" she tried again. I finally graced her with my attention. Damien said that I was a princess and I should behave like one. Not to take poop shit from anyone. But now, she will not let me do my work unless she is done.

"What?" I asked.

She raised an eyebrow and scowled. "I'm your Luna. You can't speak to me like that," she said, and for a second I was afraid of what she might do, then I remembered, even I'm a Luna. Not of this pack, but the Nightfall Pack—Damien's pack. She should respect me, too.

"That goes for you, too, Luna Morgana, even though I am a Luna, Luna of Nightfall Pack. You will address me with respect, too," I said in a confident tone. I won't let them step over me, not anymore. I will make Damien proud to call me his mate.

"Hmm, so what did Damien get you?" she asked.

"Hmm?"

"You know today is Rose Day, the start of Valentine's week. Guys get their girls roses and make them feel special," she said and giggled, or I think she attempted to giggle.

"No, he didn't get me anything. He doesn't need to. Our relationship is based on love, it's not materialistic," I said. She just shrugged and smirked.

# The Unloved Mate

"Mason got me dozens of roses, all different colours. Isn't that romantic? He is so cute! He is the best mate ever!" Morgana said, and before I could reply, she left.

I know what she is doing. She wants me to feel jealous. She is jealous that she has Mason and that he showers her with gifts. But that it won't work. I don't need Mason now, I don't want him. I have a much better mate. Damien is everything I could ask for; he is the best gift.

I continued to cook, not overthinking about her.

Strong arms wrapped around my waist, and I knew it was Damien. He buried his face in my neck and inhaled. Then he kissed my cheek and rested his chin on my shoulder.

"I'm so proud of you. I heard your conversation with Morgana. You are so confident now, and it's a perfect thing. And you are right. You are the Luna of the Nightfall Pack. You are to be respected, and those who don't, they will have another thing coming," he said. I leaned into his touch and closed my eyes.

"Hmm."

"And, I think we should go out. A change of scenery will lift your mood. You know, just a small picnic outdoors. How does that sound?"

I liked the idea. "Yes, that will be good," I said, and he leaned in for a kiss. But before our lips could meet, a clashing sound made us jump apart.

I looked around and saw an innocent-looking Nate standing over a broken plate. He looked up and blinked. He then walked away.

"Umm, so be ready at five. We will spend some time, without interruption, and have dinner. Okay?" I nodded and he kissed my head.

"`Love you, baby."

"`Love you, too."

******

## Chapter 28 – Part 2

I was ready. I was wearing a simple pink dress. I tied my hair in a messy bun, and I was done.

Damien had some business to care for, so we didn't see each other the whole time. I exited the bathroom once I was ready and saw Damien patiently waiting for me.

He saw me approaching and smiled. His eyes roamed over my body. "You look like a doll, baby, so cute." He came and hugged me. His scent was so intoxicating. Heavenly, like fresh rain.

He was wearing dark jeans and a red button-down shirt. He managed to look like a runway model, even in a simple shirt and jeans. How did I get so lucky? I don't know.

"You look good," I complimented.

He took my hand in his and led the way. "Thanks," he said and smiled. We walked out, his hand securely wrapped around my waist. He led me to his car and opened the passenger door for me. He helped me in and buckled the seat belt. He sat in the driver's seat and started driving.

"Where are we going?" I asked curiously.

"Umm, not telling. It's a surprise," he said with an amused smile.

I became excited. This will be my first surprise. I never received surprises from anyone. I squealed and mumbled an 'okay', which only made him laugh.


**An hour later...**

I hate surprises! We are on the road for an hour now, and Damien won't tell me where we are going. My patience is wearing off now, and I want to know where we are going.

"We are nearly there, baby," Damien said, and I huffed. It's been like this for so long, and I'm getting hungry now.

"Okay, we are here," Damien announced, and I instantly perked up. I tried to look outside, but Damien didn't let me.

"Wait, baby. First, we need to tie this around your pretty eyes," he said, revealing a long piece of clothing—a blindfold.

# The Unloved Mate

I pouted but closed my eyes anyway. I felt him tie the soft cloth around my head. I felt his lips on mine in a quick kiss, and I smiled.

I felt him get out of the car, and soon enough, he was at my side. He took my hand in his and guided me through the unknown path. I clung to him for my dear life the air around me was a bit cold, and I shivered. Damien wrapped his arm around me, and I leaned in his warm embrace.

After walking for five minutes, we finally stopped. Damien pulled the blindfold off my eyes, and I blinked a few times. I looked in front of me and gasped.

We were in a big garden, with lanterns hanging on the branches of trees. There was a path lined with flowers leading to a gazebo. The place was filled with white roses, my favourite.

I clasped my hand over my mouth, and my eyes widened. I turned around to face Damien but found nothing. I looked down and gasped again. Damien was on his knees, holding a bouquet of red roses in his hands with a charming smile that made me all mushy inside. I swear I melted at that sight, faster than ice.

"Oh, Damien…" I honestly don't know what to say. I am too much in shock to say anything.

"Bella, Happy Rose Day. I wanted to do something you would like, but this is the only idea that crossed my mind. I hope you like—"

Before he could continue his nervous ramble, I launched myself on him. I wrapped my arms tightly around his neck and his hands firmly on my back. "I love it! You are the best! I love you!" I said, my voice muffing slightly. He chuckled softly and pulled away. He stood up, pulled me with him, and handed me the bouquet. I gladly accepted them and inhaled the fresh scent of the roses.

"The surprise is not yet over, sweetheart."

I looked at him. There is more? "What? There is more?"

"Yup! Now turn around." I turned my back to him as he said. I could feel his presence behind me. He held a hand over my eyes, silently telling me to close them. I did. I felt something cold on my neck. I opened my eyes and looked down at my chest, only to gasp again.

## Chapter 28 – Part 2

A small ruby pendant was wrapped around my neck in a golden chain. It was simple and elegant. I loved it.

Tears stung my eyes, and I sniffed. Damien held me in his arms. He lifted my face, and I saw a glimpse of worry in his beautiful, dark eyes.

"Baby, if you don't like it, you don't have to—"

This time, I cut him off with a kiss. The kiss was anything but gentle. It was rough and needy. My hands found their way to his hair and tugged on it, earning a groan from him. Our lips moved in sync. His lips moulded mine as if made for them. I moaned when his tongue swept on my lower lip, asking for entry. I gladly parted my lips, and his tongue slipped into my mouth, exploring every inch of it.

After a few minutes, he pulled away and rested his forehead on mine. I was breathing heavily like he was. A smile broke on his lips, and then he chuckled.

"What… so… funny?" I said, still struggling to breathe.

"Nothing, just really happy."

"Oh!"

"Best day ever," he said, and I nodded in agreement.

After our little moment, we had dinner at the gazebo. I was—again—surprised when he said that he had prepared the dinner himself. He went to a restaurant he owned and cooked there so I won't get suspicious.

After dinner, we walked around the garden, talking about anything and everything. We realised it was late and we should get going. He drove while I just looked out of the window, twirling the pendant on my neck.

"When did you get this?" I asked

"The day we went to the mall when I was gone to get lunch, I saw this pendant in a jewelry store, and I thought it would look good on you. But I never got the chance to give it to you," he said with a sigh.

I rested my hand on his free hand and rubbed my thumb over his knuckles. He smiled at me, and I smiled back.

Today was the best day of my life…

# Chapter 29

**Damien's POV**

All my effort was worth it. Seeing that bright smile on her face makes my day, and being the reason behind that smile gives me satisfaction. The most challenging part was the dinner. I know nothing about cooking, but the chefs at the restaurant helped a lot. And the result was good. After dinner, I gave her the pendant I had brought for her. Her eyes reflected pure happiness. I was happy to see her like this. I want her always to be this way.

We arrived at her pack house and went straight to our room. I know she is exhausted, and I am, too. We showered one by one. Bella wore one of my T-shirts and some shorts. She was drowning in my clothes but still looked adorable.

We snuggled together in the bed, seeking warmth from each other. I pulled her closer to me, her back pushed against my chest. Her scent was like an addiction, but I don't mind being an addict.

"Goodnight, baby, sweet dreams."

"Goodnight, Damien. Dream happy," she said in a sleepy voice.

I chuckled softly at her choice of words. She was indeed an adorable baby. I kissed her cheek and closed my eyes, and after some time, sleep took over.

******

"Damien, wake up!" a soft voice said in my ear, and soft hands shook my body. I knew it was Bella, so I teased a little. I grabbed her hands and pulled her on top of me, eyes still closed. As soon as she fell on me, I closed my hands around her body so that she wouldn't get off.

"Umm, let go," she said, but her voice was muffled.

"Umm, no!" I said and gave an evil laugh.

## Chapter 29

"Damien, I can't breathe," she said and took two long breaths. I quickly let her go and held her hand.

"Sorry, are you okay? I didn't mean to—" her laugh cut me off. I narrowed my eyes at her. She tricked me. That adorable little thing, I can't even get mad at her. A small smile made its way to my lips. I hugged Bella and sighed.

"You got me worried there," I said, and she just laughed. God, I love her laugh. "You should laugh more," I said, and guess what she did? Laugh.

"Okay, now get out of bed. Today is Friday, and I have to go shopping. Remember we are visiting your parents tomorrow?" she said, and I mentally face-palmed. How could I forget?

"Oh yes, I forgot. Now that Nina is busy with Adam, I will accompany you, baby doll," I said, flicking her nose.

"Hmm, I showered already. Now, get your butt in the bathroom before I eat your breakfast." She attempts to threaten me. But she failed. How cute.

I just smiled and kissed her. She squealed at my surprise action but didn't protest. I pulled away and gave her a sheepish look.

"Get up, Damien!"

It took me less than five seconds to run to the bathroom. I showered, brushed my teeth, and whatnot before I was fully dressed to go out.

Bella wore a simple white V-neck and blue jeans. I took her hand in mine and went downstairs for breakfast. I sat on my seat and pulled Bella on my lap as always.

Joey came in and served everyone. I looked at Mason and then at Morgana. Both were engrossed in a talk with each other. I have to do something for people here. People like Joey and Bella are defenseless.

"Alpha Mason, do you realise that a child, around the age of six-seven, is being forced laboured in your pack?" I asked in a stern tone, which I use when attending serious business.

"Yes, Alpha Damien," he answered.

## The Unloved Mate

I closed my eyes and sighed. He didn't even know this act was an offense in both the human and werewolf world—such an ignorant bastard.

"Well, Alpha Mason, if you don't stop these illegal practices, then according to the werewolf law, I have to arrest you, and you will be punished or, better yet, stripped of your title," I said, my eyes still focused on Bella, as I was slowly feeding her as always. Everyone looked at me with widened eyes and mouth open.

Yes, I have the power to do that. I am an uncrowned king. My family is respected throughout the continent, even the whole world, and we were voted to become the council—a council to keep the werewolf laws in action. To keep bastards like Mason leeched.

"Y-you can't d-do that," Mason stuttered.

"Try me."

He huffed and nodded in defeat, obeying my order.

"From now on, everyone will do their shit. No one is going to do your work for you, so you better learn to do it yourself," I said and finished feeding Bella and myself.

They all nodded, and I got up with Bella. We were planning to go to the mall because she wanted to get something for my parents.

We arrived at the mall, and she started looking around for an appropriate gift for my parents. She would ask for my opinion now and then. After two hours of roaming every store, Bella finally found a suitable gift for my parents. God, shopping is tiring. Then we brought some accessories to go with the dress she was wearing at the party. It was already lunchtime by the time we were done, so we decided to eat at a small restaurant.

We were seated in a corner table. The place was packed, but not stuffy.

A waitress approached us with two menus. I guess she wore her little sister's dress. It was tiny.

The moment I saw her, I disliked her. I kept my eyes focused on my Bella sitting beside me. I took her hand in mine and caressed it.

"Hey, what would you like to have mister." The sultry voice made my head ache.

## Chapter 29

"Baby, look at the menu and tell me whatever you want," I told Bella and gave her the menu. She scanned her eyes around the menu and sighed. She bit her bottom lip and turned to me. I raised an eyebrow expectantly.

"Um, I would like a bowl of tomato soup with crisp toasted bread with a side of mixed salad. Grilled chicken with BBQ sauce with a side of green salad for Damien. That would be all. Thank you," Bella said and flashed the waitress a winning smile. The waitress took our order and left, and that's when I broke out laughing.

"That was hilarious! Did you see her face? Oh, my God, Bella. I love you." I pulled her to me and kissed her forehead.

"I hope you don't mind me ordering for you."

"Oh, hush. I like that you ordered for me. And I like what you ordered for me," I said. Our order arrived fifteen minutes later and we dug in. The food was delicious but not as good as Bella's. She serves heaven on plates.

On our way home, it was silent. No one spoke. It was not an uncomfortable silence, a peaceful one. We just held hands and smiled at each other occasionally. We reached the pack house and went straight to our room. Nate was not here today. Mom had called him to help her with some arrangements. I have to return to my pack soon, and I plan to take my Bella with me.

Tomorrow after the party, I will ask her to move to the pack house with me. I hope she says yes.

After we were refreshed, we watched a movie and cuddled on the bed. It was now time for dinner. We went down and took our seats. I noticed that the dinner was cooked by the Omegas, and everyone was serving themselves. I mentally smiled.

We ate dinner quietly. Bella's eyes started to droop and was yawning every so often. I finished dinner and carried her upstairs.

I laid her down on the bed and changed my clothes. I didn't change her clothes. I didn't want her to think I was a pervert, so I let her be. Lying beside her, I pulled her to me and rested my head in the crook of her neck. Inhaling her scent calmed me down a little.

Tomorrow, she will be meeting my pack. My parents. I am not worried about them accepting her. I'm concerned that she will accept them. What if she's afraid? What if she thinks it's too early? Will she think I'm pushing her? There are many 'what ifs'. But I guess I have to wait until tomorrow.

With that thought, I snuggled into my Bella's warmth and let the darkness take over me.

# Chapter 30

**Isabella's POV**

I was a nervous wreck. I was calm on the outside, but inside I was freaking out. I didn't know the thought of meeting Damien's parents would affect me so much.

I can't believe how calm I was yesterday. I was happily shopping for gifts for his parents, and now I think I will pass out. What if they don't like me? What if they feel I'm not worthy of Damien because I was an Omega? What if his pack hates me? Oh, God! I am going crazy.

"Baby, you ready? We have to leave..." Damien poked his head from the door and said. His voice somehow mysteriously calmed me down a little. Or maybe the fact that he will be with me the whole time. I gave myself one last look in the mirror and sighed. I took my purse and opened the door for Damien.

I wore a light pink floor-length dress. It was a theme party. Ladies have to wear gowns, and men have to wear suits. Damien chose the dress for me, and I'm really glad he did. It looks pretty good on me. I wore diamond studs and the ruby pendant that Damien gave me. It didn't match the gown, but I'll never take it off my neck. It's very special.

"Woah, you look like a princess!" Damien's voice brought me out of my thoughts. He was looking at me with wide eyes. By the time he observed me. I took the liberty to check him out.

He wore a black suit with a pink shirt and a grey tie. I can't believe he wore a pink shirt. I thought he would wear a white shirt or something. Because you know, 'guys don't wear pink.' But he said he would match with me and he selected the pink dress.

He pulled me to him and kissed me, catching me off guard. I was stunned at first but soon responded to him. After a beautiful kiss, he looped his hand in mine and escorted me downstairs.

## The Unloved Mate

Everyone was staring at us. They knew we were going to his pack, and most people assured me that no one would like me there. But Damien said his pack will like me, and his parents already love me. I believe both of them. But I think Damien is more than them, so I am not that scared, but I can't help but be nervous.

Damien opened the back door of his expensive car and closed the door behind me. Soon, he slid beside me, and the driver started to drive.

It was an hour's drive, and I was already clutching Damien's hand for dear life.

"Baby don't worry. They already love you. You have absolutely nothing to worry about. Believe me," he said, squishing me to his side. I believe him, but I don't think so in my luck. I seem to have absolutely no luck when it comes to matters like these.

"I believe you." I placed my head on his shoulder, and he stroked my hair with his large, warm hands.

"Sir, we are here."

As soon as those words left the driver's mouth, I felt my throat getting dry. I took a deep breath and closed my eyes. I opened my eyes, and Damien gave me a reassuring smile. I smiled a shaky smile.

He exited the car and came to my side to open the door. I took his outstretched hand and got out of the car, too. The driver drove off to park the car, and we stood in front of a giant stone house. It had four floors and was all white. The front door was open, and I could hear the songs playing from a distance. Damien tugged at our intertwined hands and nodded towards the house.

I walked with him up the stairs, and as soon as we reached the entrance, I resisted the urge to hide behind him.

The room was the size of a ballroom, but it had to be the living room or the hall. People were spread everywhere, mingling and drinking wine. Everyone looked so... sophisticated, so good.

We stepped in, and someone tackled me. The person squished me in their arms and let out a low squeal.

"Mom! Let her breathe! Don't kill my mate yet," Damien said, and the person, his 'mom' left me.

## Chapter 30

"Oh, my God! You look much prettier in person! That picture did no justice to your beauty, honey! You are so adorable!" she gushed out. She looked around her mid-forties. She had dark brown hair and bright blue eyes. It was an odd combination, but it looked good on her.

"Hello. It's good to meet you dear. I'm Harold, Damien's father," a man who looked somewhat like Damien said with a warm smile and extended his hand for me to shake. I shook his hand and gave him a polite nod.

"It's good to meet you, too, Sir," I said and gave a nervous smile.

"Oh, no formalities, dear. Call me Harold or Dad. We are family. You are no less than Nina for me. You both are my daughters. You being an adorable one," he said and chuckled. I felt moisture build in my eyes and smiled at him.

"Of course, honey, you are family. And family don't do formalities. Call me Lily or Mom," she said, and hugged me, a much lighter one.

I tried to control the tears in my eyes, but being the stubborn creation of God, they had to flow down my cheeks. I wiped them before anyone could notice and smiled again—a family. I had a family now. I can't ask for more.

"Mom, Dad, why don't you guys attend your guests? I want to give Bella a tour of the house real quick. We'll join you soon," Damien said, and both nodded and hugged us once more before leaving.

Damien took my hand in his and gently pulled me with him. He guided me upstairs and into a corridor with three doors. He opened the first door and motioned me to go in. I stepped in and knew it was his room.

It was just so... him.

He came up behind me and hugged me. His fresh, minty breath is fanning my neck, his hands resting on my stomach. I placed my hands on his and leaned onto him. His arms tightened around me, and he sighed.

"Why were you crying, baby?"

## The Unloved Mate

Those words got my attention. I was going to tell him I was not crying when he cut me off.

"Don't you dare lie, sweetheart. I saw those tears on your face before you wiped them off. Is something wrong? You know you can tell me."

"Nothing is wrong, Damien. It's just that, I never had an actual family before. Nothing. And now, I have everything I could ever ask for: a family, and a beautiful mate. I'm just happy. Those were happy tears," I said and flashed him a brilliant smile.

"So you think I'm beautiful?" he said, wiggling his eyebrows. I rolled my eyes and shook my head at him. Of course, he would only get that part.

"Of course you are beautiful. You are the most beautiful man I've ever seen," I replied

"Oh, God, stop now. You are the most beautiful person, baby, inside and out." He laughed and held me in his arms.

"I love you so much."

"I love you more, much more than you can think, baby." He kissed my head and continued to pepper kisses all over my face.

"Now let's go before my— our parents send a search party to find us."

I nodded and followed him out. The party was in full swing. Some guests came and greeted Damien, and he proudly introduced me as his mate. All of them were surprised at first, but soon recovered and gave us their best wishes. Everything was going fine until someone decided to ruin it for us. It was so obvious that some girl had to come and flirt with Damien. And this girl was from his pack, so I can't tell her off, not that I can tell anyone off.

"Hi, Damien. Where were you? You were gone so long. I missed you. But now that you are here, we can—"

I cleared my throat and got her attention before she could continue. Can't she see that Damien is not interested? He is busy speaking to some older man, not even looking at her.

"Oh, and you are?" she asked in a not-so-polite voice, and I felt Damien's arms tighten around me.

## Chapter 30

"Hi, I'm Isabella, Damien's mate. A pleasure to meet you." There was nothing pleasurable about meeting her.

"Stop lying, you bitc—" Before she could finish, a voice interrupted her.

"Think first before you speak, Kelly. You don't want Luna to be upset with you, do you?" Damien said coldly.

"It's Sally, not Kelly! But I am the Luna. I already sent cards to my friends for the celebration. I know I'm your mate. I can feel the pull, Damien," she said, and the crowd went silent.

"Keep your hands off my mate, Sally. We both know he is not your mate. He is mine. So it will be better if you accept the fact and leave us alone," I said in a calm tone. Damien just tightened his hands around me and planted a kiss on my forehead. As if to prove my point.

"You heard her, now scram!" Someone from the crowd shouted, and the others hooted in agreement. By now, Sally looks like a ball of fire. You could see smoke coming from her ears if you looked close enough. Her face was completely red with anger, but she knew better than to go against her pack. She turned on her heels and stormed off.

"Okay, everyone, the drama queen is gone now, so enjoy the party!" Nate yelled from what looked like a DJ setup. I saw him put on headphones, and then the music blasted from every corner.

I turned around to face Damien, with a surprised look on my face. He smirked in Nate's direction, then shifted his gaze to me before pulling me to the area where everyone was dancing.

Nate played a remix version of 'Thinking Out Loud' by Ed Sheeran. We danced like crazy for I don't know how long. Before, we could not stand straight. Damien had taken off his jacket and slung it over his shoulder. It was already one in the morning, and most of the guests had left. Damien and I went upstairs and yelled 'goodnight' to everyone.

We flung ourselves at the poor bed as soon as we entered his room. We didn't bother to change our clothes and just cuddled together.

Today went well…

# Chapter 31

**Damien's POV**

I'm happy that Bella met everyone in my pack. It's been three days since the party, and Bella already insists on meeting them again. She is ready to come with me to my pack. She is comfortable around them, and they all seem to love her.

"Dammy, what are you thinking?" Bella says softly from my side. She heard my mom calling me 'Dammy' somehow, and now she calls me that, too. But she can call me anything, so I don't protest.

We were lying on the bed with blankets dumped like a heap on top of us. Netflix playing on the TV was long forgotten, and I was playing with her hair. Those are the softest locks of hair.

"Baby, would you like to move in with me, like at my pack house?" I asked her.

She shifts in my arms to face me and flashes me a wide grin. "I would love to stay with you. But don't you think it's a bit early? I just met them not even a week ago, and if I already go and stay with them—"

"Baby, my mom is practically threatening to disown me if I don't bring you to the pack house. My dad wants to meet his 'daughter' almost every day. The pack constantly asks when their Luna will join them, and the kids are getting on their parent's nerves because they want to meet you. Now, does that convince you?" I said and flipped us over so I was on top of her, my hands on either side of her head.

"Very convincing. I will go with you, Damien," she said.

I let out a sigh of relief. She was willing to go. I cannot bear to think what would have happened if she refused.

# Chapter 31

I leaned down and planted a small kiss on her soft pink lips. It was a small kiss that lasted only about five seconds before Bella pulled away. I frowned and looked at her. Why did she pull away?

"It's time for your workout, Damien, don't you remember? Now get up!" she said enthusiastically. How can anyone be so excited about exercise?

Two days ago, we had a small argument. Our first argument. I was unable to carry her because she was putting on weight. I told her it was absolute bullshit, but she insisted on us working out together. So she could lose her extra fat and I could build more muscles. And I agreed. Now we have to go to the gym and do God knows what. But as long as she is with me, I'll bear the pain.

I got off her and went to the closet for our gym clothes. I picked out two sweatpants for both of us and a loose T-shirt for her. I went shirtless, but then I decided against it and took a plain T-shirt. I gave Bella her clothes, and she changed in the bathroom. I quickly changed in the room and filled a small gym bag with water bottles and towels.

I slipped my phone into my pocket, and then I realised something. Bella doesn't have a phone. She can mind-link us, but she needs a phone. I'll get one for her.

Bella came out of the bathroom all fresh, and we headed to the small gym in the pack house.

There were only four people there: one boy and three girls. The girls occupied the three treadmills so I don't think Bella will go there. I pulled her with me to the weightlifting area.

We lifted some weights, and Bella was huffing and puffing within twenty minutes. And I, being the incredible mate I am, helped her lift them.

After two hours of exercise, I felt good. But Bella was nowhere near feeling good. She was sprawled on the floor, drenched in sweat and breathing heavily. I lay beside her and pulled her to me. I don't care if anyone sees me like this. My Bella needs me.

"Baby, relax. When we go to our room, I will give you a good massage, and all of your pain will go away." I kissed her sweaty

## The Unloved Mate

head and got off the floor. I stretched my hands out for her, but she started groaning. I picked her up and went upstairs to our room.

I laid her there and took a quick shower. When I came back, Bella was sleeping soundly on the bed. She is really exhausted. She will never think about working out, but she doesn't need to. She is perfect.

I left her sleeping there and did some pack work on the couch.

# Chapter 32

**Isabella's POV**

I opened my eyes and squirmed under the light coming from the window. I tried to move my body, but it felt like tonnes of weight was being kept on it. Every part of my body is throbbing. I groan at the pain and wiggle a little. I will never think about exercise again, at least not weightlifting.

I felt the bed dip behind me, and a large, warm hand caressed my hair. Damien. His hands slide over to my arms and gently press on them. I turned around and faced Damien, but I saw worry and concern in his dark eyes, which made me frown.

"What happened?" I asked, sat up a little, feeling much better after his touch.

"I shouldn't have let you do all that exercise. Look at you. You are in so much pain. I'm sorry, baby," he said, taking my hands in his and rubbing my knuckles with his thumb.

"Hey, why are you saying sorry? It's not your fault. I was the one who wanted to go. Now, if you want, you can give me a foot massage and ease my pain," I joked and wiggled my eyebrows. He looked at me and pulled my legs on his lap. He started to massage them gently as if they would break.

His hands can do wonders. He is so good at it that I had to suppress the moans threatening to come out of me.

After a while, I told him to stop and lay beside me. Honestly, I'm more than okay, and now I just want to snuggle with him. He slides in beside me and wraps his arm around my waist in a spooning position. I turn around to face him and smile as I catch him staring at me.

"How are you feeling now, baby?" he asked, planting a soft, lingering kiss on my cheek.

## The Unloved Mate

"Much better after your touch. You seem to take all my pain away, Damien," I said honestly. His face showed pure happiness, which made me smile wider.

"I'm glad to know that," he said, capturing my lips in a heated kiss. He pulled me closer and cupped my jaw with one hand while the other was firmly placed on my hip. My hands slip in his hair, pulling at them lightly. A soft moan of pleasure escaped my lips, and he growled. He slowly moved on top of me, resting his weight on his elbows. His expert hand threaded my hair, and the other rubbed my waist, creating a bubbling sensation in my stomach.

He slipped his tongue in my mouth and explored every inch of it. He tasted of fresh mint. My nails dig into his back, earning a groan from him. He spread my legs with his knees and settled himself between them. He was so close. It felt good. His lips left my mouth and started kissing my jaw and neck. I moaned and bit my bottom lip as he left open mouth kisses on my neck. I turned my neck to give him more access. He licked at my sweet spot when he was supposed to mark me and bit down lightly. It will sure leave a hickey. Wrapping my legs around his waist, I rubbed myself on him earning a loud groan from him.

I couldn't help myself. It felt so right. Touching him, kissing him, and simply being in his presence. I could feel myself getting wet as the sensation in my stomach multiplied, and I closed my eyes.

"Mark me..." I whispered in Damien's ear, and he froze. He looked at me through hooded eyes filled with love and lust. Eyes darker than before and breathing heavily. His hands caressed my cheek and kissed the other.

"Are you sure? I don't want you to feel I'm rushing you," he said breathlessly. I nodded and slammed my lips to his. His actions got wild now. He kissed harder, pouring all his feelings into a single kiss. I tugged his shirt away, leaving his eight packs on full display. This only seemed to make me hotter.

I felt his hands under my T-shirt rubbing my tummy. I was a moaning mess by now, and I couldn't take the distance my clothes were creating between us. I pulled my shirt off me, leaving me

## Chapter 32

only in my sports bra. I did feel a little self-conscious, but the look of love, adoration, and lust from Damien made all the insecurities go away. I felt his erection poking my thighs, and I smiled knowing, I had this effect on him.

"I'm going to mark you now, baby. It's going to hurt a bit, but I will make all the pain go away, okay?" he said and looked at me for assurance. I nodded, and he kissed the sweet spot on my neck, making me tremble under him. He licked it several times, and I felt his sharp canines elongate.

I tilted my neck more and he bit at it. I screamed out in pain and tried to move my hand, but he pinned them down. He removed his canines from my skin and licked his mark, instantly taking away the pain and replacing it with pleasure. I opened my eyes and looked in his dark eyes, filled with worry. His hand left mine and rubbed my hips soothingly.

"I'm sorry I hurt yo—"

"Shut up," I cut him off. Why is he apologizing for marking me?

He looked at me, shocked. I sighed and pulled him closer hugging me like a giant teddy bear.

"Don't apologize for making me yours, Damien."

He buried his head on my chest and sighed. His hands wrapped tightly around me. His bare chest was covered in a thin layer of sweat and radiating heat.

I felt my eyes droop. My body suddenly felt very weak.

"Take a rest, baby. Mark took a lot of energy from your body. Sleep, I'll be here when you wake up. Sleep." His voice sounded distant in the end as I gave up and darkness overtook me.

# Chapter 33

**Damien's POV**

I woke up with a face-splitting grin on my face. My mate was sleeping soundly, buried in my arms. It's been eighteen hours since I marked her, and she has been sleeping all this time. She must be exhausted.

I can't explain the happiness and satisfaction I received when I claimed her as mine. I cannot be described. I have to inform my parents about it. They have to start preparing for the new Luna's arrival. I'm not going to waste any more time taking my Bella with me. Fuck this pack. I'm going to take her with me.

My thoughts were interrupted when my Bella shifted in my arms. I looked at her beautiful face. My wolf howled in joy looking at the new glow that decorated her face.

She grunted and shifted again, this time to face me. I pulled her closer, bringing her body as close as possible. I rubbed my hand over her very exposed hip and felt her shiver under my touch. I peppered kisses all over her face to wake her up. She needs food in her system. She has not eaten anything for so long. Moving down, I left feather kisses on her jawline and neck. I can't get enough of her. She's like a drug, making me an addict and holding me captive.

Her hold on me tightens, which means she's awake. But her eyes were still closed.

"Wake up, baby girl..." I whisper in her ear in a seductive tone. She just grunted in response and pulled me closer, if that was even possible. She angled her neck for more access. She wants more, just like me.

"You want me to continue, baby girl? Hmm?" I whispered against her soft skin and bit down gently on her neck.

# Chapter 33

I have heard that once mates are marked, they can't get their hands off each other for a few days, and then the girl goes into heat on the full moon. And I now know what it means.

I am horny as fuck. I don't want to leave this bed and stay with her all the time.

She hummed in content and released a soft, small moan. Her moan was like music to my ears, only for me. Only I can draw that sound from her. The sound is like a switch, turning me on faster than light.

I climbed on top of her, held her hands on top of her head, and kissed her. The position reminded me of yesterday when I marked her. Just thinking about it makes my pants painfully tight. God, the things she does to me. She doesn't even realise she has such an effect on me.

The kiss was cut short by an impatient knock on the door. I groaned but didn't break the kiss. Others can wait. I want to satisfy my baby. I proceed to kiss her neck, but she pulls away. I look at her in confusion.

"What happened, baby?" I asked in a daze.

She was breathing heavily and smiling. "The door. Someone is outside," she said.

"I don't care. Let's continue, baby girl," I said and leaned forward, but the door interrupted us again.

I groaned.

She giggled at my condition. She thinks it's funny? I'll show her what's funny.

I tightened my hold on her pinned hands and tickled her sides. I captured her mouth in a kiss. She was having a hard time containing her giggles. I laughed and released her. She glared at me, and I pecked her once more.

Then again, a knock on the door. I hope they don't break it. Anyway, I don't care.

Getting off the bed, I searched for my shirt thrown somewhere by Bella. I found it on the ground and slipped it on. Bella didn't make any effort to get up. She was still chilling on the bed, now

## The Unloved Mate

wide awake. I noticed she was still in her sports bra. I pulled the cover up to her chin and covered her whole body.

I opened the door, and surprise, surprise. It's Nate. I don't understand when he is here and when he is not.

He had his signature grin plastered on his face.

"Do you always have to appear at the wrong time, Nate?!" I said, I didn't bother hiding the annoyance in my voice and glared at him.

"Don't look at me like that. Your mom sent me here yesterday to deliver something, but I guess you were busy, so I came now. But again, you were busy," he explained.

"You could have come later if you realised," I growled.

"I must return tonight, so I had to do it now. Sorry. Here." He handed me a small silver treasure-like box, waved at Bella, and left muttering to himself.

I shut the door closed and walked back to my Bella. I placed the box on the nightstand and removed my shirt. With a smirk, I climbed back on the bed and on top of Bella. "Let's finish what we started." I leaned in to kiss her, but she moved making me frown.

"What? Why?"

"Damien, what did Nate tell you?" she asked, and I sighed. I dropped myself beside her and adjusted my head on her lap.

"He came to 'deliver' something Mom gave him," I said. I took Bella's left hand and placed it on my head, and she stroked my hair. "It's on the nightstand."

"Hmm. Can I see?" she asked.

"Of course, baby. It might be for you." I closed my eyes.

After a few seconds, I heard a gasp and opened my eyes. Bella was looking at something inside the box with wide eyes and a slightly open mouth.

"What is it?"

She passed the box to me. I took it and was surprised to see the golden ring in it.

The ring was a heirloom, but not the same. It has been passed on from generations in our family. To the Luna's. It was said to be a gift of peace given to the werewolves. It is only passed on to

## Chapter 33

those the pack thinks it is worthy. Once the Luna meets the pack, a vote is held. Everyone votes and gives their opinion on whether the ring should be passed to her or not. My mom couldn't wait for her arrival to do that. I knew Bella would receive it one day, but I didn't expect it to be today.

"What is this, Damien? It's not what I think it is, right?"

"It is baby. The pack chooses you," I said smiling. She was smiling too, but a sad one.

"What's wrong?" I pulled her to my side and stroked her arms.

"I can't believe it, Damien. Is this real? It all feels like a dream I never thought I would be given this much respect and love from anyone in my life. Your family and pack adore me. I don't know how to thank them for this."

"Just come home with me, baby. That's what everyone wants. I want," I said and looked down at her.

She nodded slowly. "When do you want to leave?" she asked.

"Tomorrow, maybe? If you're ready," I said, unsure if she wanted to leave this early. She untangled herself from me and ran over to the closet. She pulled out two suitcases and dropped them on the bed.

"What are you doing, baby?" I asked.

"You said we leave tomorrow. We have so much to pack, Damien. Don't be a lazy butt, and come help me!" she said and pointed her finger at me.

That brought a smile to my face. I took my shirt off the floor and passed it to her. She was still in her sports bra, and if anyone was to come in and see her like this…

I helped her pack all the stuff. It was a lot of things. The clothes, shoes, accessories, etc. Mostly Bella's stuff. I had brought one suitcase full of my things once I found Bella.

In the end, we had three big suitcases, one traveling bag, and Bella's hand purse.

Bella decided to take a shower after me. She has been in the bathroom for the last forty-five minutes. I knocked on the door, and she opened it, fully clothed.

## The Unloved Mate

"What took you so long?" I asked curiously. I turned around and faced the mirror, trying to tame my hair.

"I was just admiring my mark. Now everyone will know I'm yours, and you're mine," she said, hugging me from behind.

I smiled and looked at her through the mirror. "You have no idea how happy I am to finally mark you. And I have always been yours, baby. All yours." I kissed her head and took her hand in mine.

"Come, let's eat something. We cuddled all day, and now it's dinner time," she said, and I just chuckled.

"Can't seem to keep track of time when I'm with you, baby. I want to keep you wrapped up in my arms, never letting you go."

It was her turn to chuckle.

As usual, we sat at the dining table, with her on my lap and me feeding her.

"Alpha Mason, I have something to say."

Everyone paid attention to me now.

"Yes, Alpha Damien?"

"My mate and I will be leaving tomorrow morning. I'm taking Bella to my pack. Permanently. So I want you to cut off the links with her so I can make one," I said.

Alpha Mason looked conflicted for a few minutes. What is he waiting for? She's my mate, and I can take her by law. He can't refuse.

"B-but... okay, fine," he said, closing his eyes to cut off the link.

"Good."

******

After dinner, I cuddled Bella to sleep like I always do. She has changed so much since I met her. Now she wears my clothes, the kisses, she doesn't hesitate to scold me, and more importantly, she wears my mark. Mine.

"Goodnight, Damien. Sweet dreams."

"Goodnight, baby. Sweet dreams."

## Chapter 33

I sighed in contentment. Tomorrow, she will be sleeping in my bed. Away from this pack. Away from the people. Near me.

# Chapter 34

**Isabella's POV**

I'm not that nervous about going to the Nightfall Pack. They are all family. I had never thought I would become a Luna someday. That, too, is one of the most powerful packs in existence.

At dinner yesterday, Damien announced that we would be leaving today. When he said that, I saw an emotion flash in Mason's eyes: sadness. I don't know why he would be sad now after all that he did to me. But I didn't think about it much. One kiss from Damien makes me forget everything else.

I was standing by Damien's car while he was loading our suitcases in the trunk. No one came to say goodbye. But I guess, it's better that way. They would end up saying something that set all of us in a foul mood.

Nate stood beside me, typing furiously at his phone. He was supposed to leave yesterday, but Damien's dad told him to arrive with us. So here he is.

Damien was back by my side in no time. He opened the back door for me, and I made myself comfortable. He took the driver's seat, and Nate in the passenger seat. We didn't have breakfast before leaving. Damien said that his mom made breakfast for all of us at the pack house. So we left early so we could arrive by breakfast time.

Nate switched the radio on, and 'Like I'm Gonna Lose You' started playing. I hummed along with the song.

My life will change, but I know I will be fine as long as Damien is by my side. He is my knight in shining armour, my saving grace. He is my angel, who was sent to help me. I feel new, I feel better. Long gone is the frightened girl. Now, I'm the Alpha's girl who is unafraid of anything. I will make Damien proud to call me his mate and Luna of his pack.

## Chapter 34

With that thought, I drifted off to sleep.

"Bella, baby. Wake up," Damien said softly in my ears. I giggled when his breath tickled my ears. I felt myself being picked up in strong arms, belonging to Damien. I snuggled closer. Then I remembered we were going to his pack.

I opened my eyes and looked around. We were outside the house. But not alone. More than two hundred fifty people were standing outside the door with huge smiles. I smiled at them and jumped out of Damien's arms.

"Baby! You could have got hurt. Be careful"

Damien and I walked side by side and reached the crowd.

"Hello, everyone," Damien said.

"Hello, Alpha." The reply came from everyone.

"Now, will you keep your Luna standing outside in the sun or…" Damien said

Everyone scrambled out of the way and into the house. Damien only laughed at their tactics.

Extra sofas were placed in the big hall for everyone to sit. Harold and Lily were sitting on the couch, in a corner, chatting. Lily caught my eye, and immediately ran towards me, leaving her husband. She hugged me tightly and then released me. She sniffed me a little, and a huge smile graced her lips.

She turned towards Damien who was successfully avoiding her gaze. "You! How could you not tell me you marked her!" she seethed at her son. Damien looked at me for help, but I just giggled softly and shook my head, which caused him to glare at me.

*You will get it later, baby girl,* his voice said in my head. He had created the link between us, the first thing in the morning. Not that I complain.

*We will see, Alpha.*

I flipped my hair a little to add to my point.

"Answer me, Damien Jameson Owen!" Lily said again

"Sorry, Mom. I marked her just the day before yesterday, and we slept the whole other day. I wanted to tell you, but I never got the chance. Sorry again."

## The Unloved Mate

She sighed and turned to me, and a grin replaced her scowl. "Congratulations, dear. Now, you are the official Luna of the Nightfall Pack. Welcome home," she said and hugged me again.

It is home, indeed.

Then Harold approached us and hugged me, congratulating me.

Damien and Harold immediately engaged in talks while Lily told me about the traditional celebration for the Lunas. It must be held within a week of being marked and becoming Luna. And Lily was planning on doing it two days later. I agreed.

Damien's hand sneaked around my waist and pulled me to him.

"Mom, please excuse us. We have to unpack, and I'm sure Bella is very tired from the traveling," he said, but the mischievous glint in his eyes gave another message.

"Okay, but come down for breakfast. Everyone else will be leaving now," she said and went somewhere.

"Where is everyone going?" I asked Damien while he pulled me upstairs. Our stuff was already in our room.

"To their house, Bella. These people came here to meet you specifically. They don't stay here."

Oh!

We entered his room, and he immediately pinned me to the wall. His hands were pinning my hands on either side. He was close. I could feel his minty breath on my face.

"I told you, baby. I'll get to you later. See, I got you. I will not let you go now," he said in the most seductive voice I've ever heard.

He leaned in and placed a teasing kiss on my jaw, then my neck, and trailed a line of kisses to my shoulder.

His lips left my skin and moved closer to my lips. Our lips were only apart when someone barged in. We both sprang apart.

"Shit! I didn't lock the door!" Damien mumbled under his breath.

Lily came in with a smile, and I felt my face heat up in embarrassment. I'm sure she knew what was going on.

"Dears, breakfast is being served. Please hurry up," she said sweetly.

# Chapter 34

"You know you could have just mind-linked me or knocked on the door," Damien said, growling.

"Now, son, what's the fun in that?" she said, winking at me before leaving.

Damien quickly closed the door and made sure to lock it. I took the opportunity, fled to the bathroom, and locked the door.

A few seconds later, I heard his growl of annoyance.

"Oh, come on, baby! Not you, too!?"

# Chapter 35

**Damien's POV**

"Dears, breakfast is being served downstairs. Please hurry up," my mummy dearest said in a very sweet tone. As if she didn't barge into mine and Bella's room, interrupting our moment.

"You could have just mind-linked me, or knocked at the door," I said, growling.

"Now, honey, what would be the fun in that?" she said, and I didn't miss the wink she sent towards my mate.

The moment she left the room, I flew to the door and shut it close, locking it. I turned to face Bella with a smirk, but she was not there. I heard the bathroom click and knew she was in there.

"Come on, baby! Not you, too!?" I groaned and plopped myself on the king-size bed.

*Look at you. You're such a sweetheart, aren't you?* Dom cooed in my head.

*You are the same when it comes to our mate. You can't tease me about that, you oaf!* I shot back, to which he snorted if that was possible for a wolf.

*Oh, what a beautiful little thing she is. Our mate is a true beauty, isn't she, Damien?*

*Totally. And she is just too innocent even to notice that. She is so adorable!*

*Never in my entire existence have I thought I would agree with you, but you're right!*

*I know I'm right.*

*I knew I shouldn't have said that. I just boosted your huge ego.*
*You sure did.*

"What is taking Bella so long in the bathroom? I want to hold her again and kiss the hell out of her!"

## Chapter 35

*Why so violent, Dom? Relax, she'll be out any moment!*
*But… but…*

Bella chose that moment to come out of the bathroom and was immediately tackled on the soft rug by me.

"Why did you run into the bathroom? You had to get out, baby, eventually."

She didn't reply and just looked at me dead in the eye, fingers digging into my shoulders. That's when I noticed.

She only had a towel on.

*Oh, fuck!! What wonders would be hidden under the towel, Damien?*

*Shut the hell up. Now is not the time, Dom!*

I slowly got off her, making sure not to look down and only focus on her eyes, which was very difficult.

"Sorry," I muttered, picked up some of my clothes, and hurried into the bathroom. I banged my head on the wall. How did I not notice that before? She must have felt so uncomfortable! Oh, God!

I took a quick shower and put my clothes on. I exited the bathroom and saw Bella sitting on the bed, now fully clothed. I smiled slightly when she turned to face me.

She took my hand in hers and stood closer. She pecked my lips.

"I'm sorry. I shouldn't have done that."

"It's okay, Damien. Anyway, I'm your mate. You have full permission," she said and winked before skipping out of the room, giggling.

*Close your mouth. You look like an idiot.*

I closed my mouth and composed myself. What did she say? Did she hint to me?!

Oh, God, kill me now! This woman is driving me crazy with her tricks.

I went downstairs and took my seat. I may be the Alpha, but the head of the table seat still belongs to my father. I didn't want him sitting anywhere else.

Bella was sitting beside me, I got an idea. I placed my left hand on her right knee, rubbing the skin. Her head shot up in my direction, but I didn't glance at her and watched as everyone

# The Unloved Mate

started to take their seats. My hand kept moving up until I was dangerously close to her middle. I notice her taking a sharp intake of breath.

Once everyone was seated I planned to make her cheeks redder. I grabbed her around the waist and dropped her on my lap, making her squeal and all red. I locked her in my arms and piled food on the plate for the both of us.

The clearing of throats caught my attention. I looked up from the plate and saw everyone's amused eyes lingering on us.

"Damien, why is Isabella sitting on your lap?" Dad asked with a small smile.

"Oh, actually, we always eat like this. Even at her old pack. Isn't that right, baby?" I asked her.

She nodded and curled up in a ball, trying to hide in my shirt. That made everyone chuckle at her cuteness, and I heard my mother 'aww' at her.

I pulled her face from my shirt and held a spoonful of eggs to her mouth. I noticed her face had turned fifty shades of red. She was blushing so hard. But didn't argue about eating and curled her mouth around the spoon. How I wish her lips curled like that into mine.

I dismissed that thought as soon as it came.

During breakfast, everyone kept glancing at us with knowing smiles and smirks. It's the same thing after breakfast, too.

We were sitting on the couch right now. Everyone is engaged in some kind of talk. I was bickering with Nate about how he always manages to arrive at the wrong time. This topic must be brought up, or else Bella and I wouldn't be able to mate!

"Damien, can I speak to you for a minute, please?" A very seductive voice of my Bella whispered in my ear, making me shiver slightly.

I turned to face her and saw the most innocent look on her face. I gulped inaudibly and nodded to her. She got up and went upstairs. I did notice the way she swayed her hips.

I turned to Nate again and told him I'll be back. I excused myself and walked up the stairs calmly. As soon as I reached the

# Chapter 35

floor, I practically flew to my room. I stood before the door, mentally preparing for whatever was to come. After gathering the courage, I finally opened the door.

Bella was standing by the window, looking outside. She was long gone her jeans and T-shirt. Now, all she wore was my white dress shirt, which barely covered her mid-thigh and was see-through.

I licked my lips and took a few steps forward when her soft and seductive voice made me stop.

"You would want to lock the door, Alpha…"

And I was a goner…

# Chapter 36

**Isabella's POV**

I was nervous, very nervous. After the marking, I constantly felt horny around Damien. I didn't know if something happened to me. I spoke to Nina on Damien's phone while he was in the shower before breakfast. I explained my problem to her, and she just laughed, then said that it was normal for newly mated couples to feel horny around each other, the need to be touched by them. Also, the need to mate will be strong. And she is right.

I feel like I'm ready. To be his in every way possible. So, I dropped hints for him. But being the thickhead he is, he didn't notice.

So now, I will try a direct approach. I am probably sounding like a bitch, but I can't help myself, and Nina said that even Damien must be feeling the same, so why not?

I was standing by the window in our room, looking at the beautiful forest before me. I heard the door click open and felt Damien enter. I kept my gaze out of the window and said, "You would want to close the door, Alpha…"

I was terrified to face him, to face the rejection. I didn't know what to do if he didn't want to mate with me. But I'm sure I won't ever be able to face him.

Suddenly, I was turned around by a strong arm. Damien looked into my eyes with lust. I gulped inaudibly and placed my hands on his chest. If he rejects me, then I will face it, but now I won't back down.

His hands curve around my body, pulling me impossibly close. I stood on my tippy toes and wrapped my right hand around his shoulder, and the other remained on his chest, moving in small circles.

## Chapter 35

"Oh, baby, you got to stop, or I won't be able to resist anymore," he whispered in a husky groan.

"Then don't. Don't resist, Damien. Make me yours, in every way. I'm ready. Please..." I whisper in his ear and nibble on it.

That's when he took control. He picked me up in his arms and kissed me hard. I instinctively wrapped my legs around his waist. He started walking somewhere without breaking the heated kiss. I grabbed his face in my hands and kissed harder. He groaned, and I felt myself dip.

He laid me on the bed and stood up straight, unbuttoning his shirt. His eyes never left mine, and we both had smiles.

We went down to eat with the others after our little episode. We all sat there eating when suddenly someone asked.

"You guys finally mated, huh?"

I almost choked on my food after hearing this! How can she be so open about it? Okay, fine, I know we are werewolves, and have a different way of doing things, but still.

"Ya, I can tell. Considering the cherry colour on Isa's face," Nina said, snickered.

"Hmm. Come on with me, honey. We need to have a serious conversation," Lily said, dragging me out. Nina followed.

I'm doomed! What is she going to say?

# Chapter 37

**Damien's POV**

As soon as the girls and Mom were out of earshot, I started laughing like a madman. Oh, God, her face! I know she is scared because she will have to describe the whole mating to them, but that's not true.

Mom does this every time. Whenever a close friend or family member female mates for the first time, my Mom arranges a treat for them to celebrate, not ask for details.

Nate and Dad let out a small chuckle. After snacks, we all sprawl on the couch in the TV room and watch today's football game. They are playing horribly! I bet even Nate could do better than them. He is awful!

The game ends around six and dinner will be served around seven. I should check up on Bella.

I get off the couch and try to locate Bella. I pass Nina's room and hear some giggles and 'aws'. I stop in front of the door when I hear something.

"Oh, my God! Look at him! He is so hot! Oh, did the temperature suddenly rise, or is it just me?!" Nina's voice said. I froze in my steps and decided to listen. Then I hear Bella talking, and what she says pisses me off!

"Did you see his jawline?! Oh, God! His abs! So delicious! And his hair, I just want to run my hands through them."

Thats it! I have had enough! I broke the door open and saw Nina and Bella sitting on the floor and about dozens of photos surrounding them. They both look at me in shock. I was heaving and glaring at both of them. I was mad, furious even, but I didn't want to lash out at Bella, so I asked her.

"What is going on here? And what photos are those?"

## Chapter 37

They collected the photos and made a small bundle in the middle. Both are smiling innocently.

I took a look at the photos and almost sighed in relief when I saw only mine and Adam's pictures. That got me more confused.

Nina sighed and explained.

"We were playing a game where we had to collect all our mate's possible pictures and then shuffle them together. Then, one by one, we took out a picture, looked at it, and within ten seconds, we had to comment on it. We had almost finished, but ruined now, thanks to you."

Now I was feeling bad. But I was happy when I remembered the comment Bella made. It was for me. Does she think I'm hot?

"Damien, why did you do that? We were having so much fun. You ruined it! Now you have to sleep alone tonight. I'll sleep with Nina! Go!" Bella said in an angry tone.

I was too shocked to register her words, but when I did, I felt like I was thrown off a mountain. How could she do that to me?

I can't sleep without her!

*That sounded creepy, dude!* Dom said.

*Shut up! Not the time!*

"Bella, you can't do that! You know I won't be able to sleep all night! Please. I can explain," I said, crouching down in front of her.

"Then explain! What are you waiting for!?" Nina butted in angrily.

I'm happy Adam was not here with me, or he would be grilled. "Bella I was looking for you, and when I was going past Nina's room, I heard your giggles, so I... so I heard your conversation. And I thought you were complimenting someone else, and it didn't settle well. That's why! I'm sorry! Forgive me! Baby, I love you!"

Bella had an adorable, confused face on. It looked as if she was battling whether to forgive me or not.

"I forgive you, Damien. Only because I love you, too," she said. "But you will sleep alone today. It's your punishment for scaring us."

"Okay, then. At least, you forgave me. Can I get a kiss, please?" I said.

She leaned forward and placed her soft, luscious lips on mine. After a few minutes, she pulled away and pushed me out of the door. Before she could close the door, I pecked her lips once more.

Before closing the door, she smiled and winked at me. I sighed and went to my room. The bed was still messy from before. I pulled at the cover and sheets. I saw a red stain on the sheets. The thought that I would have hurt her made my heart uneasy. I replaced the sheet with a fresh one and threw the dirty one in the laundry. I arranged all the pillows. I have to get more pillows. These are only enough for one.

I went down for dinner and saw Bella sitting with Nina, chatting. *Baby, what are you doing there? Come here?* I mind-linked her.

*Nina wanted to speak about something. Once she is done, I'll come to you,* she said and glanced at me.

I sighed.

Once the dinner was served, Bella sat on my lap as always. At least she's not pushing me away. As usual, I fed the both of us. Now, my family didn't stare at us like an entertainment show. They got used to seeing us this way. Throughout dinner, I tried to convince her to sleep with me, but she did not budge.

Dinner was over, and everyone said their goodnight's. I walked with Bella to Nina's room and held her hand once we reached.

"Please?" I asked for the thousandth time.

She was about to say something, but Nina pulled her inside. I groaned and went to my room. I plopped myself on the bed and turned off the lights. I hugged the pillow on which Bella slept. Her faint scent lingered in the covers. I snuggled myself closer to the pillow and sighed. This is going to be a long night.

**At midnight, around 1:00…**

No matter how much I tried, sleep didn't come to me. I just closed my eyes and waited for the sun to come up so I could see my Bella again.

## Chapter 37

I heard shuffling around me and then felt the bed dip. Bella's scent hit me, and Dom howled in joy. I opened my eyes and saw Bella lying beside me. I placed the pillow behind her head, and she jumped a little.

"You're still awake?" she whispered.

"Couldn't sleep without you," I said sincerely.

"Aw, me, too. Come here!" she said and opened her arms. I didn't think twice before snuggling into her. Having her in my arms felt so right. It felt natural.

I buried my face between her neck and shoulder and breathed in her scent. She felt her doing the same. "Why are you awake?" I asked and flipped us over so that she laid on top of me.

"Same reason. Now sleep, goodnight." She yawned adorably and kissed my cheek. Her face was buried in my chest and out like a light.

I smiled and kissed her head. I could finally get some sleep now. "I love you, baby."

# Chapter 38

**Isabella's POV**

The next few days were bliss. I have completed blended into the pack. I know almost everyone now and vice versa. Damien is more loving and treats me like a baby because of what happened a few days ago. He never wants to sleep alone again.

I also made two new friends, Cole and Cameron. Both girls are very sweet. We clicked when I met them during a stroll in the shared garden. Now we are a team: Nina, me, Cole and Cameron. Even Nate joins in sometimes. We all have grown extremely close to each other. Nate has grown pretty protective over me. He said, and I quote, "Anyone who tries to hurt his Luna will receive a private ass whooping from him," but I don't think Damien will give him a chance.

Right now, I was up to no good. I knocked at my mate's office door.

He was currently meeting with some Alpha, but I was missing him too much. The longest we have been apart was for an hour. And it has been two hours since the meeting started. He mind-linked me every fifteen minutes, though.

Damien has permitted me to barge in whenever I want, but I won't do that. A faint 'come in' was heard, and I entered with a smile, which was wiped as soon as it came.

Damien was meeting with the Alpha, but the Alpha was not a he but a she. The aura around her gave away her power and authority. She was seated at the comfortable chair across from Damien, the table separating them.

I took small steps forward, Observing both of their features. The lady looked smug and held her head high, trying to hide the small blush and shyness clearly evident in her eyes.

# Chapter 38

The pungent smell of her arousal hit my nostrils, making my insides churn. I saw Damien sitting stiffly in his chair, rather uncomfortable. He avoided looking at the Alpha and kept his gaze on me while the Alpha seemed to not care about anything else.

I cleared my throat once I reached a one-hand distance from the new Alpha. Her attention was now focused on me, sizing me up and down. I suppressed a growl.

She smiled my way and then turned around to stare at my mate again.

"Hello, my name is Isabella Clark," I said, extending my hand before her. She glanced at me and then at my hand. From the corner of her eyes, she looked at Damien and then shook my hand.

"Alpha Rose Cluster," she replied shortly.

I ignored her rude behaviour and turned to my lovely mate. He pushed his chair a bit and patted his thigh. I blushed a little at the signal he sent me. I shook my head and nodded to the lady staring at him. She didn't notice the exchange of expressions between us, though.

He didn't budge and patted his thigh again. This time, I gave in. I missed him and wanted to be close. I stood in front of him and kissed his cheek. He pulled me onto his lap and kissed my lips possessively. We broke the kiss, and he adjusted me on his lap so I was entirely on top of him. I fitted perfectly in his arms. He buried my face in his neck and patted my head like a child. I giggled lowly but didn't protest.

"So, Alpha Cluster, what were you saying? You shall continue." Damien's voice was cold and emotionless—his Alpha voice.

I could not see her face but could tell that she was flushed.

"Um... yeah. So, I was saying it would be great to ally our packs. Your pack is the most powerful, and ours is the third most powerful. This alliance will make us undefeatable. And for the sake of the alliance, I have a proposal that would benefit us more."

"And what might that be?" His voice was sending shivers through my body. He sensed my discomfort and reassuringly rubbed my hips and thighs.

## The Unloved Mate

"I think we should mate." As soon as those words left her mouth, Damien growled a fierce growl.

"You dare say that again, Alpha!" he growled and placed me on the desk before standing up.

Rose stood up, too, and tried to get closer to him, but my growl stopped her midway. She gave me a harsh look but stayed away.

"Damien, darling, relax. Calm down. Look at me, look at me." I cooed at him and made him face me. His eyes were flickering between their usual dark colour and golden. His wolf was on edge.

"Baby" was all he said, and he hugged me so tight as if his life depended on it. He probably did. because that's what he always said. I'm his life.

"Alpha Damien, consider my proposal. It's better than staying with random girls. Look at you seeking comfort in this unknown... lady. Think about the power you will get. We will rule together with a beautiful family. You have not found your mate, and neither have I. If you would have, then it wouldn't go unnoticed. It is only fair that we mate. There are a lot of benefits. Our future will be like a dream, you, me, our pups, and our pack—"

That was it. I released the grip I had on Damien's hand, holding him down, and slid down the desk facing the Alpha. Damien growled because of the lack of touch, but I was too blinded to notice. Attacking an Alpha of any pack was an offense. So I held on to Damien, restraining him from causing any damage. But she went too far, dreaming of having puppies with my mate!

She has a death wish.

"You! Who do you think you are!? Are you some kind of royalty that you will strut in, state your wishes and phoof! They come true!? Well, news flash, it won't happen! Your dream future will only be a dream! And you know why? Because Damien found his mate! He found me!" I growled. Damien wrapped his hand around my stomach and inhaled my scent.

I was breathing heavily by now, and Rose looked shocked by my outburst. She was about to say something when Nate strutted in—literary strutted! It's like moving his hips side to side, and with

## Chapter 38

a slight pout to go with it. That made me laugh. All my anger died down with his simple act.

"Nate, can you please escort Alpha Cluster outside? The meeting is done." Damien's voice was calm but dangerous.

"Absolutely, Alpha! Alpha Cluster after you," Nate said professionally. Rose gave us a last glance then huffed and followed Nate.

When the door closed, Damien dropped on the chair, pulling me down with him. He kissed me slowly. It was not a rough or passionate kiss. It was soft and just about right to show how much we loved each other.

He pulled away slightly, only an inch, and rested his forehead on mine. He whispered sweet words to me. Repeating how much he loved me and would never leave me, even if I tried. Then, he said something.

"Bella, will you marry me?" he asked.

And I froze.

# Chapter 39

**Damien's POV**

The words left my mouth before I could stop them. I was pissed at the situation, but I knew what I said was true. I want to marry Bella. And I wanted to take it slow, but now I want everyone to know that I have a mate who will also be my wife.

She froze at my words. I lifted my head and looked at her. Her eyes were closed and she breathed heavily from the kiss we just shared.

"Damien…"

"Baby, I know it's too early, but please, I want everyone to know that I found my mate and that it's you. I want to show you off to everyone. That is how lucky I am to have you. Please, sweetheart. I don't want a repeat of what happened today. I want you to be recognised as the Luna of Nightfall Pack."

She just stared at me for a good few seconds before nodding. "Yes. Yes, I will marry you," she said with a smile.

A huge smile appeared on my face. "Baby, I'm so happy. You just made me the happiest man alive. This is going to be perfect!"

"Yeah, just wait till I tell everyone how you proposed. Then we'll see how perfect it will be," she said with a straight face, looking all serious.

"You won't do that, right?"

"Okay, I won't. But you must tell everyone how you proposed and where the ring is!" She wiggled her fingers in front of my face.

I kissed all her fingers and smiled. "Soon, baby. Soon."

"I should go. Cole, Cameron, and Nina wanted to go shopping for Nate's birthday," she said and slid off my lap, walking to the door. I followed.

## Chapter 39

"Hmmm, what do you think we should do for his birthday? I mean, it's his eighteenth birthday, he will find his mate. It should be special," I said.

We walked together to the kitchen, and I sat on the bar stool while she looked into the pantry.

"I guess we should do a costume party. Nate likes all that stuff. So why not?" she suggested. I guess it's not a bad idea, and Nate may enjoy it.

"I think you're right. I'll call Tanner and Susan later. The couple plan the best parties in the pack," I said and poured myself a glass of water.

"Hmmm."

"What are you looking for in the pantry?" I asked

She turned around, holding a bag full of candies. I raised my eyebrows and looked at her with judging eyes. I'm kidding.

"Candy? Seriously?"

"No one is too old for candy," she sang, plopping on my lap sideways.

She started sucking on the candy cane and making moaning sounds. Is that red and white candy that tasty?

I stopped my habit of candies when I turned twelve because it was not manly. But looking at her devouring the sugary goodness, I can't seem to hold myself back. I tried to grab a single candy, but she swatted my hand and glared at me.

"Who told you to take one?" she asked, narrowing her eyes at me.

"Uh… no one?" It came out more like a question. She gave me 'the look' and continued with her candy.

I felt determined this time. I will get my candy. But before I could do anything, Dad came in. He looked at us, or, more specifically, my mate, who didn't even notice him, too happy sucking on her candy.

"Hi, Dad. How are you this fine morning?" I said. He went to the fridge and poured a bottle of chilled orange juice into a glass.

"I'm good, son. Thanks for asking, and I can see Isa has been doing well, too," he said with a warm smile.

## The Unloved Mate

Bella smiled back and nodded happily. "I'm good."

He nodded and went back outside. I stood up carefully, holding Bella bridal style. I went upstairs to our room and opened the door. I gently threw her on the couch and stood before her, folding my arms.

"What?" she asked. She had the most innocent look right now. Wide eyes, lips slightly parted and pushed forward. It was hard to overlook, but I did somehow.

"Candy," I said. I don't know why I'm doing all this over candy. But I won't lose to her, that too for candy.

"No!" she said and turned the other way. I walked towards her and sat on the couch. I turned her to face me, and I crashed my lips to her when she did.

The sweet and tangy taste of the candy burst my taste buds. The flavour got better. She wiggled at first but gave in later. I entered my tongue in her mouth and moaned at the outburst of the taste. Different flavours mixed made it better somehow.

I pulled away and licked my lips. I finally got my candy.

# Chapter 40

**Isabella's POV**

"Let's go home now!! My legs are screaming and yelling at me to stop! Please," I yelled out to the three devils in disguise. To which they only laughed.

Right now, we are in the mall looking for a suitable gift for Nate and costumes for ourselves. The party is in two days, and everyone is excited for their Beta's birthday.

I bought a charming shirt for him that says, 'I don't wake up to impress you', and a pair of Oakley shades. Nina got him a new pair of Vans because his shoes smelled bad. Cole bought a couple of necklaces so that he could give them to her when he found his mate. And as for Cameron, she is giving him a new watch.

While we were searching for our outfits, I felt someone's hand on my shoulder. The touch burned me. I cringed and turned around. A guy was standing behind me, now facing me with a smile. The girls were too engrossed in shopping to notice.

"Who are you? And how dare you touch me." I almost growled. No one can touch me besides Damien.

His smile didn't falter, and he kept staring at me. "Hi, my name is Benson, but you can call me Ben." He extended his hand for me to shake.

I didn't want to be burned again, so I just glared at him. He chuckled and dropped his hand to his side. "I'll ask again. Who are you, and why are you talking to me?"

He didn't answer but looked me up and down. I felt disgusted by his stare but didn't lose my cool. His eyes landed on my neck, and his eyes darkened. They reflected pure anger.

"You have a mate!" he stated.

I just nodded, but from the inside, I was breaking my head from the confusion.

# The Unloved Mate

He took a few deep breaths, and his eyes changed to their normal dull blue.

"Soon enough, sweetheart, we will meet again. And when we do, situations will be different," he said, stepping back and taking off.

I was still standing there like a fool. I shook my head and decided to mind-link Damien to fix my sour mood.

*Damien!*

*Yes, baby? Are you all done with the shopping?* he said happily. He always makes me feel better.

*No, not yet. We got the gifts, but the out is still not decided."*

*Oh, can I suggest something?*

*Of course.*

*Dress like a princess. You know, like Disney princesses?*

*Why? Is there a specific reason for it?*

*Yup! I'll dress as a prince, so we'll match! How cool is that?*

*Definitely! I'll search for my dress now. See you later. I miss you, and I love you!*

*I love you, too, baby. And you have no idea how much I miss you. Come back to me soon.*

*Bye.* We said our goodbyes, and I joined the girls for the dresses.

Nina had her dress ready. She decided to be a vampire. How ironic for a werewolf to be dressed as a vampire! Cole and Cameron were still struggling. I knew what to find for myself, so I headed to the gown section. After half an hour of endless search, I found my dress. I asked the girls for their opinion and they practically threatened me to buy the dress.

It was a pink gown with a sweetheart neckline. It hugged my waist and then flared down. It had an adorable floral lace design on the waist. In all, it was perfect.

Cameron brought a Red Riding Hood costume, and Cole got a fallen angel one with black wings.

Nina called the driver that was supposed to pick us up. As soon as the SUV arrived, we stuffed our bags in the trunk and jumped in the car. By the time we reached home, we were exhausted. We spent five hours in the mall and tortured ourselves. I need some

## Chapter 40

rest. We all got our bags and said goodnight. I entered my room. And when I saw the fluffy, cloud-resembling bed, I almost cried with joy. I dropped my bags and jumped on my precious bed.

"I love you!" I screamed into the pillow.

"Aw, I love you, too, baby."

I turned my head to the side and saw a very wet Damien exiting the shower with a towel around his waist.

"I was talking to the bed," I said in a 'duh' tone.

"But I was talking to you. I missed you, won't you hug me?"

Those words brought back all my energy and I jumped him. "I missed you, too!"

He chuckled and placed me back on the ground. He went to change in the closet, and I fell on the bed.

On the way, I had dinner with the girls and told Damien not to wait for me. So now we would sleep—my favourite part of the day is when we get to sleep.

He came back wearing dark blue basketball shorts only. Not that I mind. I was next to change. I wore a pair of cute shorts and one of Damien's Giants T-shirts. I brushed my hair and tied it into a braid. I brushed my teeth and then went back to the bedroom.

Damien was already in bed. The covers were pulled up to his waist. I climbed on the bed and switched off the lamps on either side.

Damien snuggled closer to me and kissed my forehead. His touch made all my exhaustion go away. "Goodnight, baby."

"Goodnight, baby's bear," I said. I heard him chuckle.

"Baby's bear?" he asked, his voice seemed distant by now.

"Hmm, I'm your baby, and you're my bear. So baby's bear!" I said groggily.

"Okay, baby. Now sleep. You look tired."

I thought he said something else, but I was already asleep.

# Chapter 41

**Damien's POV**

"Damien! Wake up! We have to pick up your costume! Come on!" My sweet little mate screamed in my ear. Of course, she has to be excited at nine in the morning. She has been playing a significant part in planning Nate's party. And I couldn't be more proud, but she is far too enthusiastic about it.

Today is my Beta's birthday—finally, the day when he will find his mate and stop bugging Bella and me. Like seriously he has the worst timing. Just yesterday, Bella and I were in the middle of something, in a very awkward position, when he had to interrupt us. When he finds his mate, he will be busy with her.

I felt a weight on my back and groaned. Bella just loves to torture me.

"Baby, get off. I'm getting up now," I said and waited for her to get off, but she didn't.

"No, now you have to do all your work with me on your back. That's your punishment," she said. I would not consider it as a punishment. She is not heavy. And I love to carry her around like a baby.

"Okay," I said, and slowly rose myself from bed. Her legs were securely wrapped around my torso, and her arms around my neck.

I went into the bathroom and brushed my teeth. I showered last night so I won't take one now. I went to my closet next.

"Wear the blue one. It looks good on you." Bella pointed to a dark blue polo shirt. Hmm if she likes it, then I like it.

She got off my back, and I stripped quickly changing into fresh clothes.

We had breakfast and left for the costume store. Nate is not here. I sent him to the neighbouring pack for some work. Of course, that was a lie. I spoke to the Alpha to keep him occupied until evening.

## Chapter 41

We reached the store and picked up my suit, which was now fitted.

Bella said I looked like an actual prince and that she would have a hard time keeping other girls away. I laughed at that.

When we reached the pack house, everything was utter chaos! Everyone was running around, taking care of stuff. Bella excused herself to help, and I headed to our room. I placed the suit in the closet, laid on the bed, and went down to help Bella.

The decoration is perfect, and the party atmosphere is nice. The buffet is ready. Guests have started to arrive.

"Damien, let's go get ready, okay? Nate called me. He is on his way," Bella said. We started getting ready in our room.

She looked like an actual princess. Oh, my, what a beauty she is. Her long waist-length hair fell in small waves and had minimum makeup. It looks as if she just arrived from heaven. I pry my eyes off her and quickly change into my suit. I look pretty good.

Bella helped me with the tie, and I wore my shiny black shoes. My hair was slicked back with gel. We both help each other with our gloves, and we are ready.

Now all of us are waiting for the birthday boy to arrive so that we can start the party. A roar of the engine goes off, and everything becomes silent. Footsteps reach the front door, and open to reveal Nate. The lights flicker on, and everyone yells 'Happy birthday!' to him. He looks truly surprised and happy. Bella and I approach him. We hugged and wished him a happy birthday.

"Thank you so much, Damien! It means so much, really!" he said with tears in his eyes.

"It was all Bella and her squad," I said, and he nodded towards Bella. And she just smiles back.

A group of boys take him upstairs to prepare him for his party. He soon returns, all cleaned up. He was wearing a cowboy costume, which looked good on him. The party started and we cut the cake. The clock struck twelve, and the party went wild. Now is the time when Nate found his mate if she was here. He stuck his nose in the air and sniffed.

## The Unloved Mate

Everyone was looking closely as he looked around the room, searching. He started walking to the refreshments table, towards a girl, with her back towards us.

He found his mate!

She turned around. And much to our surprise, it was Cole! They stared into each other's eyes and whispered, 'mate.'

I pulled Bella closer and whispered, "Now, he will leave us alone."

"Oh, shut up! My best friends are mates! Oh, my God! I'm so happy!" she squealed.

"We have to announce our wedding too, by the way. I guess we can do it now. Everyone is here," I suggested, and she nodded.

When the crowd got over the shock of Nate and Cole being mates, I grabbed their attention and stood on the makeshift stage.

"Hello, everyone. Thank you for coming here and joining us to celebrate our Beta's birthday. I congratulate Nate and Cole for finding each other as mates. Now, I have an announcement myself. Bella and I have decided to get married. I proposed, and she said yes," I said, and there were cheers and hoots all around the room.

Soon enough, I was separated from Bella by some guests.

Someone spilled juice on my suit somewhere in the middle, and I had to go upstairs to clean it. I looked around for Bella before going. She was speaking to some lady from the pack.

I entered our room and cringed. A faint, pungent smell hit me. I looked around and saw a red piece of paper on Bella's dresser. I didn't keep it, not Bella, and no one can enter our room when we are away. That only leaves one option...

A rogue.

I snatched the red paper, and something was written in black, messy handwriting. I read it over and over again, making me more angry and overall upset.

No one dares to target my Bella! Whoever it is will pay! They don't know what they got themselves into.

The stain on my clothes was forgotten as I strode over to the hall. I stood on top of the stairs and looked down for her. She was nowhere in sight. I frowned, worry and anticipation making me

# Chapter 41

breathe heavily. I even looked in the bathrooms, kitchen, and hallways. I. Looked. Everywhere. But no sign of her. I asked around, but no one saw her. I even asked Leon, the lady she was talking to, but she said that Bella had excused herself to get some starters.

I collapsed on the floor and let out a roar. The threat was true. They took her. My Bella. They took my mate. But I won't grieve. Oh no. I was going to get her back. I will make them wish they never crossed my path. They will pity themselves as to why they were born. I will wipe their existence from the surface of the earth.

I stood up, wiping the wetness on my cheeks and standing in front of one thousand anxious werewolves. "Our pack is threatened! Your Luna is endangered. She is taken away! Whatever it takes we will bring her back!" I roared in anger.

Everyone yelled a "Yes, Alpha", and a feeling of dedication and anger replaced the party mood.

*Hold on, baby. I'm gonna find you soon. Be strong...*

\*\*\*\*\*\*\*\*\*\*

The letter:

*Hello, Alpha. I see you have a beautiful mate. I am fascinated by her beauty, and I envy you for owning her. But not for long. I shall have her. If I were you, I would keep an eye on her.*

*Yours truly,*

*Rogue*

# Chapter 42

**Isabella's POV**

The party was a success. Nate loved it and Damien announced our wedding about ten minutes ago. I was tired of talking to everyone, and my throat became dry. I need some liquid. I gulped down a glass of chilled lemonade and looked through some starters when I felt a jolt of pain in my head. My vision was clouded, and my feet wobbled. I dropped to the floor and slowly slipped into darkness.

The sound of someone yelling woke me up. I groaned when I felt pain in my head. I tried to lift my hand, but I felt a slight tug and anguishing pain. My skin was burning. It didn't take a genius to figure out that I was chained with a silver chain. I was still in my princess gown. Thankfully.

I took in my surroundings. The room I was in was dark and cold. It gave me a creepy feeling. I was leaning against the wall with my legs pressed to my chest. I felt like crying. Who are these people? What do they want from me?

The sound of the door opening set me on full alert mode—a small yellow light flickers right on top of my head. I heard footsteps coming towards me. The person came face to face with me, and I recognised him from the mall. He crouched down to my level and smiled a dirty smile showing off his ugly teeth.

"I told you we would meet again, sweetheart, didn't I? Now, you will be paying for all the pain I have endured during the past years. And the cost is much more than you can imagine." His smile became a scowl by the end of his mini-speech.

Honestly, I was not that afraid. In the beginning, I was terrified, but not anymore. I know Damien would most likely be looking for me right now, and he will be here.

"Don't get too used to the feeling of victory. You may have kidnapped me, but by doing that you have already sealed your fate,

## Chapter 42

which is death. Don't you forget who my mate is? He is coming for me, you wait," I said with confidence leaking from every word I spoke.

The look on the man's face was of hate and irrigation. He didn't hesitate to raise his hand and slap me across the face. I hissed at the burning pain on my cheek, and I could taste the rustic taste of blood on my lips.

"Now, that will remind you to keep your words in check. Think twice before speaking in front of me," he snarled and banged my head on the wall behind me before standing up. My vision blurred, and I was having difficulty keeping my eyes open.

He released me out of the silver chains with the help of heavy gloves and left the room. I thought of ways to get out of here but found none. Then I thought of mind-linking Damien. I tried to contact him, but something was stopping me. The mystery man has wolfsbane around here.

The man returned after a few minutes. He had a big metal box in his hand. He placed the box on the floor and looked at me with an evil smirk.

"Now, I will give you a glance at what you will be experiencing here during your stay. Which will be till your death," he said. The man took a big whip out of the box and wrapped it around his palm twice. "Now remember, this is only a little sneak peek of what will come." With that, he brought the whip down in full force. The harsh material of the whip tore through the skin of my arm, and I let out a scream of pain.

He showed no mercy and kept torturing me to no end. He used whips, knives, sticks, silver, and anything that could make me feel pain. When satisfied, he packed the tools and exited the room, leaving me to drown in self-pity.

My dress was badly torn, my face felt swollen all over, and my arms were decorated with cuts and bruises of all sorts. My body was aching and begging me to relieve the pain, but I couldn't. The pain in my head grew with every thought. My eyes felt heavy and weak. Black dots covered my view as I finally drifted into darkness, for the second time. This time, I woke up with my whole body throbbing in pain. I shifted and laid my head on the side wall. No sight of the man, much to my relief.

What had I ever done to receive this type of treatment? My life has always been filled with pain and hate. The only happiness I experienced was when I was with Damien.

Damien. I miss him so much. He is the best mate ever. I can't thank the moon goddess enough for pairing me with him. I don't know if I will see him again, and the thought of not saying the final goodbye made my heart clench painfully.

The thoughts made my eyes sting with hot tears that rolled down my swollen and bruised cheeks. I wiped them off and let my hands caress my dry throat. I felt something cold. The cold material of the ruby pendant Damien gave me brushed against my skin, and I couldn't hold myself. I burst into sobs. This is the gift he gave me on Valentine's Day. I remember the day perfectly—the promise to love me forever. The hope in me grew a little that he would come for me, to rescue me.

I was brought out of my thoughts by the sound of footsteps. Dread seeped through me, and I started shaking. The smirking face of the man appeared in front of me.

"How are you doing, sweetheart? Ready for more punishment?" he said and opened the box again. I crawled to the corner and pressed myself to the wall as if to disappear. He brought a silver knife this time and placed it on my swollen cheek. The touch itself burned me. He pressed the weapon with more force and it tore open the flesh of my cheek. I hissed when my salty tears mixed with my wound but could do nothing to heal it.

He kept on beating and cutting me until I was on the verge of dying. When he was satisfied with the damage, he hummed and left me alone to die.

*Where are you, Damien? Come soon…*

# Chapter 43

**Damien's POV**

All the warriors and anyone who wanted to help stood in a circle around the meeting table. I am dying inside for my baby, but I don't want to take any chances. We have to have a plan. We don't know what they are capable of, and I don't underestimate my enemies.

*That filthy rogue is going to pay!*

"Alpha, I think we should scout the lands and see if we find any traces of the rogue or our Luna," the head warrior, Cody, says.

"All right. Make groups of five each and search every inch of our land. You find anything, and I mean anything, you tell me. Nate, Ryan, Cody, and I will go to the east border. The others take the rest," I commanded and they left.

*I'll find you, baby. I promise.*

We filed out of the room and started searching instantly. The main problem is that I don't know who took her, why, and where. If I had known this is going to happen, I would have never let her out of my sight. We searched and searched for hours, and I could tell that my men were growing frustrated and tired, but they didn't show.

I was running in the forest with wind speed, on full alert for any clue. After another painful hour of running, I heard a howl—a signal from a warrior.

"Alpha! We found something behind the pack house!"

I didn't waste another nanosecond and ran towards the pack house. A small crowd of wolves was gathered around the area. I shifted into my human form and put on the shorts wrapped around my paw.

"What is it?" I asked impatiently.

"Alpha! We found some traces of blood going in that direction," a warrior said, pointing towards the dark forest.

The dark forest is called 'dark' for a reason. No one goes there. No one had the guts to explore that part of the land. Because monstrous creatures reside there, it does not belong to anyone in particular, so the rogue must have thought it was the best place to keep my baby there. Because I was hesitant to go there. But not anymore. If my baby is there, I would face anyone to bring her back to me.

"I'm going there." They looked at me with a shocked expression "I won't force any of you to come with me, but I have to go. My mate is there, and if the rogue had the balls to take my mate there, then why can't I?"

"We will go, Alpha!" Nate, Cody, Ryan, and Antonio said with a determined expressions.

"We will go, too. Our Luna should be the priority," the other guy said, and the other guy nodded in agreement. I smiled and went to the weapon room. We wore our defense suits and loaded our revolvers with silver and wolfsbane bullets. When everyone was ready, we headed to the dark forest.

"Now, I appreciate that you all decided to help and come here, but if anyone wants to back off, they can do it now. I won't mind." No one moved for a good two minutes, so I continued. "Okay, so the dark forest is not that big in the area but not that small. I'm sure that these rogues have something planned. So keep your eyes on everything and be alert. Tell me any signs of my mate, and if you find the head rogue, don't kill him. Drag him to the level thirteen cells in the warehouse."

They nodded, and we marched towards the dark forest. I don't feel frightened going in there. The only emotions in me right now are anger and disappointment. I was angry at the rogue who took my life source from me and disappointed in myself that I couldn't do anything about it. I don't know what my Bella is going through. I swear if they touch one hair on her head, he will be begging me to kill him.

We had covered about ten miles when I felt my heart race. Only her presence can make me feel this way. It gave me hope that my

# Chapter 43

Bella was close by. My steps turned into strides as I looked around, now more alert.

We searched for a long time but found nothing, although the feeling didn't stop.

"Aahh!" A small yelp was heard from a mile away. The scattered warriors followed me in that direction.

One of my warrior's legs was stuck on a wooden floor. Where did that come from? While some helped the warrior, I scrapped the grass around the plank and found a trap door.

*Damien, let me take control for a while I can sense her better,* Dom said. As much as I want to argue, I know he is right.

*Only if you give me control once we find her.*

*I promise! Now, don't waste time! I can feel she is in pain!*

*What!?*

Dom was fast in taking control.

## Dom's POV

Mate!

Mate is hurt!

That was the only thought running in my mind while my men tried to open the door. The trap was finally yanked open, and the faint smell of honey and cinnamon hit me. She's here! Mate! Mate! Not waiting for anyone, I descended the stairs. There was a big room lit with dim lights here and there.

No guards? Fishy...

Taking cautious steps I make my way around the room. Voices are coming from a room across. By now, the warriors had come down too. I motioned towards the door, and they followed me. I kicked the door open and saw about fifty rogues drinking and having fun!

My mate might be going through God knows what! And they are enjoying!? Maybe they were involved too. That made me even more mad. My men charged at them, and they were all dead within ten minutes. Puny rogues. Can't even fight! We left their corpses there and dispersed to find Bella. The anticipation was killing me. The moment I see her, I will stick to her like a leech. I can barely survive when my baby is not with me.

I entered a corridor with many metal doors. Her scent became strong here. She is here! So close! I opened every door in the corridor. Surprisingly, all were open except the last one.

A loud yelp was heard from the other side of the door. I can recognise her angelic voice anywhere. My baby! What did he do to her?

My warriors were beside me in a flash, and I kicked open the door. What I saw horrified me. The scene was enough for a lifetime of nightmares for me. My baby! My Bella!

She was chained with silver chains around her hands and legs. Her hair and dress were a mess. Her body was full of bruises. And a man standing over her with a whip in his hand. His hand stopped midair when he heard us.

"Ah, Alpha Damien. Your presence was much awaited." He chuckled. The voice sounded familiar, but I couldn't point my finger at it.

"Get him!" I ordered my warriors, and they charged. He turned around, and my breath hitched. Taking the opportunity, Damien took control.

**Damien's POV**

How could he? How could he do this to me? I was the one who helped him, and he repaid me in such a cruel way! Fine! If he wants to play dirty, then we shall! The face didn't stop my warriors from dragging him where he belonged. He didn't fight back, which confused me a little. But that can be dealt with later.

Now, my baby girl!

When they were out, I ran to her and dropped to my knees before her. She was barely conscious, and her skin was sickly pale. What did he possibly do to her in one day that made her this weak?

## Chapter 43

Her dress was tattered, and her whole face was swollen. But still, she was the most beautiful and adorable girl in the world for me. I pulled out my revolver and shot the chains. The lock on the chains broke, and I picked her up and placed her on my lap.

"Baby? Can you hear me?" I asked, cradling her face in my palm. Her swollen eyes fluttered open, and a small smile tugged on her pale, chipped lips.

"D-Damien?" she croaked. The sound broke my heart, but I nodded, pulled her face to my chest, and rocked her back and forth.

Tears welled in my eyes, but I didn't let them fall. "Yes, baby. I'm here now. No one will hurt you, I promise!" I said, and when I didn't get a response I pulled away and saw her eyes closed. I panicked and checked her breathing. She was breathing, but her pulse was low, and her heart was beating extremely slow.

I picked her up and ran towards the pack house. I mind-linked the doctor on the way and told her to get everything ready.

When I reached the pack house, I placed Bella on the bed. The doctor entered and examined Bella. Suddenly, the doctor's face paled, and her eyes widened. She looked at me with fear and then back at Bella.

"What's wrong?" I demanded.

She gulped and answered. "Alpha, whoever took our Luna, they injected her with a heavy dose of aconite. It's a very deadly poison to werewolves besides wolfsbane. I doubt she will survive."

No!

# Chapter 44

**Damien's POV**

The doctor was saying something, but I was too occupied with the pain in my heart to listen.

One of the most beautiful days in my life turned out to be the worst. Just yesterday our wedding was announced and now this. How could the moon goddess be so cruel? How could she take my only reason for living from me? Am I that bad person that I got this punishment?

"Damien! Damien!" Someone shook me, and I looked at them with emotionless faces. All my emotions faded, and only a shell remained.

Nate looked at me with an unknown emotion. His eyes were bloodshot, which shows he was crying. I looked back at my Bella. She was hooked up to multiple IV tubes and was breathing slowly.

Tears filled my eyes, and I didn't stop them from falling. No, I didn't cry out loud. My Bella would not like it if I cried, I just let the tears fall freely.

"Damien! Listen to me! Isa is not dead yet! She's breathing. Her heart was still beating. She was still here. I have heard what a mate bond can do and still think there is hope. You can bring her back. We have not given up on our Luna, so why are you giving up on your mate!" he said and left the room.

I sat closer to her bed and took her hand. They were icy, cold, and pale. Nate's words were ringing repeatedly in my head like a record...

"*We have not given up on our Luna, so why are you giving up on your mate?*"

"*I have heard what a mate bond can do, and I still think there is hope...*"

"*You can bring her back!*"

# Chapter 44

A little hope came to me. She is not dead. I will do anything to bring my baby back to me.

"Baby, it's me, Damien. Please don't leave me, come back. I need you. The pack needs you. I know what you are capable of. You have to try, princess. Come back to me, please," I said, laying my head on her stomach with her hand wrapped in mine.

For the past three days, I could not sleep. I only ate a few sandwiches Nate brought and lots of coffee to keep me awake. I spoke to her all the time and about everything. Today was no exception. I was sitting on the small chair like always, but I closed my eyes this time. As soon as I did, the heart monitor started beeping loudly. I panicked and shouted for the doctor. Sick green foam started coming out of her mouth, and I panicked even more.

The doctor told me to wait outside, and I obliged, not wanting to delay her treatment. After an hour of torturous waiting, a nurse said that I could come in. Her slow breathing was now normal, and her heart was picking up pace. And I couldn't be happier.

After some tests, the doctor said that the poison didn't settle in her body for some reason and it could be removed by performing dialysis. The green foam was the poison coming out of her body, which is a good thing.

They extracted most of the poison, but not all. I was freaking out, but the doctors said that the poison would not harm her in any way because it was in a minimal amount. She can't die from it.

She looked more healthy now. Her skin was still a bit pale, but slowly, it was gaining colour.

"Doctor, when will she wake up?"

"We don't know that, Alpha," she replied, and I nodded.

Nate entered the room with a big bouquet of daffodils and placed them in the jar next to Bella's bed. He does this every day. He said that he wants this room to smell like flowers when she wakes up and not of antiseptics and medicine.

"How you doing, Damien?" he asked

"Good. Thanks, Nate, for not giving up," I said hugging him.

## The Unloved Mate

"It's okay, Damien. What are friends for? Adam said that Nina breaks down crying every five minutes, and he wants you to speak to her," he said, and I nodded, pulling away.

"Okay, I'll speak to her tomorrow."

"Damien, when are you gonna deal with him?"

"Once my angel wakes up. And once I lay my hands on him, he will be begging to die an easier death," I said, cracking my knuckles.

"Count me in, buddy. It's been a long time since I did some damage," he said with a smirk.

I was about to reply when someone interrupted me.

"W-what d-damage?"

I turned around, and it became the happiest moment of my life. "Baby!" I ran to her side and hugged her. "Baby, you're awake. Finally!" I almost broke into tears. She hugged me back slowly. I buried my face in her neck and let her scent fill me up.

"Water," she whispered, and I carefully let her go and got a cup of water for her. I gave her the cup and sat beside her. Nate was looking at us with a happy face. "I'm happy you're awake, Luna. This man has been going crazy," he said, and Bella chuckled.

Oh, how much I missed her beautiful laugh.

"I must inform the doctors and the others," Nate said, and I nodded.

"I missed you!" Bella said with a sad smile. Those words broke my walls and spilled the tears I had been holding. All the emotions hit me like a wave—sadness, grief, dread, and now happiness.

Bella opened her arms and made a grabbing motion. I got up from the chair, sat on the bed beside her, and hugged her.

"I missed you, too. So much. Don't ever leave me again. I was so scared when the doctor said that you might not make it. I was never so scared in my life. You are my life, baby. Don't you dare die on me." I know I was rambling, but right now, the only thing on my mind was that she was awake, and I was speaking to her, this time expecting a reply.

"I know, Damien. I'm sorry."

"Don't say sorry."

# Chapter 44

Then the door opened, and the doctor came in with a notepad. She examined Bella and wrote a few things. "Everything looks good. Just take it easy now, don't do heavy work, take as much rest as you can, and take all your medication on time. You will be healthy as a horse in a week."

I nodded, and she left us alone.

Without wasting a second, I kissed her. She kissed back immediately. I waited very long to do this. I kissed her with everything in me. All the pain and happiness flowing from us. Her mouth still works wonders. She bit my lower lip and pulled at my hair. An unconscious groan escaped my throat.

"Ehem!"

We broke apart and saw all our friends and family at the door. They ran in and tackled both of us.

"Guys! She just got up! She's still weak," I said. Everyone got off.

Nina, Cole, and Cameron talked with Bella while Nate, Adam, and Ryan gave me news about the pack.

"Damien, I think now is the time. Our hands are itching to beat him. All of us want to have a go," Adam said, and others nodded.

"You are right. Now that Bella is awake, I can concentrate on making his life a living hell. Cousin or not, he will pay."

# Chapter 45

**Isabella's POV**

"Isa, I missed you so much, babe! Don't scare us like that again!" Nina said with a sad face. I just smiled, nodded, and said, "I missed you guys, too. So much!"

"Yeah, I bet you did. You know, Nina was an absolute mess. She cried every five minutes, and Adam was going crazy seeing her that way," Cole said, and Cameron let out a hearty chuckle.

I hugged all of them the best I could, and we spoke about what happened during my days in hospital.

I saw Damien coming back, and the girls bid their goodbye.

"Baby, I spoke to the doctor, and she said you can return home tomorrow. Till then, you will be under observation," he said and sat down on the bed beside me stroking my cheek. I leaned into his touch and smiled. "What did he do, princess?"

His question caught me off guard, and hesitated to answer. The pain he put me through was unbearable. The mere thought of it made my body ache in pain. "He tortured me," I said, looking down at my fingers on my lap. I felt weak, and making it nearly impossible to look him in the eye. He placed his warm fingers under my chin and made me look at him.

"What did he do?!" His words were firmer, and his eyes begged for answers.

"He... he had a big box full of tools he used. He used different kinds of whips, knives..." I said with tears in my eyes.

"That's not it, isn't it? Tell me, princess. Everything."

I sighed and began. "He dripped hot wax on my back and burned me with iron rods in the stomach. In only a day, he made me hate and feel disgusted with myself. He left hideous scars on my body, which I am ashamed of. I swear, I tried to fight him,

## Chapter 45

Damien. I did, but I couldn't do anything—" He cut me off and hugged me close to his chest. I completely broke down.

I hugged him tightly and fisted his shirt. His warm hands stroked my hair and whispered sweet nothings in my ear. This was all I needed at this time. My sobs slowly turned into hiccups, and that's when he pulled away. He wiped all the tears from my face and cupped my cheeks.

"You are so strong. You endured so much pain and still didn't give up. All the scars on your body remind you that you won and he lost. He doesn't get the satisfaction of breaking you. You are a warrior. My warrior princess," he said and gave a big kiss on my forehead.

He knew exactly what to say. His voice was calm and collected, but I knew better than that. He is going to break him and make him beg. He will make him go through pain, much worse than me. And for once, I'm not complaining.

I nodded, and he laid me down on the bed. We spoke about how he was coping without me, and judging by what he said, he was miserable. That only stacked up more guilt in my heart. Everyone was so worried and tensed for me. I should have been more careful and looked out for myself. But I didn't, which resulted in this.

Before we knew it was time for my dinner and medicine. A nurse came in with my food and medicine, kept it on my table, and instructed me to take the pills before leaving with a kind smile.

Damien insisted on feeding me because he missed me too much. He said sweet and encouraging words with every spoonful of that disgusting food. "Yes, baby, just like that", "That's my princess", "just a little more", etc.

Finally, that tasteless excuse of food was made, and now the medicine. He gave me a glass of juice and the pills. I gulped them down, and my face scrunched up in a very unlady-like expression.

Damien chuckled and flicked my nose before cleaning up all the mess I made.

"Now, it's time to rest. Have a nice sleep, baby. Good night," Damien said and tucked me in. He turned around to leave, but I grabbed his hand.

"Go home and get some sleep, too. The girls told me you didn't leave my side for a second. Please?" I asked softly. My eyes felt heavy. The medicine was showing its effect.

"But, baby, I can't leave you here all alone. I'll sleep here today. Anyway, you will be back tomorrow. I'll take a rest another time. You sleep," he said, and I knew better than arguing with him. So I just nodded and slowly drifted off to sleep.

## Damien's POV

As soon as Bella fell asleep, I called Nate to watch on her while I dealt with that bastard. I know Bella hates violence, so I would do it behind her back. But I will do it.

I was stroking her hair when Nate came in. He nodded to me and stood beside the door like a guard. I rolled my eyes at that.

I got up and walked to the door. "You know you can sit on the couch there. It will be tiring to stand here. Just be careful and keep your eyes open for any danger. She has been through enough for a free lifeline," I said and glanced one more time at my sleeping Bella.

"Absolutely."

I left the room and headed to the garage. I got in my car and sped out of the hospital to the warehouse. I reached there in less than fifteen minutes and didn't waste any time before going in. The place smelled of blood and rotten corpses. There are two hidden chambers in the forest. One for rogues and other criminals. Second, for torturous purposes. The torture chamber is where he is kept. The thirteenth level is the deadliest level of the chamber. The pain the person receives is beyond imagination.

I reached his cell, pushed the door open, and saw that Adam, Cody, and my dad were already waiting for me. The filthy being was held flat on the wall. The pure silver chains stretched his hands and legs, burning his skin.

## Chapter 45

I neared him and made him face me. His face was swollen, but not even close to what my Bella's face looked like. Her every wound will cost him a hundred.

"Why did you take her?" I asked in a calm tone, but on the inside, Dom was clawing to get control. I understand him. I want to rip this piece of shit, too, but I need answers.

"I had my reasons!" he said and spit blood on the floor.

"But we trusted you! You were my cousin! Why would you do that to me? What is wrong with you?" I was losing my patience with every passing minute. He must answer me now, or he won't remain alive for long.

"What is wrong with you, Damien? She belonged to that pack! Don't you remember? You said you would help me! But you were too much in love with her even to remember your promise!" He shouted in my face.

"I remember everything I said, and I will do it! But Bella has nothing to do with it! She is innocent! You punished them for their doing! She suffered enough. Now all she deserves is a happy life!"

"No, she doesn't. And just being a member of that Howlers Pack gave me a reason to beat her up. I don't see the reason why you kept her around so long. She is disgusti—" I cut him off by punching his already broken jaw. He said enough. He did enough.

"Now, my turn." I pulled the lever two times and heard his screams of pain as the chains stretched his arms and legs further apart. Grabbing my special whip, I slashed it across his chest. The nails in the whip tore his skin apart. I slashed it again and again until his shirt was soaked in his blood.

I didn't use silver because then he would not be able to heal and die from all the pain. But I do not want him to fall into eternal peace yet. He will die every second. He will feel the unbearable pain, then heal, only to feel it all over again.

"Cody put the restrainer on him and make sure it's tight enough to make him choke," I commanded.

Cody did what I said and felt a little satisfied, seeing him desperate for air, trashing around but unable to do anything.

*Well, buddy, that was me, when my Bella was not with me.*

## The Unloved Mate

I loosened up the belt just a little so he wouldn't die and burned the furnace in the corner. I heated the iron rod until it turned red and brought it up to his chin. He hissed from the burning sensation and turned his head from side to side. I poked the pointy end of the rod in his shoulder, and he cried out in pain. I let it cool down before I pulled it out quite harshly. I think it hurt more, but that's the whole point.

Cody removed the belt restrainer and put on a metal one. It has spikes in it. If he tried to move his neck, the spikes would go straight through his neck and chest. The furnace kept burning, so he kept on sweating and bleeding.

"I think that it's good enough for today. We will come to visit again tomorrow, cousin. Why don't you rest till then," I said, leaving the cells.

I was almost out when I realised something. Bella can't see me like this. I need to clean off the blood. I mind-linked Nate.

*Is Bella awake?*

*No, she's still sleeping but can wake up any time now. Hurry up.*

I went back to the cellar and had a quick shower before leaving again. I stripped off behind a tree and shifted into my golden wolf to reach the pack house faster. I reached there in ten minutes and shifted behind the house. I put on my clothes and ran to her room. I opened the door, and much to my relief, she was still sleeping, snuggling to the pillow like a teddy bear.

"Can I go now? Cole has been texting me all night," Nate said.

"Yeah, thanks for helping, dude. And sorry to make you stay."

"Nah, it's all right. See ya later."

He left the room, and I let out a breath. I took off my shirt, lay on the couch, and closed my eyes. I felt something beside me shifting and opened my eyes.

"Shh. Go to sleep, Damien. We'll talk later about where you were all night," Bella said, snuggling closer to my chest.

Shit!

# Chapter 46

**Damien's POV**

I could not sleep for a minute. Half the reason was that Bella was constantly shifting in her sleep and getting me all worried, and the other half was thinking if I should start training her soon. I should train her myself. It would be better that way. I will know how she's doing without being away. And after the training, she will be able to protect herself well.

My phone buzzed, and I carefully took it out of my pocket, trying not to wake Bella up. It was a text from Adam.

*I have to go back to my pack right now. Emergency. I'm taking Nina with me. I don't have all the fun with that mutt alone. I'll be back in two days. See ya.*

I rolled my eyes and replied an 'okay'.

"Good morning, Damien."

I turned my head at the voice and smiled before kissing Bella briefly.

"Good morning, baby. How are you feeling?" I asked while sitting up. I brushed a few strands of hair from Bella's face, and she smiled brightly. Even though she says she is fine, I can't but think otherwise. Seeing her in the hospital in such a state has left a scar on my heart, and I don't want anything of that sort to happen again. Ever.

"I'm good. Nora is helping a lot," she replied enthusiastically.

"I'm glad you're doing well. You should take care of yourself," I said, kissing her forehead. "Now I was thinking you should start your training soon. Maybe next week or so?" I said out of the blue.

"What?"

"I said that I want you to start training. You should be able to defend yourself when needed, baby. I will always be there, but some situations may not benefit us. That time, these trainings will help."

She nodded and kissed my lips once more before going to the bathroom. I sighed and thought about her again. After what happened that day, I can't take any chances. She was taken from under my watch, and that's a serious matter. She has to train, and I will make sure she learns everything.

She comes out of the bathroom in only a skimpy towel. I can hear her fast heartbeat all the way here, and a smirk makes its way onto my face. She avoided my gaze and rummaged through the closet. I walked towards her and wrapped my arms around her tiny waist.

"Are you trying to seduce me, princess?" I whispered in her ear, and she shivered under my touch. I love the effect I have on her.

"N-No, why would you t-think that?" she said breathlessly. I chuckled and rubbed my palms up and down her arms, and she took deep breaths.

"Do I make you nervous, baby?"

"N-No."

I laughed and tickled her sides a little. She squirmed and tried to wiggle out of my hold. I released her, still laughing, and went for a shower myself.

"I'll be right back," I yelled over my shoulder and heard a slight 'okay' from her.

After a refreshing, warm shower, I left the bathroom. Bella was looking out the window, now dressed in a mint green sweater and white shorts. I went into the closet and wore a navy blue suit and crisp white dress shirt with shiny black shoes.

Today, I was thinking about going to my office—the outside world one. I have been working from home for a long time and must see how everything is going there.

I stepped out and hugged Bella from behind. She leaned into me and sighed. I don't want to leave her.

*Then don't leave her dumbass! Bring her along!*

*Thanks for the wise advice, Dom.*

"Where are you going, Damien?" she asked.

## Chapter 46

"Office baby. I have to see how everything is going on there," I said, kissing her cheek. "Wanna come with me?"

"Can I?" she asked all excited.

"Of course you can."

"Okay, then, I'll change." She started going into the closet when I pulled her back.

"What's wrong with these? You don't have to change. Come on," I said.

"But I should look good like you do. You are wearing a suit." I just pecked her lips and smiled.

The car was waiting for us outside. Once we were in the car, Bella started fidgeting with her fingers. I frowned and held her hands in mine.

"Hey, what's wrong? Do you not feel good? Tell me." I did not try to mask my concern for her in my voice.

"I feel okay. I'm just nervous. I'm coming with you to your office in such an outfit. What will people think? What will your employees think?" She pouted her lips and looked towards the window. I almost 'awed' at her. I cupped her face in my hands and made her look at me.

"Baby, there is nothing wrong with your outfit. Besides, you're the boss here. No one can question you. And you look cute," I said, and she cracked a smile.

"You always know how to make me feel better," she commented.

"That's my job, isn't it?"

We reached the building in half an hour and exited the car before helping Bella out. We entered the building, and Bella looked around in awe.

"I should not be surprised at the beauty of this place after seeing your house. But I can't help myself."

The corner of my lips twitched as I moulded my hand in hers. Some employees greeted me and looked questioningly at Bella. I ignored them and went to the reception. I remember firing the last receptionist because of her constant flirting with the guests. So I hired a new one. Luca.

"Luca, is Mr. Charles present today?" I asked in a businessman tone.

"Hello, good afternoon, Sir. Yes, Mr. Charles is present today. I called him straight after your call."

"Good."

I nodded and walked to the elevator with Bella at my side. I pressed the top floor button and watched as the doors closed.

"Who is Mr. Charles, Damien?" Bella asked. I leaned against the wall and held Bella in front of me by her waist.

"He's my assistant. Gage Charles," I said, and buried my face in her neck, placing small kisses.

She giggled and shoved me lightly, but I didn't budge.

"You have to try harder, sweetie," I said, laughing at her attempts.

A ping sound indicated that we had reached my floor and exited the elevator.

# Chapter 47

**Damien's POV**

I kept my hand on Bella's waist while exiting the elevator. The floor here is sometimes slippery, and I don't want her to fall and hurt herself.

On the way to my cabin, Gage greeted me and asked what he was supposed to do today. This was his second day at work with me. The next day, I found my mate; since then, he has been working with Nate.

"I want the financial reports first, then I will tell you what will be next. Bring the file to my cabin," I said and walked to my cabin.

It was similar to my office back in the pack house but a little bigger. I sat on my chair, and Bella just walked around the room, touching the paintings on the wall. I sat there watching her like a creep, but she won't mind, right?

There was a knock on the door, and soon, Gage came in with a folder. He placed the folder on my table, and I asked him to leave. I started going through the documents, and I'm impressed.

After finishing the files, I looked up to see what Bella was doing and saw her sitting on the chair in front of my desk, staring at me.

"You know it's not good to stare, baby," I said, chuckling, and she just smiled.

"Yeah, as if you don't do that all the time. Don't think it unnoticed, babe." Uh, oh! I guess I got caught. I raised my hands in a surrender motion.

"Can't blame me now. It's your fault for being so beautiful." I leaned back on the chair and laughed at her expression. I opened my arms for her, and without wasting a second, she came to me. I held her on my lap and kissed her hair.

"What was in the file?" she asked, drawing circles on my suit-clad biceps.

"The financial status of the company. It shows how much profit or loss we have earned."

"Oh, is this work difficult?"

"Yes, but I am used to all this," I reply. I got off my chair, still holding Bella in my arms. I laid her on the big couch in the corner, took off my jacket, and sat down. I placed Bella's head on my lap and massaged her scalp.

She let out a content sigh and closed her eyes. "When do you want to get married?" she asked all of a sudden.

Hmm… "As soon as possible. When do you want to get married?" I asked.

"Whenever you want to," was her simple reply.

"Well, what about next month?" I suggested, and she opened her eyes. She seemed to be thinking about it.

"Not a bad idea. We should do that. I want to be Mrs. Owen as soon as possible," she said, chuckling, and placed a big kiss on her lips.

"Okay, then, I will arrange everything. You just tell me how, where, and what should be done," I said, and she nodded. She closed her eyes again, and I thought about our wedding.

Then I remembered I didn't give her the ring! I am such a stupid mate!

*That you are, I can't deny that.*

*Shut up, Dom! Not the time!*

*Well, when are you planning on giving her the ring, then? Next year? Hmm?*

*No! I will give it to her tonight. In a special way. You wait.*

*Oh, I am waiting, don't screw up like always.*

*I didn't screw up anytime! What are you talking about?*

*Well, how you proposed to her and how she could almost say 'no', I think you should be careful.*

*I hate it when you're right.*

*Which is most of the time.*

*Shut up!*

# Chapter 47

I blocked him out and formed a brilliant plan to give her the ring. Now that the wedding date is decided we have a lot to do.

The thought of being married to Bella brings an unknown sensation in my stomach. Yes, we are mates in our world, but now she will bear my surname, too. She will be recognised as Isabella Owen in everyone's eyes now.

I noticed that Bella had fallen asleep. I carefully placed a cushion below her head. I sat on my chair again and called Gage in.

He came in a few minutes later.

"I want you to set up a meeting with the Ramons on Friday morning. Inform them that the meeting should not take more than two hours, or I won't bother considering their offer even if gives me profit."

"Absolutely, Sir. Anything else, Sir?"

"Yeah, I want you to shortlist the best wedding planners and bring me the list before you go home. That's all."

He gave me a surprised look. "Not to sound nosy, Sir, but for who's wedding?" he asked cautiously. I almost laughed at his expression but kept on my emotionless face.

"My wedding, Gage," I said monotonously, trying to hide my excitement while mentioning it.

"Oh! Congratulations, Sir! Who's the lucky lady?" he asked, suddenly very excited.

I raised my eyebrow, and he composed himself. "Thank you. The lucky lady is sleeping on the couch right now." I nodded in that direction, and he noticed Bella, sleeping peacefully like a baby.

"Okay, then, Sir. The work will be done soon. Congratulations again," Gage said, and left my cabin.

A big smile took over my face as soon as he left, and I sighed, looking over at Bella.

"They think you are the lucky one. They couldn't be more wrong, baby. I'm the one lucky here," I murmured.

I got up from my chair, kneeled by the couch, and caressed her rosy cheeks. I placed a tender kiss on her lips and stared at her.

"Now, who's staring, mister?" she said, surprising me. She didn't open her eyes but chuckled.

I narrowed my eyes and climbed on top of her. Now she was fully awake and staring wide eyes at me.

"Damien! What are you doing? Get off!" she said and tried to push my chest. I balanced myself on my elbow on either side of her and kissed her everywhere: on the face, neck, and chest. She giggled in response.

She ran her hands through my hair and placed my head on her chest. I sighed and closed my eyes, savouring the moment.

"Hey, Damien! I wanted to show you this— OH, SHIT! I'M SORRY!!" Nate screamed and ran out before I could rip his head off.

And I thought he would leave us alone now…

# Chapter 48

**Isabella's POV**

After Nate's interruption, Damien went after him because 'he came in to show him something', but inside I know he went to beat him to a pulp.

Half an hour later, Damien came back satisfied and smiling, confirming my doubts.

I just stared at him. I don't have the will to fight him on this.

He climbed back on me and left feather-like kisses on my neck, and I giggled at the ticklish feeling. His lips left my neck and connected with my lips. He kissed me slowly and softly while his hand caressed my hips. Damien spread my knees apart and made himself comfortable in between. Now, he was holding his weight by his elbows and his hands in my hair.

A groan erupted from his throat, which received a moan from me in response. Damien pulled away after some time to catch our breath. His head rested on my chest, and his hands played with my hair.

I cleared my throat and pushed him back up. He got off me and helped me up. He patted my clothes and ran a hand through my hair to make it look less messy, then proceeded to tidy his suit. After that was done, we were ready to go home. But Damien said we have to wait. He spoke on his phone for a minute and then turned to me.

"Okay, we can go now." He took my hand and guided me to the elevator.

"Who were you talking to?" I asked casually. I don't care who he talks to. I trust him more than I do myself. I want to start a conversation.

## The Unloved Mate

"It was Gage. I asked him to make a list of the best wedding planners and give it to me by this time, but it seemed like it would take more time so I told him to mail it to me," he said.

With a jerk of his hands, he pulled me to him, sticking our bodies together. I laughed at his attempt and hugged him. He sighed and dropped his head on my shoulder.

"I will never get tired of this. Ever," he said.

"Tired of what?" I asked. My fingers thread his soft hair, earning a sigh from him.

"Of holding you. Being with you."

My heart melted at his reply.

"Me, too," I said, and we stood there, just holding onto each other. Loving the feeling of being so close he had to bend low to reach my height, but he didn't complain. After hugging and kissing, we finally reached the ground floor and out of the building into the car. We drive home was silent, a comfortable silence. Damien's hand wrapped securely around me, and my head on his shoulder.

Soon, we reached home, and I went straight to our bedroom to freshen up while Damien went to the kitchen to get some food for himself. I washed my face and pulled my hair in a messy bun. I changed into one of Damien's smallest T-shirts and my pink sweatpants. I padded downstairs and bumped into Damien on the way. I fell on my butt and groaned while rubbing my backside. I glared at him. While I was groaning in pain from the impact, he stood tall and strong not affected by sweet little me.

He pulled me up and held me in his arms. He brushed the bangs of hair off my face and smiled. I forgave him.

We went to the dining hall for dinner, where Nate and Damien's parents were waiting. We took our seats, or Damien took his seat and made me sit on his lap. My backside was still giving me problems, but I managed.

Damien parted his legs a little and made sit in between so that my butt won't touch the chair. I smiled gratefully at him, and he fed us, as always. He slid his hand under the table and rubbed my butt, making me gasp in shock. Everyone turned to me, giving me concerned looks.

## Chapter 48

"What happened, dear? Is something wrong?" Lily asked.

I just smiled and nodded my head. "Yeah, just the curry is a little spicy. Nothing important."

"Oh, really, baby? But I don't think the curry is that spicy." He is a dead wolf today! I turned my head and glared at him. He smirked and placed a spoonful of beans near my mouth.

I angrily ate it and ignored his attempts to talk. I stomped to our bedroom and hid under the covers quickly when dinner was over. I heard the door opening and then shutting close. Damien's smell filled the room.

I pretended to be asleep, but all of that was forgotten when he pulled the cover off me and tickled me senselessly. I giggled uncontrollably and tried to shove his hands off of me, but what could I do? He is like a mountain.

Finally, he stopped and fell on the bed beside me. He leaned on an elbow facing me.

"I'm sorry, baby." And I forgave him for almost embarrassing me in front of his family.

I flung my hand around him and pecked his lips, smiling brightly.

"Forgiven," I said and kissed him again. When we grew tired, we cuddled with each other until sleep took over.

Before going to sleep, a thought came to me. We didn't tell anyone about our wedding in a month.

# Chapter 49

**Damien's POV**

Last night, things didn't go well, and I couldn't give her the ring, but I will give it to her today.

I opened the blue velvet box and caressed the beautiful diamond ring with my thumb. I am still nervous. I know what her answer will be. She said yes before but still can't help it. I guess it's natural.

I heard a knock on my office door. I dropped the box in the drawer and sat up straight. The door opened, and a bright smile took over my face as Bella happily skipped in. I could do anything to keep that smile on her face.

"Hey, beautiful," I said, getting up from my chair. I stood close to her and hugged her. She was taken away from me by Nina and Cameron. They wanted some girl time. I could not resist three puppy dog eyes simultaneously, especially if it included Bella's.

"Hey, handsome," she replied, making me chuckle. I can't believe she's the same Bella I found in the Howlers Pack. Frightened and shy. Now look at her. The circumstances have changed her drastically, in a good way.

"How was your day?" I asked.

"It was good, but I missed you a lot," she replied with a slight frown. I gently rubbed my finger on her forehead to get rid of that frown.

"Don't frown. I don't like it when you frown. And by the way, I missed you more," I said, which made her smile.

"Hm. How was your day without me?" she asked cheekily.

"I think it went pretty well," I said, to which she pouted.

"Aw, baby, don't pout those pretty lips." And I kissed her slowly.

# Chapter 49

"But you lied. You didn't miss me at all. And here I was, missing you like I didn't see you for a year!"

"I was kidding, babe. I missed you so much. You occupied my mind all the time. I couldn't concentrate at all. Seriously."

"Really?"

"Really."

She smiled that beautiful smile and pecked my lips. "Good boy!" She patted my head and giggled. I narrowed my eyes playfully and pretended to bite her fingers.

"Let's go out, baby," I said. I had to put my plans into action now.

"What? Where?" she asked, getting up from her position on top of me.

"Somewhere."

"Tell me?"

"It's a surprise, baby," I smirked when her cheeks puffed and her mouth straightened. This is something she started doing recently. And it's damn cute. "Come on." I grabbed her hands and dragged her with me.

"But Damien! Let me get ready!"

I looked at her head to toe. She looked pretty in her seafoam green dress.

"You look good. No need to change, sweetheart," I said, kissing her forehead before dragging her again.

"According to you, I look pretty in everything!" She huffed, giving in and letting me drag her.

I opened the door of my new, sleek, black Ferrari, and she made herself comfortable. I hopped in the driver's seat and started the engine.

I slipped the ring box into my suit pocket while Bella whined like a baby. It was distracting because of all those pouts and frowns. But I managed.

After an hour of driving and Bella giving me a silent treatment, we reached our destination. I exited the car and opened the door for Bella, and she ignored me. I sighed and held her hand, to which she didn't protest.

She gasped when she saw my preparation and took small steps forward. I kneeled on one knee and held the open box in my hand. She turned around and gasped again. Now, I could see the tears filling her eyes.

"Bella, will you marry me?"

She just stood there, not making any move. My nervousness was growing with each ticked second.

"Bella?" I said.

She blinked and looked at me again. This time, a huge grin on her face and tears spilling down her rosy cheeks. "Yes! A million times, yes!" she said and jumped on me. We both fell on the cool sand, holding each other for dear life, shedding tears of happiness.

After some time, we got up, and I slid the ring on her ring finger. She looked at it with love and adoration, making me happy. I chose the right ring.

New tears fell from her eyes, and I wiped them before they could touch the ground.

"Hey, Bella, baby, don't cry. Please."

She just shook her head, hugged me tightly, and hid her face in my suit. "I'm so happy, Damien. I never thought anyone would do so much for me. You did all this for me even though I said yes already. You didn't have to," she said, still not looking at me.

I held her tiny chin and made her look at me. "Baby, I did what I wanted to, not because I had to. I will do anything that will possibly make you happy. I will do anything for you. This is nothing compared to the extent I can go for you," I said.

"How can I ever repay you, Damien? You have done so much for me. Let me do something for you in return. Let me make you happy. Please tell me what you want. I'll give it to you in a heartbeat," she said, looking into my eyes.

"All I want is for you to be happy. You don't have to repay me, baby."

"Shut up and tell me. Now!"

"Stubborn, are we?" I said, chuckling, but her stare shut me up instantly. I sighed. "Fine. Just promise me something."

"Anything."

# Chapter 49

"Tell me you will never leave me. You will always be with me when I wake up in the morning and during the day. Be next to me while I sleep. Love me forever and ever. And always smile like the beautiful ray of sunshine that you are," I said in all seriousness.

"Promise," she replied without hesitation. I smiled and kissed her.

Bella's stomach growled during our heated make-out, and her face turned red.

"Let's have dinner. Don't want my fiancée starving," I said and led her to the small setup I had made for dinner.

"I like the sound of it," she mumbled. I don't think that was meant for me to hear.

We had our dinner peacefully. We talked about our upcoming wedding mostly. I could see the excitement in her eyes when she shared the plans she made with Nina.

We revealed our wedding date in the morning, and everyone took it well. No one complained about how early the wedding was or how little time they had to prepare. Everyone was set into action within an hour.

"I like the idea of a beach wedding. What do you think?" Bella asked.

"I like whatever you like. You're the bride, baby. Your choice, my choice."

"And about the colours? I'm confused about which ones to choose."

"How about both of us choose one colour, and then we collaborate on both?" I suggested.

"That sounds good. Tell me a colour."

"Um... golden," I said. I liked the colour, so why not?

"Okay, I like that. Now, how about white? The colour of peace and purity, also matches with golden," she said.

I smiled and stole a lazy kiss from her. "Absolutely. How thoughtful."

After dinner, I took her to the small cabin by the beach and spent the night in pure bliss.

# Chapter 50

**Isabella's POV**

Yesterday was like a dream, a beautiful dream. I glanced at the stunning diamond ring on my ring finger, and a smile formed on my lips. Damien was sprawled on the bed beside me, his arm wrapped around me and facing the other side. We were still at the cabin where Damien brought us after the proposal. I lifted his arm from my stomach and got off the bed.

Picking up our clothes from different room corners, I piled them on the small couch. I took my clothes, went to the bathroom, took a nice shower, and brushed my teeth.

"Bella? Bella! Where are you?!" I heard Damien's frantic voice call out.

I came out of the bathroom and immediately went to his side.

"Baby, where did you go? I was so worried!" he said while hugging me.

"I was in the bathroom taking a shower."

"Next time, please tell me."

"Of course. But what happened?"

"I was scared that someone would take you again. I was scared," he said. He was not facing me, but I could feel his fear. I cupped his face in my hands and made him look at me.

"Hey, nothing's gonna happen to me as long as you are here. I trust you more than anyone. And besides, it's our turn to get our happily ever after. You know, get married, have loads of pups, and then grow old."

"How many pups do you want?" All the fear vanished and was replaced by the cocky smirk on his face.

"I want, um, maybe four," I said. I guess that's the most I could do.

"Hmm... I want ten," he said showing me his ten fingers.

# Chapter 50

My eyes widened, and I slapped his arm. "What do you take me for? A pup-producing machine?!"

He only chuckled and kissed me. "No, baby, I was just messing with you. I want three kids. two baby boys and one baby girl," he said seriously.

"Why?"

He laid down from his sitting position and pulled me on top of him. He shrugged his shoulders and said nothing.

After a long silence, I asked the question I wanted to ask for a long time.

"Damien, did you find out why he kidnapped me?" I felt Damien stiffen under me but then relax.

"Yeah."

"Tell me."

"Okay. His name is Benson, and he was my cousin."

I gasped, and my eyes widened. His cousin?

"Yes, he was my cousin. He wanted revenge on you for what your previous pack did. Which is wrong since you did nothing wrong."

"What happened?"

"A few years earlier, Benson's family visited us from Austria. He brought his mate with him so that she could see the whole family. One day, his mom, dad, and mate ran into the forest while he was in the office with me. Rogues attacked them but they ran. They came across your old pack and asked for help. But instead, they sided with the rogues and killed them on the side. Benson broke that day.

"He told me that he would avenge them and asked me to help him. Of course, I agreed. He left the grounds and became a rogue because of losing his mate. He has never contacted me since then and has never given me any details. I figured it was your pack when we took him to the cells."

I let the words sink in and digest them. "So it was not my fault. It was my old pack."

"Yes, baby."

"Okay."

"Okay?"

"Yes. What can we do now? The past is in the past. Now, all we have to do is live our lives happily. Don't dwell on the past," I said.

We didn't talk much after that because his mom called and yelled at him to bring me back home because she had many things to plan for the wedding.

Damien got dressed, and we left. It was 9:00 am, and breakfast was being served when we reached home.

During breakfast, Lily and I discussed the location of the wedding and how the colours that we chose would be used, etc.

After breakfast, Cole and Cameron accompanied me to the back garden. We talked and talked for a couple of hours about everything. Cole mentioned how Nate was a real sweetheart, and Cameron said she wished her mate would be like ours. And how can I forget about our wedding?

By the time we returned inside, it was noon, and the sun was on top of our heads. I went straight to our room for a shower. I feel hot all over because of the sun.

After showering, I wore one of Damien's huge T-shirts and a pair of comfy boxers. I saw a small note sticking on the mirror. It was from Damien.

*Dear Bella,*

*I'm going out with the boys and Dad for some work. You were having fun in the garden, and I didn't want to disturb you so I left a note. I'll be back in an hour or two.*

*I'll miss you, baby. Be safe.*

*Love,*
*Damien.* ♥

I shrugged, tied my hair in a messy bun, and went downstairs again. I don't feel embarrassed to go down in his clothes because every mated female here wears their mate's clothes.

# Chapter 50

I saw all the girls and Lily chatting in the living room and joined them. They told me they already planned the spa and salon appointments, and there was no time to waste.

"So, where do you want your wedding to happen?" Roza, a warrior's wife asked.

"I like Miami," I said and shrugged. Honestly, I don't care where it is held as long as it happens.

"Oh, goodie! That's a wonderful idea. Miami's a great destination. I'll start booking tickets for the guests, and we all can go by our private jet. We have to go there early to book the venues and all the reservations and als—" The front door opening cut off Lily.

The boys came in laughing their heads off, and a very flushed Damien. When they saw us, they cracked even more.

Damien came to me and hugged me, almost making me fall. I giggled when his warm breath fanned my neck.

"Baby, they are making fun of me!" he complained like a five-year-old.

"What happened, guys? Why are you making fun of him?" I raised an eyebrow at them.

"You would do too if you heard what happened," Nate said.

"Tell me!"

"Welp. We were coming back home after our work was done the whole way. He complained about how long the work took and how he missed you. By the time we reached the driveway, he was daydreaming about you, and when he came out of the car, he fell face-first into a ditch!" he explained.

"Aw. Don't laugh at him."

"See how nice my Bella is. Learn," Damien muttered, letting go of me.

"Okay, boys, time for some exciting news!" Lily squealed and clapped her hands together.

"What?" all of them asked in unison.

Which was not creepy at all. Sarcasm intended.

"We are going to Miami!!"

# Chapter 51

**Isabella's POV**

Today, we are going to meet the wedding planner and confirm everything. Cole and Nate are coming with us so that they can help. But I know they just wanted to leave the house for a while.

We were in Damien's SUV, heading to the wedding planner's office. It's scorching today, so I wore some white shorts and a sky-blue crop top, and so did Cole. We almost look the same. I was almost hesitant to wear it since most wolves don't let their mates wear revealing clothes, but to my surprise, he didn't lash out. He complimented me and kissed me for how cute I looked.

Damien is not picky when it comes to my clothes. He says I can wear anything I want. If anyone looks at me he will rip them apart. But he won't stop me from wearing what I like.

I love this boy.

Damien was driving while I was beside him in the passenger's seat, and Nate and Cole were cuddled in the back seat.

"Could you guys give it a break? I think I'm gonna be sick seeing you like this!" Damien yelled at the lovebirds, who were cuddly and kissy-kissy.

"Oh, come on, you can't tell me to stop when you are practically all over Isabella every second of the day! Even now, your hand is on her thigh!" Nate shot back.

I glanced down and saw that Damien's hand was on my thigh, dangerously high. I glared at him, and he slid his hand to my knee.

"Whatever," Damien muttered.

"We're here!" Nate yelled suddenly, making us jump. I placed my hand on my chest to calm my breath.

"Stupid!" Damien muttered under his breath and parked the car outside the office. He opened the door for me, and Nate did the same for Cole. Aw.

# Chapter 51

Damien held my waist protectively and nudged me forward. I just smiled at him and walked into the office doors. The interior of the office was pure white with grey and black furniture. It screamed professional. We approached the receptionist.

"We are here to meet Mr. Kevin. We have an appointment," Damien said in a stern tone, strict business tone.

"Of course, Mr. Owen, Mr. Kevin is in his office. You can go in now. First door to the right," he said with a warm smile. Damien started to drag me with him, but I managed to say a small thank you to the receptionist.

Because these wolves don't have manners. Bad wolves.

Nate and Cole opted to stay outside his office and do nothing.

Damien knocked on the door, and a small soft 'come in' was heard. I thought Kevin was a guy.

We entered the office and just like outside, the walls and floor were pure white. The only difference was that the furniture was very colourful. The couches were rainbow-coloured, and the chairs were pink, yellow, and orange. I almost laughed at the choice of interior. Who has such bad taste?

"Mr. Owen, oh, I've been waiting for you," the soft voice said again. I turned my head in the direction and saw a man sitting on a chair across the reasonably large desk.

His posture, voice, looks and style screamed gay. I have nothing against gays, but the way he is eye-raping my soon-to-be hubby, I think I can make an exception.

He had dirty blonde hair that reached below his ears and grey eyes. He wore a colourful shirt with a scarf around his neck.

He smiled at us, and we returned it.

"Come here, have a seat, Mr. Owen," he said which could be translated to 'I would gladly ravish you, Mr. Owen'.

I held in a scowl and plastered a fake smile on my stupid face.

We took our seats, but Damien, being Damien, made me sit between his legs. I adjusted myself a little but stopped when Damien held my hips.

"Don't, baby. Later." His voice was strained, and I wondered what happened. I moved myself a little, and then it clicked. I held in the urge to slap myself on the head. Of course, he would feel uncomfortable.

I stilled, not moving an inch so I didn't create any trouble for him. He rubbed my tummy lightly and fixed his gaze on Kevin.

"So you are the lucky bride everyone is talking about. I'm Kevin. Nice to meet you," Kevin said and extended his hand towards me.

I shook his hand. "Nice to meet you, too, Kevin. I'm Isabella." Maybe he isn't too bad.

He kissed the back of my hand.

"Pleasure is all mine. Now, do you guys have a vague idea about how you want your wedding?" he asked seriously.

"Yes, actually, we decided we wanted a beach wedding in Miami. Once we reach there, the venue will be selected, and we would like the colours golden and white to be incorporated," Damien replied.

"Hm. Sounds good. And about the dresses?" Kevin asked back

"We are flying to Miami tomorrow, so everything will be done there itself."

"Hm. Good idea, we don't have time. So what time will you guys reach there?"

"In the evening, maybe."

"So I will meet you the day after, and then we can check out the venues and the decorations. Yeah?" Kevin suggested.

We nodded and agreed.

We left after half an hour after some more discussion. Nate and Cole were making out in the car when we came back, which earned him an earful from Damien.

"Don't ever do it in my car!" he sneered one last time before throwing Nate the keys. "For punishment, you will drive."

Damien settled in the backseat and pulled me in with him.

Nate started to drive the car, and soon, we were on the main road.

I felt something wet touch my neck and turned around. I saw Damien leaning against me with a smile.

## Chapter 51

"You did a great job turning me on in there. Want to continue?" He wiggled his eyebrows suggestively. I gasped at his poor attempt to get laid and slapped his arm.

"Stupid horny wolves," I muttered and closed my eyes.

"Okay, maybe later then?" I didn't have to look at him to say he was pouting.

"Maybe," I replied. I heard him whistle lowly.

I felt drowsy and sleep started to take over. I laid my head on Damien's lap and closed my eyes.

I felt him stroke my hair and kiss my cheek. Why do I feel so sleepy? I'm not even tired.

Then sleep took over.

# Chapter 52

I had a beautiful dream. Damien's lap is always the best place to fall asleep. The security it gives me is unmatched. I know I don't have to worry about anything else while I am sleeping.

The carefree atmosphere and the happiness of finally being with the love of my life brought a smile to my face.

In the dream, I could see the bright future ahead of me. The way Damien and I would will after getting married. Our kids, as babies and as grown-ups. Of course, there will be more than one of them.

The dream was the best I've had in my entire life up until this moment. It not only gave me immense happiness but also a sense of belonging. That future is mine. I have survived those days when I wanted to die, and now I am living my best life.

The dream lasted forever. In the short span of a few hours that I slept, I dreamt of my entire life ahead. Damien's love never changed in those days. And my love for him only grew. Our kids were the best in the world. They were loved by everyone, especially their grandparents who always pampered them and spoiled them. They received everything that I did not get while growing up. The regrets that I grew up with, they will never see. For them, the world will always be a bright place where only good things happen.

Damien was the perfect father to them. I tried my best to be a good mother. And in the dream, I was successful, too. I smiled in my sleep, feeling the warmth of Damien's body against mine. I could feel his hand stroking my hair gently, and a kiss dropped on my cheek. The dream turned sweeter after that.

In that dream, I wondered how long we could go on. How long was forever? Damien had promised that he would love her forever and that they would be together until then. But how long was that? I don't know. But somehow, the dream felt endless. The love we shared kept flowing like a steady stream with no end or origin.

# Chapter 52

******

"Mom!"

A small voice woke me from my sleep. It was morning, and I was sleeping in my bed. The space next to me was empty and cold. I frowned. Weren't we in the car? When did we reach home? I wanted to call out for Damien, but another voice called out before me.

"Mom! Open the door!"

I looked towards the door of our bedroom and got off the bed. Only then I realised that I was wearing silk pajamas. On the way to the door, I glanced at my appearance in the mirror and was surprised at what I saw. The last time I saw myself in the mirror, I wasn't this old. The face in the mirror was aged. If I had to guess, it was something in the late thirties.

I frowned and opened the door. In front of the door was a restless girl. She looked very familiar and unfamiliar at the same time. The girl looked at me with her big eyes and held my hand.

"Mom, why didn't you open the door earlier?" The girl was not happy. I bent a little on my knees and caressed her head.

"What happened so early in the morning?" I said naturally as if it was something I did daily. It was surprising how familiar I was with these actions.

The little girl was not that little. Her petite body was just like mine. She was older than ten but looked like her age was no more than seven.

"It's Luca again! He broke my backpack! How will I go to school now!" The girl cried out in frustration. This was not the first time Luca had done something naughty.

"Okay, where is your dad? Did you tell him to fix it?" I said as I closed the door behind me after exiting the room. "We will get you a new one today. It's too late to get one now."

The girl became happy. "Okay! I want the same one that Rosell has! Her bag has so many stickers on it. I like it."

# The Unloved Mate

I smile and hum to her request. I went down the stairs and called out, "Damien?"

However, I saw a little boy running towards me instead of me. The girl beside me instantly went into a defense mode against the boy.

"Mom, you should scold him!" The girl pointed at the little boy who crashed into me and hugged my legs. I couldn't help but laugh.

"What did you do again, huh?" I picked up the boy in my arms and held him up to see his cute face.

The boy smiled innocently and said, "Nothing..."

The girl immediately became red. "Liar! Wait, let me tell Daddy about this! He will set you straight! That was bad. That was new. Grandpa had brought it for me a month ago, and you broke it!"

I stared at the boy's face and thought, so, this is Luca. What a cute little boy. The girl then ran up the stairs shouting, for her dad.

Feeling restless, I followed up, too. The girl went into the room that was Damien's study. Everything was the same as I remembered it. The house was where we lived, and the rooms and decor were the same. However, there were an additional number of kids, and I seemed to have grown old.

The slight restlessness didn't leave my body but grew as I approached the study. There was a sound of the little girl complaining and another deep voice humming along to her complaints, paying attention to every detail of Luca's wrongdoings.

"Okay, but he is your brother, isn't he? You should forgive him for these small mistakes. Mom and I will take you out and get you a new bag today, okay? Don't be so angry at him. You know Luca loves you. He only wants to play with his sister."

My hand stopped at the knob as I listened to Damien talking. He was precisely the same as I remember. With a smile on my face, I opened the door. Damien sat on the chair behind his desk with the little girl on his lap. The girl was clinging to his neck while puffing up her cheeks.

# Chapter 52

"Won't you say sorry to your sister?" I put Luca down and patted his head. Luca ran along and went to his sister. He poked her back and giggled.

The little girl's cheeks deflated, and she immediately slid down from Damien's lap and started to chase Luca out of the room.

I watched them as they disappeared with a smile on my face that couldn't get any better. Before I could turn around, a pair of strong arms wrapped around me from the back, and a small kiss was placed on the base of my neck. Life couldn't get any happier. This is the life I dreamt of. This is the life I want.

# Chapter 53

**Damien's POV**

Bella has been feeling very tired lately. She had fallen asleep on my lap on the way back in the car, not that I mind. But what got me worried was that the moment she got out of the car, she threw up! I pulled her hair back from her face and rubbed her back soothingly. After throwing up she couldn't even stand properly. I told Nate and Cole to go inside the house, and I'd take Bella straight to the pack doctor.

I carried her to the pack doctor and placed her on the bed.

The doctor came in shortly. "What's wrong with Luna, Alpha?" she asked while checking her pulse.

"I don't know exactly, but she has been getting really tired over small things, and she threw up when we got out of the car before she passed out. What could it be, doctor?" I said with worry, lacing my words.

"Alpha, can you please wait outside while I run some tests on Luna?" the doctor said, and I nodded.

I placed a tender kiss on Bella's forehead before leaving. I sat on the couch outside the room, my head in my hands, thinking about all the possibilities. Was it because of the hot climate? Did she eat something wrong? Maybe side effects of the medicine the doctor gave her?

"Alpha, you can go in now," a nurse told me I didn't waste any time and opened the door.

Bella was awake now and listening intently to the doctor's words.

"Bella? How are you feeling, baby?" I asked while taking a seat next to her on the bed. I kissed her cheek.

"I'm fine, Damien. More than fine, actually," she said with a smile on her face.

## Chapter 53

"I'll leave you guys alone," the doctor says, and mouths something to Bella before closing the door behind her.

"What is it?" I asked her. I want to know what was the cause of her bad health.

"Um, how do I tell you, I…" she muttered avoiding my gaze.

"What is it, baby? You know you can tell me anything," I said, making her look at me.

"Okay. But don't freak out, please. Just remember that I want this, and I'm very happy." I nodded even though I was not sure what she was saying.

She took my hand in hers and placed it on her flat tummy. I gave her a confused look. Why did she do that?

But then I felt it. A faint heartbeat. In her stomach. What does that mean? Is it real? "Bella? Is this what I think it is?" I looked at her wide eyes, and she responded with a nervous smile.

"Oh, my God! It's real? You are pregnant?!" I asked for confirmation. She nodded once again and I felt like I just died of happiness.

A big grin took over my face, and I hugged Bella tightly. Happy tears pricked my eyes and I didn't bother wiping them off. They were happy tears, and everyone should know how happy I am.

"Damien, say something," Bella said.

I pulled away and cupped her small face in my hand. "I don't have words to describe how happy you made me today. You're carrying our baby. It feels like a dream," I said, happy tears streaming down my cheeks.

Leaning in, I place a small tender kiss on her lips, then her flat stomach, for my baby.

Then the doctor came in. "Congratulations, Alpha. Luna is two weeks pregnant."

"Thank you, Doc. I can't explain how happy I am to hear this news," I said.

"Of course, but you must take good care of Luna. During the first three months of pregnancy, you have to be very careful because there are high chances that the baby can be hurt. And you have to go to the doctor for regular checkups. Your first check-up will be tomorrow," she informed us.

Hearing all those things made me feel funny in the stomach. The thought of mini me, or mini Bella running around the house made me want to cry in happiness.

"Sure, doctor. We'll take care," Bella responded.

"I have prescribed a few medicines for your nausea, but if there is even the slightest bit of trouble, don't hesitate to call me. Alpha, you can take Luna home now. I will send her diet plan to you later," she said and went out of the room.

I sighed and lay next to Bella. I rubbed her belly lightly. It will be swollen like a ball within a few months. I mentally chuckled at that.

I felt Bella's hands stroking my head and leaned into her touch.

"Damien, are you really happy? If you're doing this for me—"

I cut her off by placing my lips on hers. "Absolutely not. I am already in love with our little ball of sunshine. So discard that thought from your mind, baby," I scolded her.

"Okay," she said and giggled.

Soon, we left the hospital wing and went back to the house.

Nate and Cole, along with Cameron and my parents, head to us. We sat on the couch in front of them, I wrapped my hand on her stomach protectively. I'm already so possessive of this baby. I hope it's a tiny baby girl, just like Bella.

"Damien, would you tell us what the doctor said? We were worried," Mom asked me.

I looked at Bella for confirmation. She told me to announce it to everyone as soon as possible.

She nodded a little, and I took a deep breath. I cleared my throat and—

"You're not giving a speech here!" Nate said dryly.

"Bella is expecting!" I said loudly and clearly. Hopefully, everyone in the room heard me.

"A baby," I added as an afterthought. Wolves have weird brains. They can think of anything.

# Chapter 53

The shocked look on their face confirmed that they did hear me, and I leaned on the couch.

"Oh, my God! I'm gonna be a grandma!"

"I'm proud of you, son! I hope it's a girl!"

"I'm gonna go shopping for the baby! Tomorrow!"

"Me too, Cole! Let's go together!"

"You knocked her up! I'm proud of you, man!" Nate said.

"Bella! What happened, honey?!" Mom asked suddenly.

I turned to see tears streaming down her face. I frowned and wrapped my hands around her. I made her sit on my lap and silently told everyone to leave, which they did. "Baby, sweetie, why are you crying? Is something wrong? Are you not feeling good? Tell me," I asked and rubbed her back with one hand while the other wiped her tear-stained cheeks.

"No... nothing's wrong. These bloody... hormones are... messing with me... Damien," she managed to say. I was relieved that she was all right.

"Don't be sorry, baby, it's not your fault. And I'll be there for you always," I said. I tucked a piece of hair behind her ear and made her look at me. Her nose was running, and her eyes were red.

"Baby, don't cry. I don't like when you cry. Smile? For me?"

"Okay," she said and smiled which made me smile.

"We will get through this together," I promised.

"Damien?"

"Yes?"

"You said you would help me, right?"

"Yup!"

"Will you do what I say?" I could sense the hesitation in her voice.

"Of course. You name it, and it will be done."

"These hormones are messing with me and making me all horny. Will you help me with it?"

She didn't have to ask twice. I picked her up and sprinted to our bedroom, ready to make her forget everything.

# Chapter 54

**Isabella's POV**

In the morning, everything went in a blur. Everyone was excited about the wedding and Miami but also fussing over tiny things.

Lily informed me earlier that she had a famous designer to make wedding gowns for me, and she needed clarification, so after checking the venues, I had to go to the boutique with her. Huff! Wedding stuff is so tiring!

We arrived at our destination in Miami by evening the same day and went straight to the mansion Damien had booked for us to stay in. We are going to relax now and start working from tomorrow.

I huffed and dropped to the floor when I unpacked the last shirt from my bag. Damien said he would do it and I should only rest after the long plane journey, but I started unpacking the moment he left the room. He went out with Nate and Adam to get some things done.

I heard the door opening, but I was too tired to bother. Footsteps get closer, and Damien's scent hits me. I closed my eyes and sighed.

"Baby girl, I told you to rest, not work! Don't overexert yourself. It's not good for you and the baby," he scolded me. He picked me up and placed me on the bed. He lay beside me and put his head on my stomach.

"I can't believe we postponed the scan. Tomorrow, you will be very busy, or I would have taken you for the scan at a nearby hospital. I want to see the little thing," he whined.

"Don't worry, Damien. We can go early in the morning for the scan, and we will see the venues in the afternoon. Then you can see the little thing, okay?" I suggested and saw his eyes lit up.

## Chapter 54

"Agreed! Now I brought dinner here itself. I know how exhausted you are. Eat up all you can and have a good sleep," he said passing me the tray stacked with food.

"I'm gonna take a nice long shower. When I come back, I want at least half of the tray empty, got that?" I nodded, and he pecked my lips before he went to the bathroom.

I started eating. By the time Damien returned, I had finished most of the food. I think the baby is very hungry. Damien found it amusing, and that cost him a smack on the head by yours truly.

After having so much food, my eyes started to droop, so I lay on the bed and closed them. I felt the bed dip and Damien's large, warm arm wrap around my stomach.

"Good night, Bella," he whispered in my ear and kissed my forehead. Then he whispered, "Good night, baby", and kissed my stomach.

The next morning, Damien and I were all set for the scan. I could sense his excitement and nervousness. He had gotten an appointment from a doctor—who was a wolf, too—here in Miami itself. I buttoned the last button of my light blue shirt and sprayed some perfume.

"You done? I don't want to be late, sweetie," Damien called from the closet.

I huffed and stormed towards the closet where he was standing shirtless. I scoffed.

"Are you done? I don't want to be late, darling."

He turned around and gave me a sheepish smile. His shirt was on him in a flash, and he muttered a small sorry.

Soon we were in his car, driving to the gynaecologist. We arrived in fifteen minutes and had to wait another five minutes because she was attending to someone else.

"Mr. and Mrs. Owen?" the nurse called.

Damien and I stood up. "That's us. Can we go in now?" Damien asked, and the nurse nodded.

"Hello, Alpha Damien and Luna Isabella. You are here for your first scan, am I right?" the doctor greeted.

We both nodded.

## The Unloved Mate

"Okay, so I want you to change into this gown and lay on the small bed there. I'll get the machine ready," she tells me, and I go behind the curtain to change.

"All right, I'm done." I laid down on the bed. The doctor came in with Damien. He took my hands in his instantly.

There was a big cut on the gown on the belly area. She lifted the cloth, exposing my skin, and brought some gel.

"This will feel a little cold," the doctor warned and applied the gel to my lower stomach.

I shivered at the touch but didn't move too much. Damien's hold on my hand tightens.

She brought the small scanner rod and moved it around my skin.

"There, Mr. and Mrs. Owen, is your baby." She pointed to a small dot on the screen and I almost burst out crying. I look at Damien, but he is staring at the screen as if it's the most beautiful art in the world, and I just turn back happily.

"It is so small."

"It looks like a peanut."

Damien said at the same time. I turn my head in his direction and glare at him.

"Don't you dare call my baby a peanut!" I told him, and he shrugged.

"Do you want the printouts?" the doctor asked, and we nodded.

We thanked the doctor and went back home with happy grins on our faces. We showed everyone the pictures. They gushed about how happy they were and how the baby would get all the love in the world.

My baby is truly lucky.

Kevin showed up after breakfast. He had brought a few ideas with him that suited our plan. But still, we decided to see the places ourselves.

After four hours of continuous searching, we finally found the place we liked, and finalised it.

We booked the venue for the date and went home. Then I remembered that I had to go with Lily for the dress in an hour.

# Chapter 54

"Damien, I have to go with Lily to see the wedding dresses she ordered for me in an hour," I informed him.

"Cool. When will you be back?" he asked. He was sitting on the couch with a book in his hand, and I was beside him with my head on his shoulder.

"Don't know. Maybe an hour or even more," I replied.

"Baby girl, don't stress yourself too much, it's not good for you. Or her," he said, his book long forgotten and his undivided attention was on me.

I resisted the urge to roll my eyes at him. "We don't know if it's a girl or boy yet. What if it's a boy? Will you love him any less?" I asked him. It was a stupid question because I knew Damien would love this baby, no matter what.

"Hey! Don't say that! I will love my peanut, let it be a baby boy or baby girl, I will love them the same," he said defensively.

"I know that, Damien. I'm just teasing you. And stop calling my baby a peanut!" I almost shouted the last part.

"But it looked like a peanut," he justified. One glare from me shut him up. It's crazy how he is wrapped around my little finger, but I enjoy it too much.

I just huffed and went for a nice shower for the third time today.

Exactly after an hour, Lily came to our room, and I left with her, not without saying bye to Damien, of course.

"This is gonna be so fun!" Lily squealed. At the last moment, Cole and Nina joined us, too, and we decided to choose my dress.

**At the boutique...**

I'm confused as hell! I have two dresses in front of me, and I love both! I don't understand how other brides find the perfect dress! Both the dresses are beautiful, and I can't select any one.

"Mom! Why aren't we the designer make a dress that is a fusion of these two? Then we don't have to decide and break our heads!" Nina squealed.

"That's a good idea. I will start working on it if you want," the designer said.

"That's fantastic. Then you start your work and don't send it home, give it a call. Anyone can see it," Lily said, and finally, we headed back home.

# Chapter 55

**Damien's POV**

Today's the day. Today, my Bella will officially be mine. After weeks of planning and stressing, it's finally time.

I fixed my tie again to make sure I looked fine. I was wearing a black tux with a black tie. It usually didn't take long for me to get ready, but today, I took a good sixty-five minutes to look even presentable.

I didn't get a wink of sleep last night because Bella was held captive by the girls the whole time. We were not supposed to see each other until the wedding. It has been pure torture. I even stooped so low as to sneak into her room, but Nina kicked me out.

"Damien! Are you listening?" Adam shouted in my ear, breaking my train of thought.

"Huh? Yeah, I'm listening. What were you saying?" I asked. He sighed and shook his head. "Dude, you have been staring at this mirror for fifteen minutes. Are you narcissistic?" he asked.

"No. I'm just trying not to faint on my wedding day. By giving myself a pep talk in my mind," I replied honestly.

"Don't worry, brother. It will be fine, and I can tell if not now you will faint at the altar when you see Isa. She looks like a goddess in the dress," Jared said.

"Yup! I could pay a fortune to see that," Jacob joined him.

Why do I have to get these idiots as brothers? "Wait. Have you seen her? Did you speak to her?" I asked them, and they nodded.

"Do you have a picture?" Hope in my eyes was evident.

"Nope. Sorry. She was still getting ready, so we didn't take any pictures," Michael said, and I nodded before turning back to the mirror.

I don't look half bad.

"Honey! It's time!" my mom shouted from the other side of the door. Our mansion was an hour away from the beach venue.

We all settled in the limo. We reached the venue, and I thought, 'This is it. We made it'. Bella and I have been through everything together, and now we finally have our happy ending.

I smile and take my place at the altar. Jared stood behind me as my best man, and Jacob, Michael, and Nate, as my groomsmen.

*I'm waiting, baby...*

**Isabella's POV**

Everyone is rushing here and there, trying to get everything done perfectly, while I'm sitting on the chair in front of the mirror doing nothing and feeling completely useless. But I couldn't do anything, the girls threatened me that if I got up, they would cake my face with makeup.

So I listened.

I am already in my wedding dress, and it's truly gorgeous. My hair is in a messy bun with some strands framing my face. The girls are fussing over what kind of makeup should be done.

I looked at the clock in the room and realised I had only one hour more. One hour.

"Girls! One hour left! Fast do something! Anything!" I said.

They stopped whatever they were doing and focused on me. Within forty-five minutes, I was ready to marry the love of my life.

We settled in the limo that Damien sent earlier. The bridesmaids, Cole, Cameron, and Rozelle—one of the pack members I befriended—stood in a line before me. My maid of honour, Nina, stood by me, ready to go.

Harold came to me and planted a kiss on my forehead. He had offered to walk me down the aisle because my dad didn't want to.

"Ready, sweetheart?" he asked with a warm smile. I wrapped my arm around his and nodded.

"As ready as I will ever be," I replied.

# Chapter 55

A girl quickly gave me a bouquet of red roses, and the song started.

The girls moved forward swiftly, followed by me.

"Don't trip. Don't trip. Don't trip," I kept whispering to myself.

Harold chuckled silently and held my arm tightly. "Don't worry. I won't let my daughter fall on such a special day," he whispered.

I nodded and walked more confidently. With every step, my heart raced faster than before. Finally, my eyes landed on my beautiful mate, Damien. He looked ravishing in his black tux. A small red rose was tucked in his suit pocket, and his hair was a little messy, giving him a sexy look. He looked happy. And that's all I want. We reached the altar, and Harold handed me over to Damien, who took my hand eagerly.

"Take care of her, or I will haunt you for your entire life. And I'm not joking, son," Harold said. That's when realised how much I missed having a father in my life. But not anymore.

"Don't worry, Dad. I'll keep her like a queen," Damien promised. Looking closely, I saw water in her eyes.

I blinked back my tears. Harold kissed my cheek and went to sit down next to Lily. I stood in front of Damien as the priest started his ceremony. I didn't pay attention to anything and just kept staring at my mate.

After a lot of talking from the priest—it was time for the rings. The ring bearers, a cute girl and a boy came in with our rings. We both took our rings in our hands and repeated after the priest.

"I, Damien Owen, take you, Isabella Clark, for my lawful wife, to have and to hold from this day forward, for better, for worse, for richer, for poorer, in sickness and health, until death do us part," Damien said, slipping the ring on my finger.

"I, Isabella Clark, take you, Damien Owen, for my lawful husband, to have and to hold from this day forward for better or worse, for richer, for poorer, in sickness and health, until death do us part," I repeat and slip the ring on his finger.

"Now, you may kiss the bride," the priest said.

Damien didn't waste any more time and claimed my lips. The clapping and hooting forced us to move away. Both of us were

## The Unloved Mate

breathing heavily. He held my hand and walked me down the stage, everyone on the way blessed us.

During the reception, many people greeted us and gave us gifts. Everything was going perfectly until they showed up—my guests.

"Mason, Morgana, I'm glad you could make it," I said. Everyone was quiet as I spoke to them. I stood up, and Damien stood up with me and wrapped his hand around my stomach protectively.

"What the hell are they doing here?" he muttered.

"I invited them." He gave me a look that clearly stated, 'Are you out of your mind?!'

"Damien, I don't want to hold any grudges in the future. I want our future to be free of any negative emotions. I felt the need to do this, baby. Please," I said. His eyes softened, and he gave a slight nod.

I smiled and pecked his lips, making him smile. I turned back to my guests with a smile.

"Thanks again for coming. Enjoy yourself," I said and sat on the seat for Damien and me.

"Congratulations, Isabella. I'm happy for you," Mason said with a sad smile.

"Your happiness doesn't matter," Damien muttered, but I heard.

Both of them gave us our gifts and left. They were not comfortable. And just like that, we had our first dance.

The reception was over around 11:00 pm in the night, and I was more than just exhausted. Damien helped me get in the car because my dress was too big. I laid my head on Damien's lap and fell asleep. I am so tired.

"Baby, wake up. We have to go now," he cooed in my ear and placed kisses over my face.

I opened my eyes and sat back up. We were at the airport.

"Where are we going?" I asked

"For our honeymoon, baby. Now, we have to get going. Come on."

We were on a private jet again, but it was a different one and was decorated with flowers inside.

Chapter 55

"Where are we going for our honeymoon, Damien?" I asked, excitedly.

He chuckled and kissed me, making me forget everything. Soon, we found ourselves in the small bedroom, tangled in sheets. My wedding dress was discarded in a corner along with his clothes.

# Epilogue

**Three years later...**

**Damien's POV**

"Daddy!" My little princess voice called from the other side of the door. You know I was right; our little peanut turned out to be a girl.

During Bella's labour, I was truly scared, but the moment the nurse handed the tiny baby in my hand, I felt like I achieved everything and was at peace.

"Daddy!" Rosaline squealed and jumped on my lap. She wrapped her tiny hands around me and hugged me.

For a three-year-old, she is damn strong, I thought and hugged her back. I pulled away and kissed her cheeks repeatedly, making her giggle.

"Rose! How many times do I have to tell you not to run? You could have got hurt, baby!" Bella said while entering my office.

I placed Rose on my chair and walked towards my wife. Wrapping my arms around her swollen stomach, I quickly stole a kiss.

"How are you, baby? Is my little champ being a good boy in there?" I asked.

"Yes, I'm good, and Luca is a very good boy. But your daughter is behaving like a bad girl. She dropped a bottle of Nutella on Nate today while he was sleeping," she exclaimed.

"Oh, I'm sure he was happy about it. After all, he loves Nutella," I reasoned. Who can be mad at my princess' cute little face?

"Ugh, you always side with her. Let's have lunch. I'm starving!" she said, dragging me to the oversized couch in the corner. She picked up Rose and made her sit between us.

# Chapter 55

Having my family by my side was satisfying. After baby Rosaline's birth, Bella became very weak, but with everyone's support, we made it through.

Rosaline is everyone's little ball of sunshine. She has this unique charm around her that makes everyone happy. No one has the power to say no to her or not like her. She is treated like a princess. At such a young age, she knows her values and is respectful.

And then my boy, who is still to come into this world. We could not keep our excitement when we learned it was a boy. We already named him Luca. He is our little champ.

This is my beautiful family. Me, my lovely wife, my daughter, and my boy. Picture perfect.

"Rosaline! Don't throw your food on Daddy!" Bella said.

And a piece of chicken hit my face.

# Bonus Chapter #1

**Damien's POV**

"Daddy! Mommy! Wake up! It's Christmas!!" My four-year-old screamed from the other side of the room. I covered my ear with a pillow and snuggled more into my wife's naked body. We celebrated Christmas Eve in our way yesterday, and now all I want to do is sleep.

I felt Bella moving out of bed, but I held her tightly.

"Baby, don't leave me," I whined, but she didn't listen.

She pecked my lips and forehead once before getting off the bed. I closed my eyes again and tried to sleep.

"Mommy! Daddy! I want to open my presents!" Rosaline screamed again.

I heard the door open and tiny footsteps running inside. Soon, I was tackled by a tiny body of my daughter.

"Daddy!"

I woke up startled and faced my daughter. She had a face-splitting, which made me smile too.

"What, peanut?" I asked her. Yes, I stuck to the name. She doesn't complain, so why not?

"Daddy, I want to open my presents, but Mommy said we can't open them without you," she said with an adorable pout.

"Aw, really? Let's go then," I said and lifted her. I'm glad I wore some shorts after our activities last night.

"Daddy, Uncle Nate said he got me a big present!" she said, opening her arms wide to show how big.

"Remember to say thank you, sweetheart," I said. I placed her on the kitchen island and went to Bella, who was cooking something.

"Yes, Daddy," Rose said, diverting her attention to her toys.

I snaked my arms around Bella's tiny waist from behind and kissed her neck.

## Bonus Chapter #1

"Good morning," Bella said, turned the burner off, and faced me.

"You left me," I pouted and she kissed my pout away. I held her and deepened the kiss.

"Better?" she asked.

"That was okay. But I am up for more tonight. You know today is Christmas and all?" I offered.

"Of course. Whatever you say." Her fingers brushed my exposed chest, making me groan in pleasure. The doorbell rang, breaking our little moment.

Bella let go of me and went to open the door. I went to the fridge and gulped some milk from the carton.

"Uncle Nate! Aunty Cole!" Rose yelled. I swear she will burst my eardrums one day. How can she possibly scream so much?

I went back to our bedroom to put a shirt on before greeting them. Bella had this great idea of having a get-together for Christmas. Nate and Cole moved out of the pack house last year, and so did Cameron who found her mate around two years back. The gathering is in the evening, but knowing them, I expected them to show up in the morning.

"Hey Nate, Merry Christmas," I said and hugged him. I missed this idiot.

"Merry Christmas, Alpha." That Alpha word earned him an elbow in the ribs.

I side-hugged Cole and said Merry Christmas.

"Let's go open my presents!" Rose yelled for the thousandth time today.

"Okay, thunderball, let's go," I said. I picked her up towards the living room, where the Christmas tree was set up.

Rose wiggled out of my hold and started sorting out the presents. She had a total of nine gifts, and she was over the moon. My sweet pea, she's so innocent. She ripped open Nate's gift and gasped when she saw a doll that was as big as her.

"Nate, where did you even get that?" I whispered

"Not telling," he replied, and I dropped the matter.

## The Unloved Mate

Rose also received a cute pair of shoes from Cole, a dress from Cameron, and a tea set from Bucky—Cameron's mate. Her grandparents, my parents, gave her a doll house, which she wanted for a long time.

Then came our turn. She opened my gift first. She opened the small gift and squealed, running into my arms.

"What is it, pumpkin?" Nate asked.

"Daddy brought me tickets to Disney Land!" she squealed and kissed my cheek. "Thank you, Daddy."

"Anything for you, peanut. Now go open Mommy's present." She ran back and opened the wrap.

She took out a T-shirt that said, 'World's Best Daughter', and ran to her mom.

"I love you, Mommy," she said.

"I love you, too, darling," Bella said back.

The day went by peacefully. Others showed up, and we had a lovely time catching up with them. Yes, we meet regularly, but it's not the same as when we all lived together in the pack house. So it was fun.

The day came to an end, and everyone bid their goodbyes.

"Bye, buddy. See you tomorrow," I said to Nate and he nodded.

I closed the door and checked on Rose, who had fallen asleep an hour ago. Once I saw her sleeping in her room, I searched for my wife.

I went to our room and saw her placing clothes in the closet. I sneaked up on her and wrapped my arms around her waist.

"Where is my gift, baby? Did you forget?" I whispered. She turned around and laced her fingers around my shoulders.

"How can I forget your gift? Go lay down on the bed. I'll get it."

That got me excited, and I quickly lay down, waiting for her gift. Even though I brought a gift for her, I will give it when I receive mine.

Bella came back with a small box. "Here." She placed the box in my hand and looked at me expectantly.

"Okay."

## Bonus Chapter #1

I opened the wrapper and saw a small white box. I opened it.

It's a small plastic stick with three red lines on it.

A pregnancy test.

"Bella?" I said, not looking away from the stick. Finally, I looked at her and saw her nod.

"I'm five weeks pregnant."

"Bella!" I lunged at her, and she giggled.

"Oh, Bella, you gave me the best Christmas gift ever. I love you, baby," I said.

"I love you, too. Now, where is my gift?" she asked. She held her hand out, and I removed the box from under the pillow.

She opened it and smiled. It was a locket with our family picture in it. It also had our names on the back. Bella hugged me, then took off her diamond necklace and replaced it with the locket.

"When the baby comes, we will change the picture in your locket and engrave his or her name, too," I said, and she nodded.

We held each other all night and spoke about our family's new addition until we finally fell asleep.

# Bonus Chapter #2

**Isabella's POV**

*I* was tired from all the running. I was running from them. I don't know who they are, lurking in the shadows and giving me creeps. I can't run anymore. I'm panting and sweating heavily. But I have to run. I know I'm close, close to Damien.

I can't remember how I got into this situation. One moment, I was putting my shopping bags in the car, and the next, some guys were running behind, chasing me like prey.

I ignored the pain in my body and ran like I was on fire. I saw the house: my home. It boosted my energy, and I ran and ran. I opened the door and looked behind me. The men were gone. I sighed in relief and fell on my knees, catching my breath.

When my breathing became normal, I went around looking for my mate. The house is so empty, it's never like this. I searched the kitchen, the living room, the pool, and the library. He is usually at these places when I'm not home. He was nowhere to be seen, so I went to our bedroom.

I opened the door, and I wished I never did. Hot tears fell from my eyes on the floor. For the first time, Damien was not there to wipe them. He was there, lying on the floor, looking lifeless. I ran to him and fell on my knees. I tried to shake him and talk to him, but he did not wake up. My heart broke. My reason to live was suddenly snatched away from me.

I felt someone grab my arm and drag me away from Damien I turned around to face the masked guy, who had been chasing me around the city. I screamed and moved away. I looked at Damien for help, but his lifeless eyes just stared into nothingness. I shook my head as more tears fell.

"Damien! Help me! Damien!" I shouted in the hope that he would get up and help me. I screamed and trashed in the hands of

# Bonus Chapter #1

*my captor. How can I be so unlucky? He dragged me away until I couldn't see my mate anymore. I stopped. I stopped trying. I gave up...*

"Bella!"

"Bella, wake up! Please!"

"Baby open your eyes! Look at me!"

"No, baby. I'm here. I'm not going anywhere!"

I opened my eyes and took a long breath. I looked around and noticed I was in my room, on the bed.

"Baby!" I heard Damien say before he pulled me into a bone-crushing hug. I instantly wrapped my arms around him tightly. It was a dream— No, a nightmare.

I pulled away and searched him for any injuries. I held his face and kissed every inch of it. Then, finally, I broke down sobbing.

He placed me on his lap and stroked my hair as I let the tears fall. After some time, my sobs reduced to minor hiccups, and that's when Damien pulled away slightly.

"What happened, baby?" he asked softly.

"I had a horrible nightmare," I replied.

"Shh, you wanna talk about it?"

"It was about you, Damien. Y-you died. Then t-they took me a-away from y-you. I was so scared."

He hugged me tightly and rocked back and forth to calm me. "Shh, baby, I'm here. Nothing will happen to me or you. You don't have to worry about such things, ever," he reassured.

I nodded and closed my eyes. His words calm my nerves. His words seem so genuine. Soon, my eyes became droopy. Damien laid us on the bed and stroked my hair. I cuddled him more and placed my head on his chest.

This will never get old.

# Bonus Chapter #3

**Damien's POV**

Being an Alpha of a pack is relatively easy, but being the father of a hyperactive three-year-old girl is not. You may think that I would possess any control over my child, but in reality, it was the complete opposite.

Right now, I was being forced to go to one of Rosaline's friends' birthday party. They had also invited the parents to the party, which I find stupid. Why would they invite adults to this kind of celebration?

I had opted to go casual. I was dressed in a half-sleeve black fitted T-shirt, black jeans, and my brown jacket that Bella gifted me for our anniversary last month. I gave myself one last look in the mirror and went into the closet for my wallet and watch, but I got gifted with a very exciting scene.

Bella stood in front of the rack full of dresses, dressed only in her towel.

I felt myself getting hard down there, and I wished nothing more than to spend the night with Bella, alone.

Damn the party.

I wrapped my arms around her slim waist. She let out a slight squeal and turned around.

"Damien! Get out!" she ordered, giving me one of her 'looks'. Most of the time, it worked, but not now. Now, I was in a fun mood.

"Let's ditch the party, baby," I whispered in her left ear and nibbled on it. I could feel her fast heartbeat against my chest and her rapid breathing on my shoulder.

"No, w-we can't d-do that," she stuttered. I smirked and left small feather kisses on her bare shoulder. I have been deprived of

## Bonus Chapter #3

her for a few days because Cameron and Bucky had been visiting. But now I want her.

"But, baby, I didn't complain for the past five days. Don't you think I should be getting some, you know, for being a good boy?" I whispered seductively.

I shifted and placed my lips on her. Her taste never gets old. She responded to the kiss with the same passion. I sat on the chair in the corner, not once breaking the kiss, and pulled her between my legs. One hand cupped her face and the other on her back. My hand found the edge of the towel and undid the knot, letting the towel fall on the floor. Bella was not at all bothered that she was all naked in front of me. She was used to it. I moved my lips from hers and kissed down her throat and chest. Heaven.

Soon, my clothes were on the floor as we melted into each other, completely forgetting about the party until a slight knock and loud noise were heard. We scrambled from the floor of the closet and put on our clothes.

I patted my clothes and hair and opened the door to our room. Rosaline stood there in her princess outfit, looking all angry.

"I came to tell you that the party got cancelled," she huffed and then pouted. Aw, my poor angel.

"What? Why?" I asked with a sad face, but inside, I was jumping with joy.

"Selena's mom went into labour in the morning, so they cancelled the party." Selena was her friend whose party we were going to.

"Oh, they called now? An hour before the party? How irresponsible," I said, but Rose shook her head frantically.

"No! They called in the morning, but the maid who took the call went somewhere out and returned just now. She said she forgot to tell," she explained.

"Okay, princess. How about you get out of this dress and into some soft pajamas? Tell Jazzy to give you dinner, then go to bed. Mommy and Daddy are a little busy," I said, and she nodded. I kissed her head. "We'll see you later, peanut. Good night, and sweet dreams."

"Good night, Daddy. Say good night to Mommy, too." She ran off to find Jazzy, and I closed the door. I carried Bella out of the closet and threw her on the bed.

I climbed on top of her and smirked.

"Now, where were we?"

# Bonus Chapter #4

**Isabella's POV**

I woke up at one in the morning due to my weird craving for peanut butter in the middle of the night. I freed myself from Damien's deathly hands and padded downstairs to the kitchen. I can't skip anymore because of my huge tummy; I can't even look at my toes! There was a time when Damien had to paint my toenails for me. I feel so useless.

I reach the kitchen and open the gates to heaven, the refrigerator. Damien, being the best mate in the whole wide world, has already stacked the kitchen with the things I would possibly like to eat during my condition.

Aw, my mate is such a sweetheart!

I grab a new jar of peanut butter and a spoon and sit on the floor beside the fridge, with a lot of difficulties. Compared to other pregnant ladies, my tummy is relatively small, but I'm tiny myself. What do you expect? I still look like a fricking whale, though.

I started to feel sleepy when I finished half of the jar and curled up on the floor. I am not climbing the stairs. It's not cold since it's the middle of summer, so sleeping here won't be a problem.

I felt warm hands wrap around me. I opened one eye and saw that the person holding me was a very worried-looking Damien.

I was fully awake now, and he had my undivided attention.

"Damien? What happened?" I asked, but he just gave me the 'You're in trouble' look, and I shut up.

He carried me upstairs and laid me on the bed, covering me up to the chin with the duvet. He sat next to me and just stared.

"Will you tell me what happened?" I asked again, and this time, he sighed.

"Why were you sleeping on the floor in the kitchen?" he asked in return.

## The Unloved Mate

"I wanted to eat peanut butter, so I went to the kitchen, but fell asleep there. Too lazy to climb the stairs," I reasoned.

"You should have told me, baby, I would have brought the jar here for you. You should be careful. What if something happened to you or our baby," he said. I opened my arms, and he hugged me without hesitation. His hands wrapped around my waist and head on my chest.

"I'm sorry, but I didn't want to trouble you more than I already did. I have become so useless that I need help in everything I do. You are always so stressed because of me." I pouted.

"Aw, don't say that baby. You are not useless. It's just the pregnancy, and everyone goes through these times. We will get through it, too. Now it's already late, and you should be sleeping, not talking," he said.

He always makes me feel better. My sweetheart husband. He got off of me, laid down on the bed, and cuddled me close.

His hands around my huge tummy and head next to mine. About fifteen minutes later, I was sleeping like a log—Damien told me.

# Bonus Chapter #5

**Isabella's POV**

A loud cry woke me up from my deep slumber. I groaned and turned over but opened my eyes nonetheless. I looked beside me Damien was sleeping soundly, and I didn't want to wake him up, so I got out of our bed and slipped on his T-shirt that was lying on the floor.

Entering my baby Luca's nursery, I saw him trashing in his crib and crying. Aw, my poor baby. I picked him up and rocked him a little to calm him down. I changed his diaper and fed him. When he was satisfied and stopped crying, I paced in the room to make him fall back asleep.

I laid him on the crib and kissed his forehead once before leaving the room. I wasn't sleepy anymore, so I decided to make breakfast for everyone, considering it was already 6:00 am.

Luca was born on the twenty-first of September. He is a chubby little boy who turned six months old last week. Giving birth to him was painful, more than Rose, but it was all worth it when I cradled him in my arms. He has his daddy's dark eyes and my brown hair.

I still remember the day I went into labour. I still remember the day as if it was yesterday...


**Flashback**

*The mornings were not my favourite part of the day anymore. I had come to like mornings since Damien came into my life because I saw his beautiful face. But now, even his beautiful face didn't help. Being pregnant was not a piece of cake. I can't roll in my sleep. Cuddling with Damien is not an option. I can't even reach him*

## The Unloved Mate

*because of my football-size tummy! You will think I had experience with this because of my Rose, but no, it was different.*

*I rolled over to my side and didn't see Damien there. I got up and covered my heavily pregnant body with some clothes. I usually sleep in my bra and some sweats because I get hot quickly, much to Damien's dismay, he can't touch me.*

*I penguin walked quietly to the bathroom to brush my teeth. I saw a pink sticky note on the mirror and read it. It was from Damien.*

Baby, we ran out of bread and milk, so I'm going to the supermarket to get some. I'm taking Rose with me and will be back soon. `Love you!♥

Your love, Damien.

*I checked the time and saw that it was only 10:12 am. I decided to shower before they came back and went into the bathroom.*

*After the shower, I placed my heavy self on the sofa and watched the TV. The front door opened, and Rose ran inside with an excited Damien behind.*

*"Mommy! Mommy! See what Daddy got me!" Rose jumped up and down like a rabbit in front of me with a small box in her hand.*

*I opened the box and saw a bead bracelet with letters on it. It spelled out 'World's Best Sister'. It was truly adorable. I tied around her hand and kissed her forehead.*

*She ran to the kitchen to fill her tummy, and Damien sat beside me.*

*"How are you feeling? Is my son giving you trouble?" he asked, kissing me first and then my swollen bump. I shook my head and rested my sore feet on his lap. He lightly massaged them and hummed a random tune. He does that a lot now.*

*I fell asleep on the sofa and woke up when I felt my stomach exploding from pain. I let out a scream and tried to stand up. The sofa was soaked, but I didn't care at the moment.*

# Bonus Chapter #5

*A loud banging noise came from there, making me more breathless. Damien came rushing out of the kitchen. His flour-flavored cheeks made me almost burst into laughter. He was still wearing an apron.*

He came rushing towards me and held me in his arms. "Baby! What happened?!"

"M-my water b-broke!" I said in between deep breaths.

"What! But you're not due for another week!"

"I don't care! Take me to the hospital! I want your son out of me! Now!" I yelled as the contractions hit me.

He immediately let me go and ran around the house looking for the overnight bag. He picked me up and sat me in the backseat of his SUV. While driving, he took his apron off and called the doctor to prepare everything for our arrival.

We reached there in ten minutes with Damien's not-so-safe driving. I was immediately taken to the emergency room. By the time everything was arranged, I was ready to push. Damien was by my side, holding my hand and whispering sweet nothings in my ear, wiping my face from time to time while I screamed at him for doing this to me. This was the second time I swore at him, the first being Rose's delivery. His face was priceless.

After nine hours of pain, our son finally made it. He was quite chubby for a newborn, and that's why pushing him was so difficult. But it felt good to hold him finally.

The doctor and nurses let us with our new baby. Damien sat beside me on the bed, lightly stroking our baby's head.

"Damien, do you have any name for our baby boy?" I asked

"I thought of one. I like it."

"Tell me," I said.

"Luca? How does that sound?" he said, still smiling at our son.

"Perfect." I looked at my son and smiled. "Hi, baby Luca," I cooed.

*Later, the room was filled with all the visitors. Lily, Harold, Nate, Cole, Cameron, Bucky, Adam, Nina, and our precious Rose. Everyone visited and congratulated us...*

## The Unloved Mate

A crashing sound came from upstairs, followed by thundering footsteps. In a flash, a shirtless Damien stood in front of me.

"Good morning, sweetheart!" I said cheerfully as if he was not glaring at me.

"Good morning to you, baby, but would you care to explain why you left the bed? You know I want to see your face first thing in the morning," he said and sighed.

I love how he always wishes me, even though he is not in a good mood.

I wrapped my hands around his neck and pulled myself up to kiss him. He lifted me by my legs and kissed me. I hopped back down but kept my hands around his neck. "I'm sorry, but Luca's cries woke me up, and then I thought I would make breakfast. It won't happen again. Promise," I said.

"I forgive you this time, Mrs Owen, but not again. I don't like not waking up next to you. The bed felt cold," he said and kissed me again.

"When is Rose coming back? I miss her," I whined and detached myself from my sexy mate. He sat on the barstool and sighed.

"Nate said he would drop her off in the evening today. I miss her too, but I got to spend alone time with you," he said. He walked around the table and came behind me, where I was fixing our plates. His lips assaulted the skin around my neck, and it was very difficult to keep myself from moaning in pleasure.

He turned me around and kissed me hard on the lips. Sometimes, I feel this wolf will never be satisfied. We just made love last night, and he is here for more. But I'm not complaining.

We were both at a point where we couldn't hold ourselves back. My hands went to the waistband of his pajamas, and pulled them down as his hands slipped under my shorts.

"Aahh!" Luca's cries made us jump apart. Still, in a daze, I fixed myself up and gave Damien one last peck before hurrying toward Luca's room. But I didn't miss Damien say...

# Bonus Chapter #5

"Sometimes, it feels like we have another Nate in our life. Ugh! Cold shower, here I come."

## ABOUT THE AUTHOR

Hello, I am Sharda Pathak, also known by my penname Skylar. I am an author based in Maharashtra, India who started Writing at the age of eighteen while still in college.

After a few years of struggling with mainstream education and writing as a side hustle, I decided to do what I liked for a living. I am 22, with more than twenty novels created out of my imagination.

I am an avid reader with a passion for fantasy and romance, and the two elements are often incorporated into the stories I create.

You can also check her works on www.dreame.com.

# ABOUT DREAME

*Established in 2018 and headquartered in Singapore, Dreame is a global hub for creativity and fascinating stories of all kinds in many different genres and themes.*

*Our goal is to unite an open, vibrant, and diverse ecosystem for storytellers and readers around the world.*

*Available in over 20 languages and 100 countries, we are dedicated to bringing quality and rich content for tens of millions of readers to enjoy.*

*We are committed to discover the endless possibilities behind every story and provide an ultimate platform for readers to connect with the authors, inspire each other, and share their thoughts anytime, anywhere.*

*Join the journey with Dreame, and let creativity enrich our lives!*

Printed in Great Britain
by Amazon